HOME COMING

A. AMERICAN

CHAPTER 1

A FTER WAKING UP, THAD STAYED in the bed. The room was quiet; only the soft sound of Mary breathing beside him disturbed the silence. Light filtering through the blinds cut across the room in sharp beams. Thad watched as tiny particles of dust drifted in and out of the beams in a silent dance. Slowly turning his head to the side, he saw Mary's bare shoulders. They were covered in only a sheet and he could see her form lying beneath it.

A pang of guilt swept over him. The image of Anita and Tony came into his mind. He'd had such a hard time dealing with his feelings for Mary and the ever-present memory of their loss. But he wasn't disrespecting them. He carried their memory every day with him and thought of them often. And he would never forget them. Looking again at Mary, he thought, *no, this isn't wrong.* He loved Mary. It wasn't the same love he had for Anita and never would be. But it was just as strong, and he would give Mary as much as he gave Anita.

Moving slowly, Thad slipped out of the bed and pulled his pants on. Glancing back to make sure Mary was still asleep, he eased out of the room and quietly closed the door. He made his way through the kitchen, which was now a useless space in the house. Modern kitchens simply were not designed to function without the luxury of power and running water. It didn't matter though. Thad had adapted to the new reality a long time ago.

In preparing the house for him and Mary, he'd installed an elevated water tank to supply the house. So, the sinks and toilets worked. You could take a shower, but the pressure was weak. He didn't have another of the large tanks like the one sitting in the road not far from his house. Instead, he'd connected two fifty-five-gallon drums together and put them on a platform, eight feet off the ground. He connected the output to the house in the same manner as previously, using a garden hose to tie into the hose bib outside the bathroom. And that bathroom was his next stop.

After taking care of nature's requirements, he picked up a bowl of eggs sitting on the kitchen counter and went out the back door. The house was small, which was fine with him, but it had a terrific patio on the back of the house. Unlike most of the houses in the area, this one was concrete block sitting on a footer directly on the ground. The patio was a solid poured cement pad.

Thad set the eggs on a table and pulled a Weber grill away from the wall. He dropped a double handful of pine needles into the bottom of it and lit them with a lighter. He waited for those to burn away and the small pieces of oak he'd piled onto it to turn into a sustainable fire. Once it was ready, he put the grill top on and placed a cast iron skillet on it. Taking a spoonful of bacon fat from a Mason jar, he banged it on the side of the skillet and waited for it to melt down.

While the fat was melting, he went back in the house and collected the rest of his breakfast materials. Miss Kay had given him a loaf of bread the night before when he and Mary left to go home. It was in a basket with a small jar of butter and jar of jelly from Gina. There was also a small piece of bacon wrapped in a towel. As Thad sliced the bacon, he smiled to himself, remembering how people used to react to food being left on the counter overnight. Today, no one would throw something out that sat out overnight.

With the bacon sliced, he laid the strips in the grease. He liked to add a little extra grease to the pan when cooking bacon. It would be added to by the bacon he was cooking and create a nice skillet to cook his eggs in. As the bacon popped and hissed, he sliced up the bread. It would go on the grill later for a light toasting. Then he filled a percolator from the sink and spooned some coffee into it. The grounds had been a gift from the old man and he smiled as he watched the dark grounds fall into the basket. He couldn't help but wonder how it ate the old man up to give it away.

The coffee finally boiled as he was toasting the bread. Two plates sat on the table with eggs and bacon. Initially, he intended to wake Mary up and have her join him for breakfast on the patio. Then he had another idea and went into the kitchen to go through the cupboards. In the back of one, he found a tray that would suit his needs. It was the kind you'd use in the oven, but this morning it would carry Mary's breakfast to her in bed.

He carried the little tray carefully towards the bedroom. At the door, he fumbled for a minute, watching the coffee as it sloshed slightly. Getting the door open, he saw Mary roll over and smile. Seeing the tray, she sat up. The sheet fell away, exposing her breasts. She quickly blushed and pulled it up. Thad smiled at her embarrassment and said, "It's ok. I think I know what they look like now."

Mary looked down and smiled again. "I guess you do," she replied and let the sheet fall away. Thad carried the tray over to her and placed it on her lap. "This looks really good," she said as she picked up the fork.

"I hope you like it," Thad replied as he leaned over. Mary looked up and he kissed her.

She looked around and asked, "Where's yours?"

"I could only find one tray. Mine is on the table out on the patio."

She looked at the tray, "This is very nice," and then added, "but I'd rather eat with you. Take it out there and I'll get dressed and join you."

Thad nodded. "That was my first idea. But I thought this would be nice."

"It is nice. Very sweet of you," Mary replied and held the tray up. "Take this out there and I'll be right out." As Thad took the tray, she grabbed the coffee cup, "I'll keep this."

Thad smiled, "I'll wait for you."

Mary jumped out of the bed, sipping on the coffee. The sheet trailed behind her, falling away as she made her way to the bathroom. Thad stood for a minute watching her bare backside until she closed the door behind her. He then carried the tray back out to the patio and waited for Mary. It didn't take her long. She came out of the house in a small thin sun dress and sat down closely beside him.

Taking a bite from a piece of bacon, Mary smiled at Thad, "This is wonderful." She looked around the yard and added, "It's better than the other house."

Thad sipped his coffee, "It was kind of crowded there. You really like this house?"

She nodded eagerly, "Yes! Very much. I like the back porch and the house is nice and small. It won't be hard to keep clean."

"It'd be better if we had some power," Thad said.

Placing one of her eggs on a piece of toast, Mary replied, "It would be. But it's fine for now. Now that they have power to town, maybe we'll get some too."

"Morgan said they were going to run it out here. He told them there wasn't any hurry. But they said they're going to do it anyway."

"Morgan should just let them do what they want. He always seems worried about other people doing things for him, like he doesn't deserve it or something," Mary replied.

Thad mopped an egg yolk on his plate with a piece of toast. "That's Morgan. He'll go out of his way for anyone but doesn't want anyone to do it for him."

"He always seems worried," Mary added.

Thad finished his breakfast and took a sip of coffee. "That's just his way. If anything bad happens, he beats himself up over it. Like it was his fault. Like all this is his fault. He needs to relax a little."

Mary tapped Thad's mug with her own, "I agree with that. He certainly needs to relax."

Thad stood up and took the plates. "What do you want to do today?" He asked.

Mary rocked her head back and forth. "I don't know." Then she gave him a devilish smile. "We could go back to bed if you want."

Thad smiled and looked at the plates in his hands. "Should I wash these first?"

Mary stood up and whispered into his ear, "They'll wait." Thad left the plates on the kitchen counter and followed Mary back to the bedroom.

The other newlyweds had also chosen themselves a place to live. It wasn't the best choice tactically, and Aric had been told so by several people. It was on the back road of the neighborhood, past Danny's house. His was the closest to it and it was still a fair walk to get there. If something happened, they would be on their own until help arrived.

But Fred liked the house. It was a small log home, single story with a loft. The house had an open design and full porch wrapping all the way around it. This allowed the windows to be open all the time, as direct sunlight never came in them to heat up the interior. In northern latitudes, you wanted a southern exposure to allow this light in to warm the place in winter. You didn't need that in Florida. Any benefit from a southern exposure in winter was trumped by the broiling heat it created in summer. And summer lasted a lot longer than winter down in Florida.

The little house had wood floors, which had obvious advantages when there was no electricity. A broom still worked. Aric had spent time cleaning the place up. Whoever had lived there had left a long time ago, and when he first went in, it was like looking at a snapshot of a life interrupted. Dirty dishes had been left in the sink. A pile of dirty clothes sat in front of the washer. All the cabinets in the house were open as a result of the several trips made through the house in the months after the Day. But nothing had ever been damaged because the group that went through the houses was always very careful. At the time, open windows that rain could blow in through were closed, as were doors that had been left standing open. The houses were secured in the thought they may be needed later; and that turned out to be really good foresight.

This morning, the morning after her wedding, Fred wasn't feeling well. She was still in bed and Aric checked on her occasionally as he tended to chores around the house. He'd helped Thad put the water drums on the roof of his house and Thad was supposed to come down sometime today and help Aric get the two drums they scrounged up onto the roof of his new home. You could live without power. You could live without running water. But living with running water was a lot nicer. Not to mention, having the drums on the roof outside kept the water in them warm. Later in the summer, that water would get hot. But it kept the toilets working and it allowed for basic washing and general use.

Aric walked into the bedroom and sat on the side of the bed. "How you feeling?"

Fred rolled over onto her back. "I'm tired of throwing up."

Aric glanced down into the bucket he'd placed beside the bed for her. "Looks like you've been busy."

With absolutely no effort, she slapped his shoulder. "Shut up. Don't remind me. I wish I had some crackers or something."

Aric patted her thigh under the sheet, "I do too."

A knock at the door got his attention. "Let me go see who that is."

"Whoever it is, tell them I'm not here."

Opening the door, Aric was surprised to see Miss Kay and Jess standing on the porch. Kay held a large bowl with a plastic lid and Jess carried a pan covered with a towel. "Hey," was all he could manage.

Jess cocked her head to the side and asked, "You going to invite us in?"

Stepping back and pulling the door open, Aric replied, "Oh sure, come in."

As Kay passed Aric, she stopped to hug him, having to go up on her toes to do so. "Good morning, sweetheart. How is your wife this morning?" Kay couldn't help but smile as she asked.

"She's still in bed I'm afraid," Aric replied as he hugged her.

Jess set the pan on the kitchen counter and asked, "She still getting sick?"

Aric nodded. "Yeah. She's having a rough time with it."

Kay made her way to the kitchen, placing the bowl on the counter. "This should make her feel better," she said as she pulled the lid off the bowl. Aric leaned over to see a clear broth in it.

"What is that?" He asked.

"It's bone broth. It'll make her feel better," Kay replied.

"So will these," Jess said as she pulled the towel off the pan. It was filled with small thinly sliced pieces of bread. Jess picked one up, "Not quite as good as crackers, but it's the best we can do."

Aric took the piece from her and took a bite. He nodded his head, "It's like melba toast."

Kay was filling a bowl with broth. "Exactly. I can't make crackers, but I can make melba toast."

Aric motioned with the last bite of the toast, "She's going to like this. Thank you for bringing it over."

Kay smiled and replied, "Let's go check on our mother-to-be."

Fred was sitting up in the bed when they walked in. She smiled when she saw Kay and Jess, trying to look upbeat. "You didn't have to bring that over here."

Kay shooshed her. "You need your strength and something to help your tummy out." She set the bowl on the nightstand. "You drink as much of that as you can."

"And these should help too," Jess said as she handed Fred a small stack of the toast.

Fred immediately ate a piece of the small bread. "Thank you for this. I really wanted some crackers, but, you know something, these are better than crackers."

"I'll make sure you have some every day. You just pick them up at supper time and bring them home, so you'll have them in the morning." Kay sat down on the edge of the bed. "And don't worry. This nausea won't last forever. It'll stop soon."

Taking another bite of toast, "Not soon enough."

Kay laughed and patted her leg. "You'll be alright." "And what are you doing today, Aric, besides taking care of Fred?"

"We're getting the water drums installed on the roof today."

"Good!" Kay excitedly replied. "You'll have to have running water when it's time for the baby."

"That's the plan," Aric responded.

Kay stood up and announced, "Alright. I'll leave you alone." "Take care of yourself, Fred; and if you need anything, anything at all, you just let me know."

Fred held out a hand and Kay took it. "I will." "I'll send Aric if I need anything."

"Good."

Fred looked at Jess and asked, "Can you stay a while?"

Jess looked at Miss Kay, who gave her a dismissive wave. "You stay here. I can get myself back. I still know how to drive a truck."

"Ok. I'll stay here with Fred for a while then."

Kay said her goodbyes, gave Aric another hug, and left. Aric had a real soft spot for the older woman. Growing up, his own mother had worked a lot. She was very focused on her career and he was often left to fend for himself. It was how he'd developed a love of the outdoors, spending most of his time outside to be away from the empty house. His father was very much like his mother, also consumed with his career. Aric had often wondered as a young boy why they'd even bothered to have a kid. Was he a mistake? An accident?

But Miss Kay was so unlike his own mother as to be her total opposite. He imagined her as a mother, always there, looking out for her children. He couldn't imagine her any other way. He almost thought of her as being smothering, very active and engaged in the lives of her kids. And it made him smile. He loved the old woman and was thankful that his son would only know her as his grandmother. And what a fine one she would be.

"Hey, babe. I'm going to go out and work on the water system," Aric said.

"Ok. Just be careful. I don't need you falling off the roof."

He smiled and leaned in and kissed her. "Don't worry. I won't."

Since their house was so far from the others, he'd taken one of the four-wheelers as his own. Not that anyone cared. There were plenty of them around. Gas was certainly an issue, but for now, they had plenty. He'd also found a yard cart at one of the houses in the neighborhood and rigged a hitch up on the ATV so he could pull it. The addition made the four-wheeler even more handy. Hopping on it, he started it and sped down the drive towards the gate.

I was under the hood of the Suburban reconnecting the batteries. Focusing on what I was doing, I wasn't paying much attention to anything else and that's why I didn't hear Dalton's big ass walk up behind me until he whispered, practically in my ear, "What are you doing, Morgan?"

I jumped, banging my elbow on the hinge of the hood. "Son of a bitch!" I shouted. "Why the hell are you sneaking up on me?"

Dalton shrugged, "I wasn't sneaking. I just walked up. A train could sneak up on your ass. You really should work on that, you know."

Rubbing my elbow, I shook my head. "I'm going to hang a cow bell around your neck."

He smiled, "That's what the world needs, more cow bells."

Turning my attention back to the battery I was connecting, I asked, "What the hell do you want?"

"How's the vinegar doing?"

"It ain't ready yet."

"Have you checked it?"

I shook my head. "No. It ain't ready yet."

"I want to check it."

"Then go check it," I replied, annoyed. My elbow was throbbing. Wasn't a damn thing funny about it.

Dalton looked at the house. "Is Mel in there?"

"No, she and the girls are over at Danny's."

"Alright. I'm gonna go check it out."

"I'll be done in a minute and I'll meet you inside."

Dalton wandered off towards the house and I wrapped up connecting the battery. Once it was reconnected, I checked the other one to make sure it was also good and climbed in behind the wheel of the truck. Holding my breath, I turned the key. The truck turned over a couple of times before catching. The old Cummins rumbled in its typical way, blowing some smoke for a bit before settling down to a smooth idle. Satisfied that the truck would run, for a while anyway, I shut it off. Closing the hood, I headed for the house.

Dalton had the cheese cloth off the big crock. He was on his knees looking down into it, a finger in his mouth. "How is it?" I asked.

Without looking up, he replied, "Tastes like shit."

"Shit like vinegar? Or shit like shit?"

"It's sour. But it ain't vinegar. Not yet anyway."

"I told you it wasn't ready yet."

He pulled the cheese cloth back over the open top and stretched my homemade rubber band around it. Standing up, he looked down at the crock. "This chemistry crap isn't that much fun."

I patted his back and said, "It's like the old Heinz commercials, patience."

He looked over his shoulder at me, "I ain't got any."

I laughed. "Yeah, me neither."

We walked back outside. I had some tools to put away. "What are you going to do today?"

Dalton stopped and looked up into the trees. "Not much. Nothing really planned. I was over at the old man's place this morning and he's in a bitchy mood."

"About what?"

He shrugged, "Something on the radio. Said it sounds like there are other units operating in the area and he's trying to figure out who the hell they are and why he doesn't know about them."

I laughed. "That old fucker needs to relax."

As we talked, Aric pulled up on a four-wheeler. "Nice wagon," Dalton said.

Aric looked over his shoulder and replied, "I like it."

"What's up?" I asked.

"Thad was going to come help me get the water tank up on the roof of the house. I stopped by his place but didn't see him."

"Did you knock on the door?" I asked.

"No. I didn't want to bother them. Ya know."

I laughed. "You got a point there."

"Yeah, you already got the prize out of your box. He's probably still eating cereal," Dalton added.

Aric and I looked at one another, then I slowly turned to look at Dalton. "What in the hell are we talking about?"

Dalton looked at me, then at Aric. "You mean neither one of you knows what I mean? You don't get it?"

I shrugged, "I get it. It just doesn't make any sense."

Dalton looked at Aric and asked, "Do you get it?"

Shrugging, Aric replied, "Kinda."

Dalton shook his head. "You people are hopeless."

"Right now, I'm waterless. Can you guys come help me get the tanks up there?"

"Sure, why not," I said. "We're not doing anything right now."

Dalton looked at Aric, "Chemistry is a slow process."

Aric looked at me for more. "Ignore Gigantor this morning. He's off his meds."

We were at Aric's house working on the tanks when Thad showed up. We'd already managed to get the two barrels on the roof and were cutting a piece of plywood to make a platform for them. A two-by-four would be screwed to the plywood on the down slope side to give the barrels a flat place on the roof.

"Well, well, look who's finally out of bed!" I shouted down from the roof.

Thad smiled and waved as he climbed out of the little red truck. "Hey, guys. Sorry I'm late. I got tied up."

Dalton was leaned over the piece of plywood about to cut it with a Skill Saw as a small Honda generator hummed in the background. He straightened up when he heard Thad.

"I didn't know Mary was into that kind of thing. Who gets tied up, you or her?" Dalton belly-laughed.

Aric and I both started to laugh. I whistled loudly from the roof, just to add to Thad's embarrassment. He opened his mouth to say something and stopped. Instead, he just put his face in his hands and shook his head. This, of course, got us to laughing even harder.

"Don't worry about them, Thad," Dalton said. Sensing some relief, Thad looked up and smiled before Dalton continued. "I can teach you some knots if you need."

Aric and I both started to laugh again, and Thad shook his head. "You boys is a mess!"

"What's all this racket out here? I thought you guys were supposed to be working?" Jess said from the porch. She was leaning against a post and Fred was beside her. Aric looked up, "Hey, babe. You look better. Are you feeling better?"

Fred nodded, and Jess replied, "She'd feel better if she didn't have to pee in a bucket."

"She should he happy she has a bucket to pee in!" I shouted down from my perch on the roof.

"And having a window to throw it out!" Dalton added with a laugh.

Jess leaned out from the porch and looked up. "Who's up there?"

"I'll never tell!" I called back.

"Don't make me come up there!"

"Ain't nothing up here but work. I think I'm safe," I shouted and leaned out where I could see her.

I had a big smile on my face and Jess rolled her eyes. "I should have known."

"If you don't mind," I said, "we have work to do."

"Then quit goofing off and get to it!"

"You talk like you're the one that's married now," I said as I rubbed my chin. "When's that going to happen anyway?"

Jess gave me the finger and disappeared. Aric looked up, "I think you pissed her off."

"She'll get over it. Now, hand me that bucket of blackjack."

Dalton cut the plywood and the two-by-four for the platform. While he and Aric worked on that, Thad climbed up onto the roof. I was using a scrap piece of wood to spread the black tar on the shingles where we would screw the platform down. The drums would sit on the roof over the porch, but we still didn't want any leaks. Dalton passed the platform up and Thad and I secured it to the roof once the tar was all in place. Eventually, we would pipe it into the house. For now, we used a garden hose and connected the drums to a hose bib on the side of the house.

"I'll go get the water tank and we'll get this thing filled," Thad said. "It's at Danny's. I left it there with a hose running in it to fill it. Should be about full now."

"While you do that, we'll get the barrels secured," I replied.

To give the barrels some support and to keep them from being blown off the roof if they got low and a wind kicked up, we used some additional two-by-fours to strap them down. I called down measurements to Dalton that he'd cut, and Aric would pass up. When I finished, there was a piece of lumber running up the outside of each barrel that was screwed into one running across the top. Just something to keep them from tipping off the roof.

When I finished, I took off my hat and wiped my forehead with a bandanna. It was hot, and it wasn't even noon yet. "It's hot as balls up here," I called down.

"It ain't just up there. It's hot everywhere," Dalton replied.

"And only going to get worse," Aric added.

I looked up into the sky, then around the neighborhood. "You know, we should go swimming."

"Smashing idea!" Dalton shouted back.

"Yeah!" Aric replied. "Let's go to one of the springs or something."

"Alexander isn't that far away," I said. "Last time we were there, there was only one person. And he's not around anymore."

"What happened to him?" Dalton asked. I looked down with raised eyebrows and he got the idea. "Ah," he replied with a knowing nod.

Thad pulled up with the tanker in tow. As we were getting the hose up to the roof, we told him about the idea to go to the spring.

"When you want to do that?" He asked.

"Today!" I shouted.

Thad laughed. "You think them women are going to be ready to do something like that today? With no notice?" He laughed again and said, "You better rethink that idea."

"He's right," Dalton said as he pulled the starter rope on the trash pump to push the water to the barrels.

As we were discussing how the ladies were sure to put the squash on our idea, Sarge pulled up in his Hummer. Getting out, he walked over to the porch and looked around. After a minute, he shouted, "Morgan! We need to go to town."

"What for?"

"We need to talk to Sheffield. I have an idea to get rid of those commies once and for all."

"What do you need me for?" I asked.

He looked up at me and shook his head. "Because I said so!" Then he looked around and asked, "Where's your rifle?"

"At the house. I don't need it here to put a water barrel on the roof."

He looked around the other guys and asked, "Where the hell are your rifles?"

Dalton held up his AK. "Got mine, Top."

Aric looked at the house and said, "Mine's in there."

Then he looked at Thad and asked, "What about you? You leave yours at home too?" Thad smiled and nodded slowly. The old man shook his head and started in on us. "What fucking good are they going to do you at home? When you need it, there ain't no time to go get it! What the hell's wrong with all of you? Is there some collective case of dumbass going on here all of a sudden?"

"Calm down," I said. "What the hell's wrong with you this morning? Someone piss in your coffee?"

"Calm down? You want me to calm down? Tell me this then, dickhole. What's happened in the last couple of days to make things different? So that we don't need to keep our rifles close?" He looked around, but no one said anything. "Did you forget what happened at the park?"

That pissed me off. "No. Some of us helped dig the grave."

The old man pointed at me and shouted, "Did you enjoy it? Do you want to dig more?" When I didn't answer, he continued. "If you don't want to dig any more graves, then you assholes better get your shit wired tight! Now get your ass off that roof! We got to go to town."

I climbed down and walked over to the Hummer without saying anything to him. I climbed into the truck and waited. He spoke with the rest of the guys for a minute, then got in behind the wheel. Looking over, he asked, "You all butt-hurt now?"

"Hardly," I shot back.

"Then stop moping like a fat kid that had his candy stolen."

"I'll make you a deal. You shut the hell up and drive and I'll stop *moping,*" I replied with as much sarcasm as I could muster.

"No deal. I'm not going to shut up. We need to talk," he replied as he started the truck and backed out of the driveway.

Thad was looking at us and I waved at him. He smiled, shook his head and waved. Without looking over, I asked, "What the hell do you want to talk about?"

As we bounced down the road under a cloudless sky, he said, "We've got to get rid of those fucking commies."

"That's your job," I replied with a snort.

The old man looked over at me, total disgust on his face. Then he focused back on the road as we rounded the corner and headed towards Danny's house. After a moment, he spoke. In a voice nearly devoid of inflection, he asked, "What in the hell's gotten into everyone lately? Mikey is not acting like himself. All of you out this morning and not a damn gun among you." He looked over and genuinely asked, "What the hell is going on?"

Looking out the window, I replied, "We're tired. The attack on the park was hard on everyone."

"So, what are you going to do? Sit down and wait to die? Hide under the covers and hope the monsters go away?"

Finally, I looked over at him. "It's just that every time we get a leg up, something happens to knock us down. It's kinda depressing."

Sarge stopped the truck in the road. "But you can't just give up. You know, in the Before, there were a lot of people that were always looking for someone else to handle their shit. Always waiting for the government to come take care of them. Those days are gone. You have to take care of your own shit now. All you have to rely on is yourself and your friends. And we're lucky. We have an awesome group of folks here. Think about them and taking care of them, just as they are you."

"You really think you need to tell *me* that?"

"No. But I do think from time to time you need to be reminded."

I thought about that for a minute. He was right, and I knew it. But it was also easy to want to forget it all for a while. "Well played," was all I replied.

Sarge smiled and said, "Glad to have you back, old buddy. Now, let's go talk to Sheffield about getting rid of those commies."

"Stop by the house so I can get my kit."

The old man looked over and smiled, "Did you actually think I was going to take you to town like this?"

We pulled into the yard to find Mel and the kids out front.

They were all looking up into the trees. I got out and looked up, asking, "What's going on?"

Little Bit pointed up and said, "Something is making a ruckus up there."

I smiled and rubbed her head, asking, "A ruckus huh? Where did you learn that word?"

Mel laughed and said, "I asked her the same thing."

Little Bit shrugged, "Listen to it. It's making a ruckus."

There was a squeaking coming from somewhere in the tree. From over my shoulder, Sarge asked, "What's this now?"

Little Bit took his hand and said, "Something's up there. Can you hear it?"

Sarge smiled as he looked down at her and replied, "Sure can. What do you want to bet it's a baby squirrel?"

Little Bit's face lit up, "Really? It's a baby?" Then she and Edie held hands and jumped around shouting, "It's a baby! It's a baby."

Sarge pointed up into the tree and said, "There it is, right there."

I looked up and spotted the tiny gray form squirming around in a clump of leaves. Little Bit took a sharp breath and said, "Oh no, it's going to fall!"

We all watched as it wriggled around and did indeed fall. Mel and the kids all let out a squeal. Without thinking, I pulled my hat off, reached out and the little guy dropped right into it. There were cheers from everyone as I took him out of the hat. The poor little guy had ants all over him and I wiped them away and looked him over. His eyes were still closed, but he did have a coat of fine fur and looked good, other than the ants.

"Can I hold him! I want to hold him!" Little Bit shouted.

Handing her the tiny creature, I said, "Be careful."

Mel knelt down beside her said, "Gentle, be real gentle with it."

Edie and Jace gathered around to rub its head with a finger as they all giggled and squealed. Little Bit looked up at Mel and asked, "Can we keep it?"

Mel scooped it up from her hand and held the little guy up in front of her face. "I don't know what we'd feed it."

"That's easy," Sarge replied, "Baby formula. He won't eat much, and we can spare enough for the little guy."

"That's a good idea," Mel replied. "I have an eyedropper I can feed him with."

"What are we going to name him?" Little Bit asked.

"I think you already did," Mel replied. Little Bit looked up confused and Mel said, "Ruckus! Why don't we call him Ruckus?"

The kids all laughed out loud and Little Bit danced around, "I love it! We have a baby squirrel named Ruckus!"

"That's a fine name for a limb rat," Sarge replied with a smile.

Mel took the little rodent into the house and the kids followed her. Sarge looked at me and said, "Hurry up and get your shit."

"Yeah, yeah," I replied as I headed into the house.

Mel was in the kitchen with the kids. She'd found a box and was putting a couple of small towels in it for the baby limb rat. "Hey, babe, I'm going to town with Mr. Personality out there."

She looked up and smiled, "Alright."

"We won't be long."

She held the squirrel up in front of her and in a babyish voice said, "Ok, we're going to go find you some food."

I grabbed my gear up and dropped the vest on over my head as I headed out the door. Sarge was waiting in the truck when

I climbed in and we headed down the road. Sarge slowed as we came to the bunker where a couple of Guard guys were on duty. We had six of them here and they were all good people. They seemed to genuinely enjoy being here as opposed to the armory.

"What's up?" I asked Chris Yates. He was a good guy to have around as he was a medic and took some of the pressure off Doc.

"Just enjoying the sunshine."

I laughed, "You're in the right place for it! Where's Wallner?"

"He's goofing off somewhere. He has the night shift later."

I nodded. "Good deal. You guys need anything?"

Chris shook his head, "No, we're good here."

Sarge leaned forward and barked, "Good! Then get your ass back to work!"

I rolled my eyes and Chris smiled, replying, "Roger that, Top!"

As we rode towards town, I asked, "So what's up? What are you thinking about doing with those commies?"

Sarge glanced over before starting into it. "What happened at the park was just the opening salvo. The commies are going to try and drive a wedge into the community. To sow distrust and fear. That way, when they decide the time is right, they'll step in as the saviors. This is the exact same shit we did in the Middle East, Africa, Asia, just pick a place."

I took the words in slowly. It made me think of Dad, something I hadn't done in a long time now. He was a crew chief and door-gunner on scout helicopters in Vietnam. He'd seen his share of this sort of thing. In a time when the people of this country didn't even pretend to support the troops or the mission that detached politicians gave them.

My mind wandered off the topic and focused on Mom and Dad. I wondered how they were doing. Dad was a tough old man and I thought, hoped, he and Mom were doing alright. I imagined them working the river for food. He loved to fish and was really good at it. Doing it for fun is one thing but doing it every day to feed yourself made it something else entirely.

My thoughts were interrupted by Sarge barking at me. "You paying attention over there?"

Rousing myself, I said, "Sorry. I was thinking about my Mom and Dad."

He nodded and asked, "They live over on the St Johns, right?"

"Yeah. That's where he retired to. The old man loved to fish, and it was the perfect place."

"You should go over there and check on them."

I nodded. "I want to. There's just been so much going on."

"We can make time," he said. Then Sarge looked over and said, "It's important, you know."

I nodded. "It is. I'll make the time soon. Back to the original topic. What's the deal with the Russians?"

"It ain't just Russians."

"I know, I know, there's Cubans too. Now answer my question."

Sarge looked over at me. A half grin cut his face. "I think I can get a B1 bomber to hit them. It'll blast them all to hell. One run and that's it."

I took an exaggerated look out the windshield, at the sky. "So, where's the bomber? What's the hold up?"

"It ain't that simple, dipshit."

I leaned against the door, resting my elbow on it. "Enlighten me."

"We need to get eyes on them first. I want to make sure that all of them are actually there. At least most of them." He smiled, "When we were at Eglin, I picked up a piece of equipment for this very thing. A laser designator. Once we have eyes on them and Bone is in the air, we can paint the target and they'll drop some big ass smart bombs on them."

I thought about it for a minute. I'd seen YouTube videos of this sort of thing. I had an idea of what he was talking about. "So, what are waiting on?"

"That's why we're on our way to see Sheffield."

"And why am I here?"

Sarge looked over and shook his head. "I know you really just think of yourself as the Sheriff. But you are a very important part of this here. It's more than you want, I know that. Everyone knows it. But you always step up to the plate. You're here because I want you here." He slowed the truck and stopped in the road. "I need your help, Morgan. It's that simple."

I nodded. "You saved my life once. I guess I owe you. I've got your back."

The old man smiled and reached out and gave my shoulder a squeeze. "I know you do."

We'd stopped on the road between Altoona and Umatilla. We were sitting just before the old Pizza Hut. Sitting in the road, just past it, was the bucket truck. I smiled, "Looks like Baker is running power out this way."

Sarge nodded and put the truck in gear. "Looks that way."

We stopped at the truck and I got out. There was a crowd of people gathered across the street from the truck. Terry was up in the bucket and Baker and Eric were on the ground. I walked over to Baker and looked up the pole. "You're uh, moving the wrong direction, you know." I pointed down the road towards Eustis and added, "Eustis is that way."

She was stripped down to just a t-shirt with her hair pulled back in a ponytail. She was looking up at Terry as well and didn't look away when she replied. "That job is done. Now we're heading this way."

I nodded and looked around. "Uh huh. And where are you headed, this way?"

"You know where we're going, asshole. We're going to get the power up to your neighborhood first, then we're going to come back and start checking side lines and restoring power to Umatilla."

"You have all the parts to pull this off?"

Baker laughed, "Hell no! But we're scavenging parts as we go. We'll make it happen."

Sarge had made his way over and said, "Of course you will!"

"Hey," I said to Baker, "We're going to Alexander Springs tomorrow. You guys should come with us."

"What?" Sarge asked.

"You heard me," I replied.

From up in the bucket, Terry shouted down, "Hell yes, we'll go! I could use a day off and swimming sounds like a damn fine way to spend that day!"

"When were you going to tell me about this little field trip?" Sarge asked.

"I would've earlier this morning. But you had your ass in a knot."

"Whaaaat?" Baker asked in exaggeration. Looking at Sarge, she said, "You had your ass in a knot? But you're such a people person."

If Baker had been a man, Sarge would have had plenty to say to her. But he held his tongue and worked his jaw. His eyes narrowed as Baker smiled at him, waiting for his response. Finally, he spit on the ground and walked away. Baker laughed and said, "See you next time, Top."

I looked over my shoulder as the old man walked away. Turning back to Baker, I said, "You guys come out to the house tomorrow morning and we'll head up to Alexander. It'll be fun. We've got some meat we'll grill, make a day of it."

"Sounds good to me," Baker said.

"Me too," Eric added.

"Alright then, I'll see you tomorrow. I guess we have shit to do." Looking up the pole, I shouted to Terry, "See you tomorrow! Bring a swim suit and no banana hammock!"

"Eww!" Baker shouted.

I laughed and headed for the truck where Sarge was waiting, fuming. Climbing in, I looked over and asked, "You get your ass in a knot again?"

"Fuck you, asshole. You're a dick. You know that?" He shot back.

I nodded, "So that's what you wanted to say to Baker. Whadda you got for me?"

As he started the truck, the old man shot back, "That was for you! I wouldn't talk to a woman like that!"

I laughed. "Yeah, ok, it's your lie, you tell it. Let's get to town so we can get back to the house."

We didn't talk for the rest of the way to the armory. Rolling in behind the building, we hopped out and I followed the old man inside. Sheffield was waiting for us in the conference room when we came in and took a seat.

"Morning, fellers." Sarge said as he sat down.

"Morning," Livingston replied.

"What's on your mind," Sheffield asked.

Sarge sat drumming his fingers on the table for a moment before answering him. "I've been on the horn with Eglin. They want to eliminate the commie issue here in Central Florida."

"And what do they suggest we do?" Livingston asked.

Sarge looked up and smiled. "They want to hit them with a B1. One strike and wipe them out."

Sheffield was obviously surprised. "What?"

The old man nodded and replied, "You heard me."

"Holy shit," Livingston added.

"Holy shit indeed," Sarge said. "But it's the best way for us to get rid of them, with nearly no risk to our people."

"What the hell are they waiting on then?" Sheffield asked.

"We need to get some people over there and put eyes on 'em. I picked up a laser when I was up north. They want us to get people in place and paint the target, so there's no chance of a miss."

"Let's get some folks out there then. I've been really worried about this. If they hit us once, they'll hit us again," Sheffield said.

Sarge nodded, "We're going to. In a couple of days, I'm going to send Mike and Ted out to identify the target. That'll give Eglin a couple of days to get the strike organized as well. Things aren't as easy as they once used to be."

"That's great," Livingston said. "If this works, then we will be rid of the last threat we have."

"That's the idea," Sarge replied. "I'll stay in touch with you as we work this thing up. Just keep your patrols out in case they try sneaking in. You still have people out on 441?"

Sheffield nodded. "Oh yeah. They're doing forty-eight-hour watches. Six men are out at a time."

"Good. Keep that up. If this works, in a couple of days, we can all relax."

"Damn, I hope so," Sheffield replied.

Sarge got to his feet, "We'll see you boys in a couple of days. You need anything?"

Sheffield shook his head. "No, we're good."

"Where's Cecil?"

"I saw him on his tractor this morning headed towards his corn patch," Livingston said.

"Alright, I'll check on him on the way back."

I followed the old man out, without having said a single word in the meeting. Why had I come? In the Hummer I asked that question.

"Say, Colonel. Why the hell was I there again?"

The old man shot daggers at me. "I already told you not to call me that."

Seeing he was irritated made me smile. "That's beside the point. No one said a word to me and I didn't have shit to offer on the situation. So, why was I there?"

"Just shut up and sit there," he barked back at me. Looking out through the windshield, he shook his head.

I laughed to myself but didn't push it. He was already irritated. We found Cecil in the cornfield. The corn was tall, over your head. Cecil was sitting in the seat of his tractor, under the shade of the only oak tree around.

Seeing us pull up, Cecil smiled his typical broad smile and waved before climbing down from the machine. "Morning, Linus, Morgan. What sort of trouble are you two up to today?"

"Oh, whatever we can find," Sarge replied with a smile.

"I'm just here to carry his golf clubs," I said.

Sarge shot me a look, "Oh, dry up, Nancy."

Cecil laughed. "Glad to see you boys are good as usual."

I looked out over the cornfield. "Looks like the corn is about ready to harvest."

Cecil nodded and shaded his eyes to look out across the field. "Yes, it is!" He said with pride. "We'll have to get some folks out here soon to get it all picked." He walked out into the field and pulled an ear from a stalk and peeled the husk back. Inside was a beautiful golden ear of corn. He took a bite of it and smiled, juice dripping down his chin. "Oh yeah. It's about ready."

"That's a whole lot of food," I said.

"We'll pick some now, to eat fresh. The rest we'll leave to dry on the stalk," Cecil said. "This really isn't fit to eat fresh, but it'll be a nice change."

I took the ear from him and took a bite. "It's sweet." Looking up, I added, "But it is tough."

Cecil nodded. "It's something different, so it don't taste so bad. But you wouldn't want to eat a bunch of it."

"Gimme that thing," Sarge said, holding his hand out. I handed him the ear and he took a bite. Nodding as he chewed the tough kernels, he said, "Yeah. I wouldn't want to have to live on the stuff."

"Hey, Cecil, we're going up to Alexander Springs tomorrow," I said, "you should go with us."

He thought about it for a minute. "I'd like to. But I don't have any way to get out there." He slapped the tractor and said, "It'd be a long ride on this thing."

"Damn right it would," I said with a laugh. "How about I come pick you up in the morning."

He smiled that broad toothy smile again. "That'd be fine. I'd like that. A change of scenery would be really nice."

"Bring some shorts and you can go for a swim," Sarge said.

Cecil laughed. "I don't own any short pants. And I ain't done no swimming in a long time. But I'd be happy to sit on the side of the spring and soak my feet."

Sarge smiled, "That sounds like a deal. We'll collect you in the morning." We said goodbye and headed back to the Hummer.

"I think this will be good, taking a break from things," I said as we headed back towards the ranch.

The old man nodded. "Some down time would be good.

But I'm sending Mike and Teddy out to put an eyeball on those commies. In a day or so, we'll hit 'em."

"That should piss Mike off," I replied with a laugh.

Sarge looked over at me and smiled, "Good."

I was dropped off at the house and went inside. Mel and the all the kids were sitting in the living room, passing the little squirrel around. An eye dropper sat on the table with a small cup, a little formula still in it.

"How's he doing?" I asked when I came in.

"He was really hungry!" Little Bit shouted.

"Did he eat a lot?"

Mel looked up, "Yes he did. I think he'll be fine. I need a cage for him."

"I'll see what I can find," I answered, thinking that was one more thing I'd have to deal with. "Tomorrow, we're going to Alexander Springs for the day. I think we could all use a day to swim and relax."

"Really?" Taylor asked. I nodded, and she clapped her hands as she got up. "I need to go find a bathing suit!"

Lee Ann, not as much into swimming as her sister, surprised me when she too jumped up to go find something to wear. Little Bit was the most excited, as little kids usually were; and she jumped around the living room with exuberant anticipation.

"What time are we leaving?" Mel asked.

I shrugged, "I don't know. When everyone is ready, I guess."

"Are we taking food?"

"I think Thad was going to take some meat to grill or something."

Mel stood up and put the little limb rat in a box. "I'll go talk to Kay and see what we can come up with."

She took Little Bit and they headed next door, leaving me alone in the living room. With everyone now occupied, I decided to go find Mike. Leaving the house, I walked towards the home he shared with Ted, Ronnie and Sarge. The dogs labored to their feet and trotted after me as I walked down the driveway toward the road.

It was a scorching hot day. The sun was high in the cloudless sky. As I walked, sweat began to run down my neck and back. I was already regretting taking the walk. I looked back to see the dogs standing in the road panting. I guess they were smarter than I was because they lingered in the road for a moment, then Meat Head turned and headed back to the house. Drake was immediately on his trail. I laughed and thought of Little Sister as I continued to walk in the direction of the bunker.

Summer days in Florida can be miserable. When the humidity gets up and the temps rise, you'll sweat like a lawyer in hell; but it doesn't evaporate, just pools up on your skin until it either soaks everything you're wearing or drips off. Either way, it really sucks. I tugged at the plate carrier, trying to get some air under it. But doing so allowed the incredible funk that always built up under it to escape and I turned my head to gasp for an unpolluted breath. *Shit, that stinks!* I muttered to myself.

Imagine wearing the same gym clothes every day, all day, and working out to the max. That would give you an idea of what it was like. Oh, and you never washed any of it. Yeah, now you're getting the picture. I felt for all the people that ever served in any of our desert wars for what they had to endure.

I found Wallner in a lounge chair under the tarp of at the rear of the bunker. He was stripped down to his waist and sweat covered his pasty white bare chest. As I came up, I put a hand up to shield my eyes from the glare.

"Damn, man. Put on a shirt or something. It's like looking directly at the sun!"

With his hat pulled down over his eyes, he mumbled, "It's too damn hot. Too hot to even think."

"Well, tomorrow we're going to Alexander Springs."

Before I could finish the statement, he bolted upright in his chair and shouted, "Really?" Jumping to his feet, he said, "Hot damn! A day of swimming sounds nice. Back at the armory, we would swim in the lake. But someone had to stand guard for gators and the water smelled like shit and was as warm as piss."

I laughed. "Yeah, I know what that's like. But the spring will be nice and cool. Clean, clear water. That will be great."

Then his expression changed. "Shit."

"What?"

"I know someone is going to have to stay behind to provide security."

I nodded. "Three someone's."

Wallner rubbed the stubble on his chin. "We'll draw straws. Three of us get to go; three have to stay behind."

"That's up to you guys."

He nodded. "We'll sort it out." Then looked at me and said, "Man, I'm looking forward to this."

"If, you get to go."

He gave me a mischievous smile, "Yeah, *if* I get to go."

"I don't want to know," I said with wave of my hand as I walked off.

I found Mike in a lawn chair in the front yard of the house. He was lying there, butt naked, sunning himself. The tall grass came up to the bottom of the chair and it looked as though he were floating on it. I stopped short when I saw him and said, "Would you put some damn clothes on?"

He was wearing sunglasses and I couldn't see his eyes. But his head rocked towards me and he replied, "Why? I'm getting a tan."

"There's some parts that shouldn't ever see the sun."

He adjusted the head of the chair to lie flat and rolled over, putting his pale ass in the air. "There. You happy now?"

I half laughed to myself and walked over and fell into the grass beside him. Resting back on my arms I looked over and asked, "You alright?"

I expected some smart-ass reply. But he was quiet for a moment, then said, "I'm fucking bored, Morgan. I joined the Army to visit far-away exotic lands, meet interesting people and kill them in a most terrifying manner. This was fun for a while. But, I'm getting bored to death. I need something to do and I don't mean standing at the damn bunker either. There ain't shit going to happen there."

"You seen the old man today?"

"This morning."

"Then you don't know what you're about to do?"

He sat up quickly, knocking the sunglasses askew. "No. What is it? Do I get to take my tank?"

"I don't know about your tank. But he's lining up a strike against the Russians at the auto auction. Said he's got a B1 bomber strike planned. You and Ted are supposed to go over there and put a laser or something on the target."

He jumped to his feet and shouted, "Hot damn!"

I turned my head, "Put something on, would you?"

Mike looked down and smiled. Putting his hands behind his head, he started to gyrate his hips, shouting, "Helicopter, helicopter, helicopter!"

Dalton's voice boomed from the road, "You're doing it wrong! You have to have something to swing to pull that off."

Mike looked at him and smiled, "You wanna go for a ride?"

Dalton walked across the yard and snorted, "That little thing couldn't even get my interest up."

Mike snatched the sunglasses from his face and pointed at Dalton with them, "You'd fall in love. Hey! We got a mission!"

"What sort of mission?"

As we were talking, Sarge pulled up in his Hummer. He sat in the driver's seat, shaking his head. Mike started walking towards the truck and the old man shouted, "You better go put some damned clothes on before you even think about talking to me! Who the hell walks around naked? What the hell is wrong with you?"

"You know the difference between naked and nekkid?" I asked. No one answered, so I continued. "You're naked when you ain't got any clothes on. You're nekkid when you ain't got any clothes on and you're up to something!"

"He better get some clothes on his nekkid ass!" Sarge shouted.

Mike turned and sprinted for the house. He came back out with boots on his feet and a pair of shorts. He was pulling a t-shirt on as he walked across the yard. "So, what's this mission?"

The old man climbed out of the truck and jabbed a finger at Mike again, "I better never catch you running around in your birthday suit again. If I do, I'll grab you by the stem and take you on a tour of the neighborhood, got it?"

"Yeah, yeah. What's the mission? I'm fucking dying here. I'm so bored I can't even jackoff anymore." Sarge dropped his face into his hand and shook his head.

"What's the word, Top?" Dalton asked.

I leaned in close to Dalton and said, "It's Colonel. But you got to say it with a thick southern accent."

Sarge slowly lifted his face from his hand and looked at me. Straight faced and through gritted teeth, he said, "Morgan, you do not want to start any shit with me right now." Then, ignoring Mike, he looked at Dalton. "We're going to set up on the commies at their base of operation. Mark them with a laser so a B1 can drop some serious hurt on their asses."

"You have the laser?"

Sarge cocked his head to the side and asked, "And just how the hell would we do it if we didn't? Stop being a dumbass, Dalton."

"Are we taking the big gun?" Mike asked.

"Hell no, shithead. You have to sneak in there and paint the target. You think they won't see that big bastard come rolling up? Get your head out of your ass. You'll take the war wagon. Get in somewhere so you can have eyes on the target and wait for the Bone."

"Who's going?" Dalton asked.

The old man pointed at him, "You, numb nuts, and Teddy."

Mike tuned and sprinted for the house, "I'll get my shit!"

"Tell Teddy to bring his ass out here!" Sarge barked after him. Then, looking at Dalton, he said, "This is important, Dalton. You guys need to stay out of sight. We're not going there to get into a gunfight. If that happens, then the mission is a failure. We're going to have one shot at this. If Bone can't drop on the first pass, there won't be a second attempt."

Dalton nodded as Ted came out of the house. Sarge filled him in on the mission and handed him a piece of paper. "Here's everyone's callsign. I'm Swamp Rat one, you're two. Eustis is Gator Hole and the B1 flight is Bone one and two. They'll contact you when they're in route and let you know when to light up the target." He pointed at the house and said, "Keep his ass outta trouble. No shooting or any other bullshit."

Reading the paper, Ted nodded. "He'll be alright. He likes to play the jackass part up, but he's a pro."

"What about after the strike?" Dalton asked. "We cleared hot on anyone left walking?"

Sarge nodded without hesitation. "Anyone you see upright after the strike is a fair target."

"Can I get that M1 of yours then? It'll give me some reach out and touch someone range."

Sarge nodded, "Come on inside and I'll get it for you. Teddy, you get your shit together and get ready to go. I want you guys in place with eyes on by this evening."

"Roger that, boss." Ted replied as he walked away.

As Dalton followed Sarge into the house, I said, "Alright guys. I'm gonna take off." Turning to head up the road, I added, "Since there's no reason for me to be here."

As he walked into the house, Sarge called out over his shoulder, "Dry up, Nancy!" It made me smile.

CHAPTER 2

THE AUTO AUCTION SAT ON a huge lot at the intersections of Highway 50 and the 42-toll road in Ocoee. It occupied over one hundred fifty acres, a huge area. Fortunately for the guys, most of the communist forces were gathered around one large metal building. But there were several positions scattered around the facility as well as perimeter patrols.

It'd taken hours for them to get to the area. Caution was the word of the day and it made Ted lay out a surreptitious route. The final approach was made along the shores of Story Lake to the northeast of the compound. The buggy was too large and loud to get too close to the target area and was left in the garage of an abandoned house. Actually, every house in the area was abandoned and appeared to have been empty for some time.

The three men closed the final distance on foot around midnight. Numerous stops were made to watch and listen. NVGs and thermal optics were used to look for any hidden observation posts. Dalton spotted one and the men adjusted their route to keep distance and obstacles between them and the manned position.

In the early hours of the morning, the three men chose a position that would allow them to observe the activity yet be far enough away to provide some security. The spot they chose was a small clump of trees at the edge of a residential area. The lack of people cutting the grass and keeping the weeds at bay had allowed nature to reclaim what was once hers. It provided great concealment, but little cover. It was hoped cover wouldn't be an issue.

"I'll take the first watch," Ted whispered. "You two get some sleep."

Dalton nodded, used his pack as a pillow to get comfortable. He was asleep almost immediately. It took Mike a little longer. He fidgeted, tossed and turned until Ted told him to knock it off and get some sleep. "You're up next," he said over his shoulder.

The Russian and Cuban forces were not very concerned about the possibility of attack from the looks of the place. While they did have a defensive position set up, they also had the place lit up like Times Square. From his position, Ted couldn't hear the generators but knew there must be a couple running. Two separate areas were well lighted. One was the large building where the auctions took place. The cars would roll in at one end and leave the other end of the building... sold, in most cases.

The bulk of activity was concentrated around this building. There was additional activity around another smaller building not far from the first. Since he was lying on the ground, Ted couldn't see any armor that may be gathered there; but he was certain there was plenty of it. Surveying the target, he began to worry that the strike they were preparing to make wouldn't be sufficient to do the job. There was just too much real estate. But he'd find out soon enough.

The trip to the springs looked like the Clampetts going on vacation. We had a string of trucks all loaded with people. There was also a cooler and brightly colored inflatables for the kids. Everyone was in good spirits; even the old man was smiling as he sped past us on the way to the spring. My girls were in the backseat of the Suburban laughing and talking. They had swim masks around their necks and were ready to get in the water.

We'd spent the morning getting things ready. Thad prepared burgers and Miss Kay baked some buns. There was a precious bottle of mustard, several bottles combined into one, and a little ketchup. There was no cheese, but we did have some lettuce and tomatoes. No matter, they were sure to be amazing. I'd made sweet tea, enough to fill the five-gallon water keg. We'd frozen a gallon jug of water and dropped it in to chill the brew.

We rode down the road with all the windows open. It was like standing in front of the oven with the door open, but we enjoyed it all the same. I couldn't help but smile; the excitement was infectious. When we made the turn to head towards the spring, I could hear everyone in the other trucks whooping and hollering. I went wide in the turn and pulled abreast of Thad. He looked out, smiling as usual. I pressed the throttle and passed him. The little red pick-up didn't have the ass to keep pace with the Cummins.

Jamie and Ian were bringing up the rear in one of the MRAPs. The old man thought it would be a good idea to have some muscle with us, just in case things went sideways. Jess and Doc rode with them and I could hear them cussing on the radio about everyone leaving them behind. Sarge came over the radio and called for everyone to slow down. He cussed me when I sped past him. They could wait; we were going swimming!

But I did slow a bit, enough to keep them in sight. I wasn't worried about the big armored truck getting in trouble, but the Suburban would be a prime target for someone not paying attention to the line of vehicles coming up behind me. The worry was wasted though. It was a beautiful day and we didn't encounter any trouble.

I drove right past the little pay station. I used to call it a ranger station. But it was no longer that. The Forestry Service had contracted the operation of the parks to a private company long ago. Naturally, it got a lot more expensive to visit what was supposed to be public land. The land belonged to the people..... if they could afford to get in.

At the swimming area, I got out and took down a section of the split rail fence that bordered the spring. I wanted to drive down to the water, keep the trucks close. I wound the truck through the trees, sometimes on the sidewalk, sometimes on the grass, until we were down near the beach. The park was empty, we had it all to ourselves. Before I was stopped all the way, the doors flew open and the kids bolted for the water.

Getting out, I laughed as they all ran into the water and dove head-first into the crystal-clear spring. Mel walked to the front of the truck and watched them. Still watching the kids, I said, "Remember how long it used to take them to get into the water?"

She looked over at me. "It's still going to take me that long."

I held out my hand as Thad pulled to a stop beside the Suburban. "Come on, *babe*. Let's go swimming."

It wasn't long before everyone was in the water. Everyone except the old man. He, Miss Kay and Cecil were sitting on the stone wall that surrounded the near side of the spring with their pants rolled up and their bare feet in the water. Mel and I waded into the cool water. She never did like going to the spring. Well, she did, but she hated the *getting in* part. Florida springs stay at seventy-two degrees year-round. In the summer, that means at least a twenty-degree difference. To say it was brisk was an understatement.

Mel and I held hands as we waded out into the water. Her breath was short and in quick gasps as she tried to hold her stomach out of the water. But it was useless, and I had to laugh. "Come on, babe. Just get in."

"You get in!" She shouted back.

Glancing over my shoulder at the rest of our group as they all dashed for the water, I said, "Ok." And I turned and dove in.

The water was cold, but awesome. I swam through the cool water as far as I could hold my breath before surfacing. When I came up, I saw Mel was with Jess and Fred. They were watching the kids who were all clinging to a bright pink raft, trying to clamor aboard. Aric and Thad were both swimming as hard as they could, racing one another towards the bubbling spring.

Coming up, I waved at Mel. She waved back, and I started towards the gurgling water. Getting to the giant crack in the ground where the cool water issued forth, I found Wallner there with two of the Guardsmen. I smiled and splashed water in his face, "So, you did make it."

He smiled, took a mouthful of water and spit it into the air like a fountain. "Yes, I did! Man, this feels good!"

Thad and Aric were splashing each other in a fury of spray. Everywhere you looked, people were laughing and smiling. It was just the break we needed. I looked towards the shore and saw Perez sitting under a tree, smoking of course. He was barefoot and down to his t-shirt. I saw Danny in the shallow water, sitting in water up to his chin. The kids' raft had found its way to him and he was spinning them around. Hearing another truck, I looked up to see Baker, Terry, Scott and Eric running for the water. They'd driven the bucket truck all the way out here and were quickly in the water with everyone else.

We spent the day like this. At some point, Thad left the water to start cooking. I headed for the shore, stopping to kiss

Mel on my way and to splash the kids chasing minnows along the bank. Catching up to Thad, I told him I'd collect some wood for the fire. We were going to use one of the grills at the park. It didn't take long to get the wood. The park had numerous hardwood trees, and their limbs littered the ground.

We loaded the grill with wood and kept feeding it until there was a heavy bed of coals. Then Thad started cooking. I left that part to him. Partly because he was so good at it, but mainly because he enjoyed it. "You got this?" I asked.

Thad nodded as he shook some sort of spice onto the patties of meat as they dripped fat into the flames. "Oh yeah. This ain't nothing."

"You need anything?"

He shook his head. "No, looks like I got everything I need."

Miss Kay came over as I was walking away, "You go swim, Morgan. We got this."

I smiled, "Just let me know if you need anything."

I waded back out into the water and sat down, resting on my ass with my feet coming up to the surface. Mel swam up to me and took up the same position. "This is really nice."

I nodded as I worked my arms through the water to hold myself upright. "Yes, it is. I wish we lived here. Could you imagine being able to come here every day?"

"That'd be nice. But I ain't moving out here."

As we discussed how nice it would be to have unlimited access to the spring, Miss Kay called out that lunch was ready. An afternoon of swimming had created intense appetites, and everyone was immediately headed for shore. We gathered under the shade of the big trees, sitting on blankets or beach towels.

Enormous burgers were passed out and Kay surprised everyone with a batch of homemade mayo. It was a huge hit, adding a new taste to what would have otherwise been a pretty bland meal. As we ate, the old man kept his radio at hand. I was sure he'd been keeping in touch with the guys as they lay in whatever hide they'd found or made overlooking the commies. I thought of those guys, what they were doing while we were here carrying on as if we didn't have a care in the world.

Thad and Mary sat close together, laughing and talking. Aric lay on the ground, his head in Fred's lap. Mel and I sat with the girls on a blanket she'd brought. The kids ate quickly, wanting to get back into the water. The scene was interrupted by the sound of a machine. A big one.

I and many others rose to our feet as the sound grew louder. We were all looking to the south, over the trees. Something was flying our direction.

"What is that?" Fred asked.

"It ain't one of ours," Sarge replied.

In the distance, it came into view. A very large helicopter slowly came over the horizon. Sarge was shielding his eyes with a hand and announced, "Everyone stay still!"

"What is that?" Thad asked.

"It's a Russian MI-24 attack helicopter, a Hind."

Aric snatched up his rifle and raised it. Sarge slapped it down. "Don't even think about shooting at that damn thing! You out of your mind? That thing is heavily armored. Your rifle wouldn't even crack the glass."

The big helicopter turned lazily in the sky south of us, headed to the south. Sarge picked the radio and called Sheffield in Eustis. Sheffield said they could see it, that it came from south of them and was heading back towards town. They stayed on the radio as the copter flew directly over Bay Street and out of town. Ted came over the radio and said they didn't see the bird but would keep their eyes open for it.

"This can't be good," Sarge said as he put the radio aside.

I'm really glad we hid the MRAP under the trees; if they had seen it, they probably would have attacked.

"Should we leave?" Miss Kay asked.

"I don't think so," Sarge said. "They didn't do anything. I'm surprised they didn't shoot up Eustis. Kind of worries me, actually."

Seeing the menacing Russian helicopter put a damper on things for a while. But it didn't last too long, and soon we were all back in the water. I'd brought a couple of fishing poles and spent some time casting a line. The lack of people in the area for so long had brought the fish back into the spring and the fishing was good.

Thad and I were fishing along the bank, where the spring discharges to form the river that runs through the forest to eventually reach the St Johns. We were catching blue gills and small bass and having a grand time.

Thad was reeling in a large bass and laughing. "This is the best fishing I've had in a long time!"

"It's the *only* fishing we've had in a long time!" I replied as I got a solid strike and set the hook on a blue gill so fat I couldn't wrap my hand around it.

Tossing the fish into the cooler we'd brought the burgers in, I said, "Looks like we've got about all we can carry home."

Thad lifted his bass out of the water. It was at least three pounds; and as he removed the treble hook on the Rapala plug, he said, "Yeah, this one won't even fit in. I can't close the top!"

"Looks like we'll have a hell of a fish fry."

"Fresh fish will be nice."

Thad lifted the cooler with a grunt. "Damn, this is heavy!"

I slapped him on the back, "It's been a good day, buddy."

I looked up into the sky. The sun was starting to drop, and the heat was finally letting up. Down by the water, it was cool and the scenery pleasant to the eye. "A damn fine day."

Thad nudged me with an elbow, nearly knocking me over. "It sure was. We need to do this more often." His mood shifted slightly, and he added, "There's more to life than just surviving. You got to take time to live too or there's no sense in surviving."

"You couldn't be more right, my friend." I looked at him and smiled, "We need to remember that. Let's do this sort of thing more often. Next time, let's go to the wayside on Juniper Run."

"Where's that?"

"Straight up nineteen, north of forty. It's a nice wide place in the river. Most of it is knee deep but there are deeper pockets. It used to be a fun place to go till the Forestry Service shut it down because the rednecks would leave too much trash, beer bottles and shit like that."

"I think we should do something like this once a week. Give everyone something to look forward to."

"Sounds like a plan," I said as I set the cooler on the picnic table beside the grill.

"What's a plan?" Sarge asked.

"We need to do something like this once a week. No reason not to," I replied.

Sarge thought about it for a minute. He looked out at the spring where Perez was standing in the water with his pants legs rolled up. He was leaned over splashing the cool water on his arms and wiping the back of his neck. He nodded his head and said, "I think that's a fine idea. Everyone's had a great time today. It's good to get out and have a change of scenery."

"Oh, my Lord!" Miss Kay said. "Look at all these fish!"

Thad smiled. "Yes ma'am. Me and Morgan loaded the box."

"We'll have a wonderful fish fry tomorrow night. Nothing

beats fresh fish," Kay said. "I've got everything we need. I'll even make cornbread."

"I'll fix us up a pot of green beans, like Momma used to make," Thad added.

"That'd be wonderful, Thad. You are a good cook."

Thad blushed, as was his custom when paid a compliment. "I learned from Momma and my grandmother."

Kay patted his shoulder, "They taught you well."

As the light began to fade, we pulled out of the springs on our way home. There was no hurry this time as we again rode with the windows open. After spending all day in the water, we were much cooler and the air blowing by us felt pleasant. When we turned onto Highway 19, it was nearly sunset, and the stars were beginning to come out. The sky was clear, so I was surprised when I heard the distant sound of thunder.

Looking at Mel, I asked, "Do you hear that?"

"Sounds like thunder," she replied as she looked up. "But I don't see any clouds."

Before I could answer, the radio crackled to life.

During World War II the Soviets developed a new weapon, the Katyusha multiple rocket launcher. The weapon terrified the Germans that came under its fire. They called it Stalin's organ because of its resemblance to a pipe organ. The rockets made a terrible screaming sound when launched and instilled fear in the hearts of anyone that heard it.

The weapon has been steadily upgraded over the years. The current system is called the Grad. In Russian it means hail and is a good description of what the weapon does. The current version carries forty rockets that are a little longer than nine feet. They can carry a variety of warheads with a range of between twelve and nineteen miles. The warheads ranged from high explosive to incendiary.

The thunder we were hearing was from three of these units sitting on the eastern shore of Lake Beauclair just south of Eustis. Each machine fired its forty-rocket load, one-hundred-twenty rockets. They carried a mixed load, two with high explosive warheads and the last with the incendiary type.

Sarge called for a halt and we stopped in the middle of the road. Everyone got out of the vehicles and stood in the road looking south. We couldn't see Eustis from where we were, but we could clearly hear it.

"What is that awful noise?" Kay asked.

The old man stood looking south and replied, "It's artillery hitting Eustis from the sound of it. I think that helicopter we saw earlier was getting solid coordinates."

Cecil gave out a low whistle, "It sounds like hell."

Sarge nodded. "It is." He looked around and called Doc. "Get in the MRAP; we're going to town."

Chris Yates had drawn a straw to come on this trip as well and he moved quickly to collect his gear and follow Doc.

I ran to the Suburban and grabbed my gear. I was in shorts and flip flops, but I was going too. Mel didn't question me when I kissed her, saying, "I'll be back as soon as I can."

She nodded and looked down the road, in the direction of the sound. "I'll get the girls home and wait for you."

I climbed into the back of the MRAP with Perez, Ian, Doc, Aric and Cecil. Jamie was driving as usual. As we drove towards the sounds of the still-rumbling explosions, Doc started going through his bag. He asked who had tourniquets on them. I started to pull mine out, but he stopped me. "Keep it. You'll probably find someone to use it on."

The sound of thunder stopped as we passed through Umatilla. But Eustis was now just ahead, and I heard Jamie take a sharp breath. "Oh my God."

I leaned forward and saw what shocked her. It looked like the road disappeared into a wall of flames. Thick columns of smoke rose high into the sky and the dark horizon was illuminated with the light of the fires consuming Eustis. I'd seen videos like this. Videos of neighborhoods decimated by combat in far flung places around the world. But it was the kind of thing I saw on TV, not in my community.

We found the guards at the barricade on the north side of town in a ditch on the side of the road, near where the old man had fished a gator out of the canal. The stunned men and two women climbed up out of the ditch when we stopped. They were obviously in shock and stared down the road towards town.

As evening was already approaching, the heavy smoke blocked out even more of the fading light, casting a sense of doom over everything. As Americans, we weren't used to seeing this sort of thing on our own land. Of course, we knew it happened and that our own military conducted just this sort of operation around the world; but it was always *over there.* Never was it here. Never had any American town been exposed to destruction on this level, not since the Civil War.

The troops at the barricade were awestruck. None of the rockets made their way this far. They were concentrated on the Eustis area. Notoriously inaccurate, it was just a roll of the dice that none of them found their way this far north. We stopped and talked with the wide-eyed soldiers.

"Anyone been into town yet?" Sarge asked.

The Guardsmen shook their heads. "No. We've been taking cover in the culvert. I've never seen anything like it. No one can be alive in there," he said, looking into town.

Sarge looked down the road. A thick column of dense black smoke was climbing high into the sky from the burning diesel fuel of the bladder located beside the armory. "It ain't going to be pretty, but we need to go in there."

He told the Guardsmen to stay at the barricade and we made our way into the inferno that was Eustis. The Grad rockets were not what you'd call a precision munition. I don't know what the failure rate is, but we had to maneuver around an unexploded rocket, its fins protruding out of the asphalt in the middle of Bay Street.

When the armory came into view, my heart sank. The building was utterly destroyed and a flaming pyre. Several bodies lay in the street in front of what was left of the building. And upon closer inspection, there were more bodies and, more disturbingly, pieces of bodies everywhere. Some were charred corpses. Reminiscent of the figures left after the eruption of Pompei. But these were still smoking. Their lips, if they had any, were curled back in a sneer, revealing their teeth. It was impossible to discern man from woman. They were simply ghastly, charred apparitions of people, like three dimensional shadows.

The fires were so intense it was difficult to get close to several places. The police department was no longer there. A vague outline of the building was still on the ground, but nothing more than two feet tall protruded above the surface. The county administration building, our courthouse, was also ablaze. I worried for Mitch and Michelle.

Every structure in town was either damaged or destroyed. The roads were blasted and cratered. It wasn't the Eustis I knew. We drove over to the clinic. The military grade tents that housed our only medical service were no longer there. Tattered pieces of canvas and shattered medical equipment littered the ground. The first recognizable body I found was a man in medical scrubs.

He was lying in the road, not far from the clinic. He was very clearly dead, but I saw no obvious injuries.

But there were survivors. They appeared out of the flaming and charred ruins of the town. Always in shock, sometimes injured, sometimes not. Some were naked, their clothes either blasted or burned off. We began collecting the wounded in the park. It was a large open area where nothing was burning, though rockets had also fallen there. There were craters blasted into the lawn. The bandshell had taken a hit too, blasting away more than half of the dome. But, it was the best we could do at the time.

I was knelt down beside a woman. She'd caught a blast on her left side and been horribly injured. Though her left side was blackened from the explosion and there were terrible wounds covering her entire left side, she was still conscious. Her left leg was missing just above the knee and I fumbled with my tourniquet to get it out. She tried to speak, but a large hole in her cheek prevented her from forming anything intelligible. She was hard to look at.

I couldn't say anything to her. What could I say? *You're going to be alright?* I knew better than that. There was no way we could save her. Feeling a hand on my shoulder, I looked back to see Doc standing over me; and he shook his head. I looked back to the woman and said, "We can't just leave her like this."

"There's nothing we can do for her. We don't have the resources to help her."

"But, we can't just let her suffer."

"We're going to have to make some very hard decisions." It was Sarge. He'd walked up as Doc and I talked.

"Like what?" I asked.

The old man looked around the burning town, then said, "We don't have the resources to save most of these people.

So, we either let them suffer until they die, or put 'em out of their misery."

"You mean shoot them?" I asked. And I looked at Doc, expecting him to argue the point.

But he didn't. "It's the humane thing to do. As much as I hate the thought of it. We can't help them and they're suffering terribly. It would be best to stop the suffering as quick as we can."

I looked at the woman. It didn't appear she was registering what we were talking about. It also didn't appear she was completely conscious. I looked closely at her now. With the missing leg, she was also missing most of the fingers on her left hand. The left side of her face was horribly disfigured with most of her cheek blasted away, so I could see into her mouth where several teeth were also missing. Even if we could save her, what sort of life would she possibly have? Reconstructive surgery was out of the question. There was no way to get her a prosthetic leg. It was a simple fact that modern medicine as we'd all come to know it, no longer existed.

I slowly rose to my feet and looked at Doc, "You sure there's nothing we can do?"

He looked at her and shook his head. "Not for her. There are others we can save, but anyone wounded this severely, no. There's no saving her."

As Doc spoke a pistol shot rang out down the street. I looked in the direction of the shot. "Looks like the others have already figured this out."

"I've already talked to them all. No one likes it, Morgan," Sarge said. "But it's the reality of it. It's what we're going to have to do."

I nodded and looked down at the woman lying on the street. "I'm sorry," I said as I drew my pistol and lowered it. Her life ended with the report of the Springfield. I felt ill and relieved at the same time. Sick at the thought of having to shoot her lying in the street, relieved at knowing she wasn't suffering any longer. She was the first, but sadly there would be many after her. It was a very, very long night.

When the sun started to break the horizon, I was standing in the front yard of a house on East Ward Street changing magazines in my pistol. I dropped the empty mag into the dump pouch where it clanged against the other two already there. We'd cleared the area of the business district earlier in the night and had moved into the surrounding residential areas.

The ranks of rescuers swelled overnight as people pulled themselves out of their shocked state and came out to help. So, I wasn't surprised when a man walked towards me from the street. It took me a minute to recognize him.

"Hi, Morgan," Alex the Canadian traveler I'd found at the Publix, said.

"Oh, hey, Alex."

He looked at the pistol I was holding and said, "Hell of a night, huh?"

I nodded, "Yeah. And it ain't over yet."

"I see that. Are you still moving the wounded to the park?"

As I holstered the pistol, I replied, "The ones we think we can help."

He nodded, understanding just what I meant. "Where you headed now?"

I was tired and thirsty. "I'm going to head back towards the armory. We couldn't go through it last night because it was still burning. And I need a drink of water."

"Care if I walk with you?"

"You're welcome to join me," I replied as I stepped out onto the road. We walked in silence for a bit, then I asked, "Where were you last night?"

"I found a house on the side of the lake no one was living in. It's a really nice place, right on the water, and I've been trying to fix it up to make life a little easier under the current conditions."

I smiled, genuinely happy. "That's great. Glad you found a place."

He stretched out a leg and pulled up on the jeans he wore. "There were even some clothes there that fit me."

"Sounds like things are looking up for you."

He gave a nervous laugh. "They kind of were."

The rest of our group was at the armory when we got there. They were already picking through the still-smoking remains of the buildings. A line of charred corpses was laid out in the street, many of which didn't even look like people. Just black stumps. Then there was the smell. Seeing Perez, I went over to him.

"Give me a couple of your smokes," I said, holding my hand out.

He was leaned over raking through a smoldering pile with an E-tool. "You picked a bad time to start," he replied as he stood up. Shaking two out of the pack, he handed them to me.

I broke the filters off and handed the rest back to him. "I'm not," I said as I stuck the filters into my nostrils. "Just need something to help with the fucking smell."

Perez nodded and looked around. "Yeah. You'll get used to it."

"I hope not. Thanks for these," I said as I walked off.

Perez lit up one of the filter-less fags and replied, "Not a problem." And he went back to work picking through the debris.

I found Cecil and the old man standing over several bodies laid out near the rear of what was left of the building. Walking up, I looked down and asked, "Is this Sheffield?" I knew there was no chance in hell he was still alive.

Doc nodded as he wiped a singed dog tag off with a rag and handed it to me along with another. They were Livingston and Sheffield's tags. I looked down at the two blackened and shrunken forms lying on the ground. It was hard to imagine it was the two men I had known so well. They certainly didn't look like themselves now. Moments like this hit really hard.

"We don't have an accurate count of how many were here," Sarge said. "But so far, we've found eighteen bodies. There are some at the barricade and a couple out on pickets who were lucky to avoid this massacre. I don't know how many more we'll find alive."

"Plus, the guys we have back at the ranch," I said.

"At least we saved them," Sarge replied.

"Cecil, did your house make it?" I asked.

"Just some broken windows. Nothing serious."

I nodded, "Good."

"Anyone have a count on the dead?" Cecil asked.

"It has to be over a hundred," Sarge replied.

"Way over," I added.

"We got a week's buryin' ahead of us," Cecil replied.

"We're going to have to do mass graves. I hate to say it, but it's the only way," Doc replied. "And we're going to have to do it soon. Like, we should start today."

As we were talking, Mitch and Michelle walked up. "Wow, am I ever glad to see you two are alright," I said.

"We were at home and we hid in the bunker," Michelle replied.

"This is unbelievable," Mitch said. "We saw so many bodies on our way here."

Sarge nodded. "There's a bunch. We're going to have to get started burying them soon. We were just talking about it."

"Where are the wounded?" Michelle asked.

"They're at the park. I was about to head that way," Doc replied.

"Come on," Sarge said, "We'll all walk over there."

As we made our way towards the park, I stopped at the MRAP for a drink. My canteen had run out hours ago and I was dry. I replenished it from a water keg we kept in the MRAP. While I was doing that, a man walked up. He was obviously agitated. "Why do some of these people have bullet wounds to their heads?"

Capping the canteen, I turned around. I was tired and not in the mood for the conversation. "We did what we could. Some people were so injured we couldn't save them. It was more humane to stop their suffering than to let them die slowly."

"So, you just shot them? What the hell gives you the right to decide to do that?" The man asked, furious at the realization.

"We couldn't help them," I replied, feeling overwhelmed.

Then the man shoved me back against the truck and screamed into my face, "You just executed wounded people! You sick bastards!"

He had a hold on my vest in double-handed grip. Without even thinking about it, I brought one arm up and over his, using my elbow to break his grip. Then drove the same elbow into the side of his head, knocking him to the ground. I reached down and grabbed the man, screaming into his face.

"And what would you have done? Where were you last night? We were out here all fucking night! You think I liked this? Come here you son of a bitch!" I dragged the man across the pavement as he tried to get his feet under him. I pulled him over to the first woman, the one I was trying to help when Doc walked up behind me. I shoved him to the ground beside her body and grabbed a handful of his hair, turning his head to look at her.

"And what would you have done for her? Look at her! What the fuck do you think you would have done for her?" I was still screaming at the man when some guys grabbed me and pulled me off him. It was Aric and Doc.

Sarge walked over and pulled the man to his feet. He dusted him off and said, "If you want to help, come to the park with us. The people there, we think we can save." The man was bewildered and looked around. "I know this is hard," Sarge continued, "but the clinic was destroyed and most of the staff there killed as well. The ones that are left, wounded even, are helping." He pointed towards the park and continued. "Burn victims need a lot of fluid. That's usually done through IV; well, we don't have any of that now. It was all destroyed. If burn victims don't get fluids, they die of dehydration. It's not the burns that kill them. Would you rather these people lie here and dry up and die? Or would you rather see their suffering end quickly?"

The man regained his composure and looked around. He slowly nodded his head. "I see why you did it now. I understand." He looked at me and apologized, "Sorry for jumping your ass, Sheriff." He rubbed the side of his head and added, "You've got a hell of an elbow."

"Sorry it came to that," I replied. "It's been a long night, one that we will never forget, I think."

"None of us will," Sarge added.

We all walked to the park. The wounded were lying on the ground wherever they could. Family members had joined many of them there. In many cases, they used pieces of debris as fans to keep the flies away from their wounds. There was a lot of crying and sadness in the park. In many cases, the wounded lying in the park were the sole survivors of a family. Or surviving family was with them, telling them of those that perished. Parents wept for dead children, husbands for wives and vice versa. It was a mournful place to witness.

"We need to move these people," Doc said. "We can't just leave them out here exposed like this."

A female in filthy medical scrubs was nearby and heard the comment. Her head was wrapped in a blood-soaked bandage, but she was still there assisting the wounded. "We need to move them to the high school. I sent someone over there earlier to check it out and it's in good shape. It's undamaged and the gym would make a good place to keep them. It's even stocked with cots, for use as an evacuation shelter. There are people over there setting them up now."

"What's your name?" Sarge asked.

She stood up, gently touching the bandage on her head. "Tina Beck."

"That's good thinking, Tina. I'm glad to have you here. You alright to keep going? That head wound looks pretty bad."

"It's nothing. Just a scalp wound. They bleed profusely but I'm fine. Besides, we need all the help we can get."

"Amen, sister," Sarge replied. He looked at Cecil and asked, "Can you get a trailer for your tractor? It'd make moving all these wounded a lot easier. I'd like to have all of them in the gym today."

Cecil nodded, "I've got a big one we've been using out at the farm. If someone can give me a ride out there, I'll bring it back."

We'd found one Hummer in town that had somehow survived. It had some shrapnel damage but was operational. I told Cecil I'd carry him over to the farm to retrieve the tractor and we headed off towards the truck. As we walked, Cecil was quiet. And that was fine with me. But after a while, he spoke.

"Morgan, I'm so sorry you guys had to do that today. Me,

I couldn't do it and I'm sorry I wasn't any help. It was a hell of a thing."

"You helped Cecil. I saw you helping to get the wounded to the park. You were there picking through the burned-out buildings. I wouldn't wish what we had to do today on anyone and don't hold it against them if they couldn't. Hell, I barely could."

"You know, I spent some time in Vietnam. Take it from someone that's been there, my friend, this isn't over for you. It's going to be with you for a long time. Now, I know you're a tough son of a bitch," he paused and looked at me, "but promise me you won't try to keep it bottled up. Talk to someone about it. You're going to need to. If you try to hold it all in, it'll eat you from the inside out." Looking at me again, he added, "Take it from the voice of experience. You ever need to talk about it, just come find me. I'll listen as long as you need to talk."

Cecil and I couldn't be more different. We were from different generations and there was a wide gap in our ages. He was a black man that grew up in Lake County Florida, not always a hospitable place for his race. But good people are good people and his offer moved me. I stepped closer to him and put my arm around his shoulder.

"That means a lot me, really. I know I'm still in shock over it and it'll all come out soon enough. You and I will be talking in the future, I think." I looked at him and added, "I'm fortunate to call you a friend."

He smiled, as he was prone to do, and replied, "I know you'd do it for me. You'd do it for anyone that needed it. But sometimes you need a shoulder to lean on too. You've got more of them than you know. You're highly thought of around here. People see you as a source of reliability, something they can count on. You're not alone."

"Neither are you. Hell, you're a far more valuable asset to the community than I am." I walked in silence for a moment before saying, "You know what really pisses me off? We just managed to get the power back into town. Things were looking up, and now this. I'm sure the breakers are all tripped at the plant. We're going to have to disconnect the lines running south."

"I'd wager Baker and her crew are at the plant doing just that right now."

We arrived at the truck and climbed in. I drove Cecil out to the farm and he mounted the tractor; the trailer was already attached, and we headed back to town. I rolled along slowly behind the old machine. It gave me time to think, think about the night before and what we'd done. But the more I thought about it, the more I realized it was the right thing to do.

We were so spoiled in our previous lives. Anything you wanted was a mouse-click away. If you were injured, state of the art medical care would come to you! All it took was for someone to make a phone call, and then highly skilled personnel would arrive on the scene, stabilize your injury and load you into an ambulance. They would already be communicating with a hospital and when you arrived, a team of specialists would be waiting to treat you.

Contrast that to now, where there is no help coming. The few trained personnel we had were either killed or injured. Hospital? No such thing exists today. We had a military tent to treat our most severely wounded in, and even that was destroyed. The precious supply of drugs we had were gone. The few pieces of medical equipment that could help keep someone alive were also destroyed. There is no *they*. *They* are no longer coming to your aid. You are on your own now. And the people whose suffering we mercifully ended last night were in no condition to help themselves and there just aren't enough people around to care for them. As horrible as it was, it was the best thing we could do.

Cecil drove the tractor into the park where people were waiting to get them loaded immediately. Many of them were in severe pain and some were unconscious. Missing limbs and blast wounds were common. I didn't know how some of these people would survive their wounds. But they were deemed worth the effort and we would do our best.

As the trailer was being loaded, I had a couple of the walking wounded get into the truck. Once the trailer was loaded, we headed for the school. I was surprised when we pulled up to see Jess and Thad. They immediately started moving the wounded from the trailer into the gym where cots were set up for them.

I helped a man with a nasty wound to his right leg into the gym. Settling him onto a cot, I caught up with Thad. "Hey, buddy. When did you guys get here?"

"We came last night. When you guys didn't come back, we figured it was a bad deal and you'd need help."

"You were right about that. Thanks for coming out."

"It's what we've got to do."

We moved the rest of the wounded into the gym and made them as comfortable as possible. We had no painkillers to offer them and those that were in pain and still conscious suffered terribly. We were short on bandages as well and many wounds were wrapped in whatever was at hand. I made a mental note to go out and try to find some usnea. It's a yellowish lichen often called Old Man's Beard. The Seminole Indians used it for bandages and it has very strong antimicrobial properties. It wasn't much, but it would be something.

I was walking out of the gym when Jess stopped me. "You look like shit. You need to go home and get some sleep."

"You looked in a mirror lately?" I asked.

When Jess was irritated, she'd cross her arms over her chest and cock her hip to the side. She adopted this pose now and replied, "You know what I mean, smartass. You need to go get some sleep."

I nodded. "I'm tired for sure."

"Then go home and sleep. There's enough people here to take care of the wounded."

I looked around and replied, "Let me find the old man and I'll probably head back."

She pointed to the door, "He's out there talking with Cecil."

"Thanks Jess. Thanks for looking out for me."

With a smirk, she replied, "Someone has to. Because you're obviously not going to do it."

I shook my head and gave her shoulder a squeeze before heading out the door. Sarge and Cecil were standing by the tractor. I leaned against the tractor and let out a breath.

"You look tired, Morgan," Cecil said.

"You mean he looks like shit," Sarge offered.

"You're both right, I guess. Now that we've got most of the people moved, I'm headed home. I need some sleep."

"That's a good idea. We're all probably going to head back soon. Mitch is organizing folks here in town to tend to the wounded. Doc and the staff that survived are going to do what they can for the wounded. We can live without you for a while," Sarge replied.

"Alright. I'll see you back at the ranch," I said with a wave.

I went over to the Hummer I'd driven earlier and took it back to the house. There were a lot of people in Umatilla standing in the road and looking to the south. I'm sure word was spreading, but they could clearly see the smoke that still rose into the sky from some of the buildings. A couple of people stepped out into the road, as if to stop me and talk. But I swerved around them and continued on. I wasn't in a chatting mood. I was exhausted and wanted to go climb into my bed.

As I approached Altoona, storm clouds gathered on the horizon. Rain was on the way and, as bad as it was, my first thought was that it would wash the blood and smell off the streets in town. As I passed the market, people stopped and watched as I went by. I didn't pull in. No doubt that they also had questions; and I wasn't stopping to answer theirs either. When I rolled by the bunker I waved at the guys, not even stopping there.

I parked the Hummer in front of the house and got out. Meat Head and Drake were there, tails wagging and tongues lolling. They made me smile and I knelt down to pet their heads. Drake came up, sat down in front of me and put his paw on my knee. When I reached up to scratch his ears, he pawed at my hand. He was an interesting dog and I wondered what he was like in the Before.

Meat Head rolled over on his back and I rubbed his belly as he moaned. A habit he had when he was being petted or scratched. As I was messing with the dogs, Danny walked up. He announced his presence in typical Danny manner, "Yo," was all he said.

Looking up from the dogs, I replied. "Hey, man. How's the mitt?"

He looked at his hand. Doc had done a pretty good job of sewing it back together. Yet, you couldn't help but notice the missing fingers. He worked his thumb and fingers and replied, "It's good. But every time I look at it, it's like something out of an alien movie. You know, they always had three fingers."

I smiled, "I can see that. But if you open your mouth and another little head comes out, I'm shooting you in the face."

Danny laughed, then his expression changed. "How bad was it?"

"Worse than you can imagine, buddy. All of downtown Eustis is gone. It took one hell of a pounding."

"How bad were the casualties?"

I thought about how to answer that question for a moment. "Terrible. It's hard to imagine what high explosives can do to a human body." I looked up at him and added, "I don't have to imagine anymore."

He nodded. "I know what you mean. So, what's the next move?"

I stood up and looked up into the sky. "Well, the old man is supposedly organizing a bomber strike that should wipe out the commies."

"When's that going to happen?"

"Any time. Well, I'm beat, buddy. I need some sleep. I'll see you tomorrow."

"Go get some rest. I'll catch you later."

I went into the house to find Mel sitting on the couch feeding the little limb rat. She looked up when I came in and smiled. Then the smile faded, and she wrinkled her nose.

"Hey, baby. I'm glad you're back; but you really stink. Can you go outside and take all that off, so I can wash it later?"

I looked down at myself. I was covered in soot and gore, the gore not so easily seen through the black soot. "That's probably a good idea. Sorry, I wasn't thinking. How's the little guy doing?"

Mel looked at Ruckus, holding him up in front of her face, nose to nose. In a baby voice, she said, "He's fine. Aren't you?" Looking back at me, she added, "He's eating and pooping, that's all he has to do."

"Are his eyes open yet?"

"No, it'll be another couple of weeks."

It made me smile. I don't know why. "Good. Glad he's alright." I stripped off my armor and set it on the floor beside the door before going back outside. My feet were black as coal, I didn't have the best footwear on for a day like today. And that black extended up my legs to above my knees. My shorts and shirt were also covered in various contaminates. Peeling the clothes off, I dropped them into a pile by the door and walked back inside, naked.

When I came in, Mel looked at me shocked. "Good thing the girls aren't here!"

"Oh," I replied, "I hadn't thought about that. Yeah, good thing."

As Mel got up off the couch, she said, "Go take a shower and I'll get you a glass of tea and something to eat. I'm sure you're hungry."

"Yeah, I'm hungry. But I'm really thirsty."

"Go on to the shower; you really stink. I'll bring you some water in a sec."

I nodded and headed for the bathroom. In the Before, I would turn the shower on and let it run until the hot water made it from the heater to the shower. A hot shower was one of life's greatest luxuries as far as I was concerned, one I hadn't had in some time. So, when I turned the water on in the shower, I stepped in immediately. The water was bracing, but it felt good. Using the small piece of soap, I still hadn't found another piece, I scrubbed myself clean. The water ran black down the drain and it took some time to get all the crud scraped off my body. But eventually the water ran clear down the drain and I shut it off and stepped out to towel off.

There was a glass of ice water sitting on the vanity and I took it and greedily gulped it down. It was damn cold, and good. Going into the bedroom, I found clothes laid out on the bed and another glass of tea on the nightstand. It made me smile, Mel was always looking out for me. As I consumed more tea, I remembered joking back in the day about the magic tea jug. It was magic because I could pour the last glass of tea from it, set it on the counter and come back later to find it in the fridge, full. It was a running joke between me and Mel about the tea fairies.

Clean and dressed, I came out, tea in hand and sat down on the couch. Mel was in the kitchen and I asked, "Where are the girls?"

"Little Bit is over at Danny's and the other two are down at Fred's house. They got bored and wanted to go keep her company since Aric was in town."

"I imagine he's back now. Everyone was headed home when I left. Folks from town were going to take care of the injured. I just needed some sleep."

"Eat something first, then go lie down."

She came out of the kitchen with a sausage biscuit on a plate and handed it to me. It was nice having flour and being able to make bread stuff. And I love biscuits. The sausage was from one of our hogs that Thad butchered. Spices were hard to come by, but it was still good. Really good. As I ate, Mel sat down on the couch and pulled my leg into her lap. She started to rub my foot, and it felt so good.

We didn't talk as I ate, she just rubbed my foot and calf and I enjoyed the biscuit. I was afraid to say anything because I didn't want to have to go into what we'd done. I wasn't sure how Mel would take to the thought of executing the wounded. But she never asked anything. Never said a word. When I finished the snack, Mel took the plate and said, "Go to bed for a while. You want me to wake you up later?"

I stretched. "No, let me sleep until the crack of when-the-fuck ever."

CHAPTER 3

T HE OLD MAN SAT TAPPING his foot on the floor, radio mic in one hand and a cup of coffee in the other. He stared at the radio, willing it to issue a sound. He was impatient and getting more irritated by the minute. Bone One should be on station now and he wasn't hearing anything. Just as he was raising the mic to his mouth, the speaker crackled. A calm, cool voice came over the speaker. Air Force pilots always impressed the old man with how laid back and at ease they were, no matter what was happening.

Bone One, Swamp Rat one.

"Go for Swamp Rat."

Swamp Rat, we're about three minutes out. Are your people out of the target area?

"Roger that Bone. They're ready to laze the target."

Swamp Rat, have them light it up.

"Swamp Rat Two, paint the target. Bone is in-bound."

We copy, Swamp Rat One. Target is lit.

Swamp Rat Two, get small. Get in a hole if you got one. Weapons are loose, ten seconds.

Instinctively, the old man looked at his watch. For their part, Ted whispered the weapons were on their way and they had ten seconds. Mike was holding the laser on the target and asked,

"Why are we doing this? They can fly those things through an open window. Why the hell are we lying our here in weeds?"

"The GPS system has been compromised. There are gaps in coverage and we don't want one of those gaps to appear when we have JDAMs on their way in. This is foolproof." Ted thought about what he said and added, "Even with you running the thing."

There came a sudden tearing sound, followed immediately by several intense explosions. The auto auction disappeared in a massive cloud of dust, smoke and flame. All six of the weapons impacted within a fraction of a second of one another.

Bone One, all weapons on target.

Roger that, Swamp Rat.

"Holy shit," Dalton said absent mindedly.

Ted looked over and asked, "You never seen one before?"

"No. First time. And that shockwave, it compressed my chest and popped my ears."

"Yeah, shoulda told you to keep your mouth open. You might get some dirt in it, but it beats that pressure squeezing your head."

The plan was simple. Bone One would drop its payload. When the target came back into view, Ted would do a damage assessment. If the strike wasn't one hundred percent successful, Bone Two would come in and finish off whatever was left. Ted was watching the dust settle, waiting for the visibility to improve. After several minutes, the dust settled enough that Ted could make out some figures moving in the target area.

Picking up the radio, he keyed the mic. *Bone Two, we still have hostiles at the target site.*

Roger that, Swamp Rat. We'll be in position in about seven minutes.

Roger, Bone. Bring the hate.

Meanwhile, Dalton was watching the target location through the scope of the M1A. As visibility improved, he was able to make out individuals moving about the carnage created by the strike. That is until the rifle barked, scaring Ted.

"What the hell are you doing?" Ted practically shouted.

Without moving the weapon from his head, Dalton replied. "He said it was open season on anyone left standing after the strike."

"There's another strike inbound. You need to stop that shit."

The rifle barked again, and Dalton replied, "This is just confusing them even more. They're already more befuddled than a twelve-year-old boy in a whore house. They can't tell where the shots are coming from."

Swamp Rat, weapons inbound. You've got about twelve seconds.

Roger that, Bone. Thank you.

The Russian and Cuban troops that survived the initial strike were trying to get their shit together. They hadn't yet wrapped their heads around just what happened and, as a result, were out in the open trying to aid the wounded and recover equipment. Because of this, when the next flight of weapons streaked in, there was nothing they could do, and they fell like blades of grass before the scythe.

Good bombs, Bone Two. Good bombs.

Copy that, Swamp Rat. Good luck.

Swamp Rat Two, Swamp Rat one. Maintain your current position. We're coming in with the green machine to clean up.

Copy that. Standing by.

Mel sat on the edge of the bed and woke me up. I rolled over and looked at her. "Sorry to wake you up, but Linus is here and wants to talk to you."

Sitting up, I rubbed my eyes and tried to get my head together. I was groggy. "How long have I been asleep?"

"You slept all night. I was going to let you sleep until you woke up as you had requested, but he just showed up."

Swinging my legs out of the bed, I pulled on a pair of pants, not bothering to put on any drawers. Pulling a shirt on as I walked out of the bedroom, I found Sarge standing in the living room.

"What's up?" I asked.

"We need to roll. The bombers hit the commies. We're going to take our tank down there and make sure there's no one left alive." The old man looked at Mel when he made the last statement.

"How'd it go?" I asked.

"Looks like we smoked their asses. But we need to go in on the ground and make sure. The guys are still there. Dalton is plinking at a couple he's seen moving around. But we'll go in with the big green machine and wipe out what's left."

I nodded. "Alright Let me get my boots on and grab my kit."

I picked up my boots and sat on the couch. Mel came out of the bedroom and handed me a pair of socks. "Thanks, babe." After getting dressed and collecting my gear, I took Mel's hand.

"I'll be back when we're done. This shouldn't be a big deal. The bombers have already smashed them."

She leaned in and kissed me. "If this is what we have to do to live peacefully, then go do it. Just be careful."

"I won't let him get hurt, Mel." Sarge said.

The look on her face said she didn't believe him. But neither of them said anything about it. As I headed for the door, Little Bit ran up and handed me a large travel mug. "Here, daddy; here's some tea for you."

Taking the cup, I rubbed her head and said, "Thank you, sweetie; this is just what I needed."

The tank wasn't parked in the yard. It was too big to get through the gate and sat on the street out front idling. Behind it sat an MRAP and I could see Thad behind the wheel.

"Who's driving that thing?" I asked, pointing at the tank.

"Jamie. She has to drive everything, or she gets pissed. Ian's in there too and I'll be on the gun. You're going to ride with Thad and man the turret in the truck. Perez and Aric are there as well. We're going to set up on the overpass where we can look down onto the target. Anything that moves will get hit. You look for personnel and I'll handle vehicles."

"Works for me," I replied as I broke away to head to the truck.

I went to the back and climbed in. Thad turned and looked back at me, that typical smile spread across his face. "Mornin', Sheriff."

"You ready to go mop these assholes up?" I asked.

The smile faded, "Let's get it over with." As he spoke, the tank in front of us lurched and began to roll. Thad turned and put the big truck in gear and we followed it out onto highway nineteen.

Jamie had the pedal to the metal and it was all the truck could do to keep up with her. I was surprised at just how fast the big green machine could go.

"Damn, Thad. She's going to leave us in the dust."

Thad was coaxing every bit he could manage out of the big truck. "Naw, she ain't getting away."

We flew past the market in Altoona and were soon approaching the one in Umatilla. Unlike Altoona, I actually had a chance to look out here and saw quite a crowd. The people stopped what they were doing and pointed as we passed them at nearly sixty miles an hour.

Ted's voice crackled over the radio. *Swamp Rat one, there are a couple pieces of armor starting to move around. We've stopped taking pot shots at them until you arrive.*

Roger that, Sarge replied. *Just stay out of sight until we get there. Tell Dalton to lay off that Springfield for now. He'll get plenty of chances later.*

"You ready for this?" Aric asked.

With a shrug, I replied, "It needs to be done. I want to be able to sleep at night."

Dalton had already laid the rifle aside. He knew what was coming and didn't want their position discovered before the real firepower arrived. In the meantime, he busied himself by sharpening his kukri. Mike was lying beside him and lowered the binoculars he was looking through.

"What the hell are you going to do with that?" Mike asked.

Dalton shrugged, "No sense in wasting ammo."

Mike looked at the blade, then back at Dalton, "You just gonna chop their heads off?"

"Whatever it takes to get the job done." Mike shook his head and returned his attention to the binoculars.

"When the old man gets here and starts tossing HE rounds into them, we'll move in. Him blasting shit with that gun will distract their attention," Ted said.

"This is bullshit. He did this on purpose," Mike grumbled.

"Did what?" Ted asked.

Mike waved his hand around. "This. Got me out here lying

in the fucking weeds while he drives my tank up and starts blasting shit with it. Bullshit I tell you."

———✶——✶——✶——✶——✶——

We followed the old man down 441, both vehicles were being pushed to their max. I sat in the back for a long time, then decided to climb up into the turret. The truck we were in had a mark nineteen grenade launcher on it. I liked the weapon and took a few minutes to make sure it was ready to go. I was struck by the situation, sitting in the top of this truck with a weapon like this in my hands. The world was certainly getting stranger. I watched the thick column of smoke that was rising in the sky ahead of us. It made me feel good to know it was communist equipment burning this time.

The tank didn't go up the on-ramp to the toll road. Instead, it passed under it and went up the off-ramp. In this way, we'd be on the same side of the road as the auto auction. I slapped the top cover closed on the weapon; it was ready to go, and I dipped down inside the truck. Grabbing a helmet, I pulled it on my head and strapped it to my chin. There was a good possibility of taking fire and I wanted all the protection I could get.

As we bounced down the road, my pulse began to quicken. I hated this part, the waiting for shit to start. The anticipation was always nerve racking; and in a way, I just wanted to get on with it. While at the same time, I just wanted to go home. But this had to be done and I wanted some revenge as well. I was already thinking of walking through the area and putting wounded Russian and Cuban soldiers down. Of course, it wasn't going to be that easy. They weren't just going to lie there and let me shoot 'em.

Two minutes, Sarge said over the radio.

Leaning down, I looked at Aric. "Wake Perez up. The show's about to start."

"I'm awake. You can't sleep for shit in these things," he replied.

I looked forward and saw the turret on the tank start to swing to the left as it slowed. Thad slowed as well and soon we were just creeping along. I couldn't see the area fully when the tank fired the first time. The blast surprised me, and I jumped as the spent casing was ejected out the rear of the gun, landing on the road with a clang.

Poking my head back up, I looked out and could now see the compound. There was an odd tracked vehicle with flames spewing from the top of it down there. I assumed it was the target of the shell just fired.

Thad, Sarge called, *pull around us so Morgan can get that grenade launcher into action.*

The truck jerked, and we rolled around the tank. Now, I could see the entire facility. There were people moving around down there and I swung the weapon around and fired a shot. It fell short and I adjusted and fired another. It landed close to a group of three men and they all went down. Having their range, I fired three more and watched as the grenades impacted around them, tossing them around like rags.

I was scanning for targets, looking for anyone moving and turning the mark nineteen on them. The weapon was amazing and would spit grenades with surprising speed and accuracy. We started taking some small arms fire; I could hear the rounds as they passed overhead. The cracking and popping was like that of an angry insect and I ignored it.

Aric and Thad were calling out targets for us as well. If they saw anyone move, they'd let me know. Perez was sitting in the back by the door, his carbine resting between his legs. He was smoking the short butt of a cigarette. A very short butt.

"You out of those things?" Aric asked him.

Perez looked at the stub in his fingers and nodded. Then he smiled, "But Russians like to smoke."

Aric smiled and shook his head, "That's why you're here."

"Just a side benefit," Perez replied with a shrug.

Another armored vehicle rounded a corner. The rear doors on it swung wildly as the driver maneuvered the bulky machine. The tank thundered again, and the round missed, impacting a car. But the old man wasn't waiting and immediately fired another. This one found its mark and blasted the turret from the machine. It rolled forward as flames shot out of every opening on it.

I saw a puff in the distance and immediately turned the weapon on it. The RPG fired from the position whistled past the tank. The gunner wouldn't get another chance as I dropped four grenades on him.

"Aric! I need ammo!" I called down.

Aric, having cans ready with their lids removed and waiting, handed one up. I slid it into the tray and opened the top cover and got the weapon reloaded. As I was doing so, Sarge called on the radio and told us to make our way down to the compound. Aric prepared several more cans for me before moving to the rear of the truck. As we began to make our way down to the lot, he and Perez sat by the door, their carbines ready.

It took us a little maneuvering to get down into the lot. The auto auction is on a large piece of open land. This is good in that it doesn't provide a lot of cover. Bad, in that this lot is full of cars which do offer the surviving commies some concealment. But the bombs Bone One and Two dropped had set most of the cars ablaze. It was kind of odd to watch the fire as it moved across the acres of parked cars, like some kind of surreal forest fire. Only instead of a forest of trees, it was a lot full of cars.

Periodically, the big gun would fire. It's hard to describe what a gun of that caliber going off is like. There's the noise of course. An ear shattering boom that is followed by a concussive wave that takes the air from your lungs. It compresses your ears and you can feel it in your lungs. Dust is kicked up from every surface for a large area around the gun. It just jumps into the air. Then the round impacts its target. There's a flash and another bang, and debris is flung into the air. Sometimes, stuff was set on fire as the old man was firing HE rounds at general targets. I witnessed him hit two more pieces of armor. For these, he fired AP rounds, causing hunks of armor to fly into the air and fountains of flame to erupt from the stricken vehicles.

On more than one, I saw wounded men roll out of the armor. They were either in flames or their clothes were smoking. All of them were severely wounded. I took no pity on them and added a couple of the forty-millimeter grenades to insure they were eliminated. The entire time, I envisioned the carnage left behind in Eustis. Every one of these men here was getting what they deserved.

Throughout the smoke and flames, I could occasionally see figures moving, running. These men weren't interested in mounting an organized defense. They were trying to get the hell out of the target area. Whenever I saw movement, I would fire at it. And I got really good at it in short order and would see bodies cartwheeling through the air. Others would simply collapse where they stood. And it felt good. I got a rush every time I saw them fall.

After a while, the radio crackled. It was Sarge. *Teddy, start moving in from your side. We're going to work in from our side. I don't want a single one of these bastards to make it out.*

Roger that, Top. We're moving.

Thad, start working your way through the lot. Morgan, you kill anyone you see.

"With pleasure," I replied.

"You ready to move?" Thad asked over his shoulder.

"Let's get this over with," I replied.

Thad put the truck in gear and began to move through the shattered remains of the auto auction. I ducked down and grabbed my carbine to have it in the turret with me. The mark nineteen was a fantastic weapon but wasn't much good for close-in work. And I fully anticipated having to engage some close targets.

Dalton, Ted and Mike emerged from their hide and started to move towards the auction. The three men spread out, keeping about ten meters between them and rifles at the ready. They entered the east side of the compound and immediately encountered a group of four Cuban soldiers running for their lives. They'd dropped their rifles and gear and were simply trying to get out of Dodge. As soon as Dalton saw them, he started firing his AK. Mike and Ted quickly joined in, and the four men were cut down. They were the first of many to follow.

While the airstrike had done an amazing job, there were still people alive, though only a couple dozen. But we had to exterminate them. That's right, exterminate. What else can you do to people that commit such crimes as shelling a town full of civilians?

As they moved through the yard, the men would come across wounded Russian and Cuban soldiers. Dalton didn't waste ammo on the wounded. Many of them would ask for help. He came across a Cuban soldier with severe wounds, his left leg blasted away above the knee and shrapnel wounds to his abdomen.

He held a hand up and begged, "Por favor, ayúdame."

Dalton leaned over and whispered, "Deberías haberte quedado en Cuba." And with a flick of his wrist, he cut the man's throat from ear to ear.

And that's how it went for the rest of the day. We moved through the compound, dispatching the wounded. There were a couple of firefights. Thankfully, the incoming fire was ineffective, and we didn't suffer any casualties. On those couple of occasions, I used my carbine. I'd dismounted and was walking through the lot looking for men that needed to be put down. But I wasn't using my carbine for that work. Instead, I used the tomahawk that Dalton had made for me. It saved ammo and helped quench the rage building inside me.

But killing a man with an edged weapon isn't a clean business, and by late afternoon, I was covered in blood. I hadn't noticed it, but when I came upon Dalton, he paused and looked at me. Reaching into his pocket, he took out a rag and handed it to me, saying, "Wipe your face."

I took it and did as he said and was shocked at what I saw. "Damn," I said and looked down at myself. I looked awful. I was covered in blood from my boots to my face. Even my carbine was dripping blood. As I mopped at the blood, trying to remove it, Sarge walked up.

"Holy hell, Morgan. You look like shit. What the hell have you been doing? You're supposed to kill them, not wear 'em like a suit."

I looked down at the tomahawk and replied, "I have been. It's not easy."

The old man was gripping his Colt and glanced at it, "Like

hell. Just shoot the bastards in the head. It's quick and clean. What you're doing is a little fucked up." A couple of shots rang out not far from us and I looked over to see Jamie standing over a prone body. She was calmly changing magazines in her rifle, taking the time to put the spent one in a dump pouch on her belt.

Looking down at the hawk again, I said, "I guess you're right." And I wiped the bloody weapon on my pants before tucking it back into my belt and drawing my Springfield.

For the rest of the day, I used my pistol. There's a kind of disconnect when using a handgun for the task. With the hawk, it's personal. You have to get close and use physical force to drive the blade into the man. And it often took more than one blow. Not that I cared at the moment. But Sarge's words pulled me back from the brink. Another advantage to using the pistol, it sped up the process and I was able to move much faster, and it didn't require nearly the same amount of energy.

By early evening, the shooting had died down. The sun was dipping towards the horizon, but the fires provided plenty of light, though the smoke did obscure it, adding to the surreal scene. I was tired, bone tired, in a weary kind of way. Stopping to lean against a burned-out car, Thad walked up beside me.

I looked at him and asked, "How are you holding up, buddy?"

"It needed to be done. I didn't enjoy it, I didn't hate it. It was just something that needed to happen."

I nodded, "That's a good way to look at it. I think I'll use it."

"I'm worried about you," Thad said softly and shook his head. "We're all angry, but this," he pointed at me and the horror covering me, "this isn't healthy. You going to be alright?"

I nodded. "Yeah. I was caught up in it for a minute. But

Dalton and Sarge pulled me back from the brink, I guess you could say."

"Good. But I'm going to keep an eye on you. You're my friend, Morgan and I'm worried about you."

"Thank you, Thad," I said and offered my hand. He looked at it, hesitating. Then I looked at it. There was blood all over it, so I wiped it on my pants and offered it again. This time, he smiled and took it as I asked, "Better?"

"Much better."

Sarge, Ted, Mike and Dalton wandered over to us. Sarge looked around at the carnage that surrounded us. "Looks like it's done. I think this is finally over."

"There's a shit load of material we need to recover here," Dalton said.

"I'm not fucking with it today. It's getting late and I'm tired," I said.

Aric, Ian and Jamie walked up. "What are we going to do with all this shit lying around?" Jamie asked. "There's a mountain of hardware here."

"I guess we'll come back tomorrow and collect it all. There's shit here we don't have any need for. But we should at least secure it so no one else gets their hands on it," Sarge replied.

"We hope we have no need for it," Dalton said.

"Indeed," Thad added.

Sarge nodded and said, "Alright then, let's head back to the ranch. We'll come back tomorrow with some manpower and trucks to haul all this out of here."

"We can't just leave all this here overnight. Someone needs to stay behind and make sure no one tries to sneak in and take any of it," Jamie replied.

"Any volunteers?" The old man asked.

"We'll stay," Ian said. "With all the racket that's gone on

here tonight, I doubt anyone will come in. Just leave us all the water and MREs you have. Ammo too, just in case."

"I'll stay too. Perez is going to stay as well," Aric added.

I laughed, "He's busy picking through the bodies for smokes, isn't he?"

Aric nodded with a smile. Jamie took a pack of Russian smokes from her pocket and lit one. "They've got a lot of them."

Sarge nodded. "Alright. We'll be back in the morning. You guys just hold the fort until we get back."

"I'm staying too," Dalton said. "I think there are still a couple of guys sneaking around out there, and I want to find them."

"There are a couple of cases of MREs in the truck. I'll go grab you one," Thad said.

"I'll help you," I added. "There's a jug of water in the back as well. And ammo."

Thad and I walked off towards where we had left the truck. It was sitting with the rear door open, just as we had left it. I grabbed a Jerry can of water and sling-bag full of mags and hung it over my shoulder. Thad grabbed the case of meals and we started back towards the group.

"I hope this is the end of it," I said as I adjusted the strap of the bag on my shoulder.

"I pray to God it is too, Morgan. It just seems to be a never-ending nightmare."

I certainly understood what he meant. "Me too. I just want to try and get things back to normal. To improve life a little." I held the carbine up and added, "I'm tired of having to use this. I wish I could put it down and never pick it up again."

With his free hand, Thad reached over and patted my back. "That day will come. We're getting closer to it. This, as bad as it seems, is a big step in that direction."

I looked around at the burning, smoking ruins. "You know, you're right. This really should be the end of major issues. I mean, what else could there be? You know, on this level."

Thad's smile wasn't there this time. But he wasn't particularly distraught either. "All we can do is keep going. Keep putting one foot in front of the other. I learned that a long time ago."

I knew what he meant, what he was talking about. But I wasn't about to bring it up. "You're right, buddy. What's the alternative? Sit down and wait to die? That's not going to happen. Like Jeff Goldblum says in Jurassic Park, *life will find a way*. That's what we're doing now. Just finding a way."

Now, Thad smiled. "I like that movie. I'd like to watch it." Then he looked me over. "When we get home, come to my house. I don't want Mel and the girls to see you like this. Leave these clothes at my house and I'll wash them for you." He grimaced and shook his head, "You look like something out of a chainsaw horror movie."

I looked down at myself. He was right of course. I did look horrible. Nodding, I replied. "Thanks, man. I'll do that. I didn't really want to go home looking like this either."

We dropped the ammo, water and food off, said our goodbyes and headed back to the truck. Walking back, I asked Thad if he wanted me to drive. "No," he replied and wrinkled his nose. "You'll get that gore all over the driver's seat. You sit in the back. I'll drive."

I smiled. "If you insist."

He laughed, "I do! Now get in the back."

I climbed in the back of the truck and stretched out as best I could. I felt the truck move and then quickly fell asleep. I woke up when Thad opened the rear door. It startled me, and I sat up in confusion before I realized where I was.

"We back already?" I asked.

"You been back here snoring like a freight train taking a gravel road," Thad replied with a laugh. "Come inside and change your clothes."

While we were talking, Mary came out of the house. It was dark, and she carried a small LED lantern. Seeing her, Thad brightened. She came up and put her arm around him. He leaned over and kissed the top of her head.

"Morgan is going to come inside and change his clothes. Can you find something for him to wear in the stuff we put away?"

"Of course," Mary replied. "Come with me, Morgan. Let's get you out of those dirty clothes. You leave those here and I'll wash them for you."

"You don't have to do that," I replied as I took my gear off.

"Nonsense. It's no bother. I know you don't want to go home looking like this."

"Thank you," I replied. I wanted to give her a hug but didn't want to touch her with the clothes I had on.

I went inside with her and she told me to go to the bathroom and take my clothes off. I did as she said and tossed them into the tub. I took a moment to wash my face and arms and looked considerably better. Mary knocked at the door and I cracked it open, so she could hand me a t-shirt and a pair of jeans. I had no idea who they belonged to, or rather, who they *had* belonged to. But it didn't matter. They were clean, and they fit, and I quickly dressed and came out.

Mary smiled when she saw me and said, "You look much better."

"I feel better. You don't have to wash that stuff. I'll come by tomorrow and pick it up and wash it myself."

"It's no bother. I'll take care of it. I know you don't want Mel seeing you like this. Just go home and get some rest."

I walked outside and found Thad getting his things out of the truck. I thanked him for looking out for me and for driving while I slept. He told me not to worry about it. We agreed to get together in the morning for what we expected to be another long day. I left Thad and Mary, giving her a hug now that I was cleaner, and headed home.

It was dark, and I could hear the Stryker moving around somewhere towards the old man's place. I smiled, thinking of Mikey driving it around, probably still pissed he missed the opportunity to fire the big gun at real targets. I was looking forward to going back to the auction tomorrow, just so I could screw with him about it.

The dogs met me in the road. Meat Head and Drake were off on their nightly patrol, I guessed. I took a minute to rub their heads as they sat with tongues lolling in the road. But they were anxious to get on with whatever it was they were up to, and they quickly disappeared into the night. I envied them in a way. They came and went as they wanted with no thought of tomorrow. Or so I thought. We still fed them every day, they weren't going hungry by any means. Yet, every night, they would disappear and return before the dawn.

While out walking, I had to pass my house. Aric stayed at the site and I needed to let Fred know. I'm sure she was sitting up waiting on him. It was a bit of a walk to the house that she and Aric shared. I could have driven down, grabbing an ATV or even the Suburban, but I was enjoying the time alone. Walking in the dark quiet of night felt good. The only sound was my boots on the road. I looked up at all the stars. To imagine all those stars could have planets around them just like our sun was amazing. What did those planets look like? What kind of life lived on them. I always liked astronomy, just wasn't smart enough to get into it.

The house was dark as I approached it. Getting closer, I could finally see a little light coming from what I assumed was the bedroom. I was relieved that Fred was probably still awake. I stepped up onto the porch and knocked on the door. There was a thud, then a quick shuffling inside as the light moved from room to room. The door jerked open and Fred was there with a smile on her face. Seeing me, it faded as fear washed over her.

Realizing what she was thinking, I reacted quickly, "No, no, no, Fred. Everything is fine. I just wanted to let you know that Aric is staying out overnight. We have to secure the site until the morning and he stayed behind."

Her face changed, and she wiped a tear from her eye. "You scared me. I thought," she paused, "I don't know what I thought."

I felt bad, then had to evaluate her response to my appearance. Does everyone think of me as the angel of death? I mean, I get it, but shit, I hope not. "Well, don't worry. He's not there alone and everything will be fine. He'll be back tomorrow. I just didn't want you sitting up all night waiting on him."

She smiled. "Thank you for that."

"You need anything?"

Fred looked back over her shoulder, then back at me. "No. I'm good. Jess and Kay were here a little while ago. I guess I'll go to bed. I was sitting up waiting on Aric."

"Alright. If you need anything, just let me know. You have the radio, right?" We'd given Aric a radio to keep at his house. He lived the farthest away from everyone else and we wanted him to have a way to call for help should the need arise.

She held it up. "Right here. I'll be fine. I'm going to bed."

"Alright then. Good night." I replied and waved as I stepped off the porch and headed home.

When I arrived at the house, all was dark. I was expecting

Mel to be sitting up waiting on me but was happy when I saw she wasn't. It meant she'd gone to bed and hadn't sat up all night worrying. I came in quietly and closed the door behind me. Using my flashlight, I made my way to the bedroom and went into the bathroom to take a shower. I didn't want her to see me in my current state. I may have changed clothes, but I was still a mess. The water was cold but felt good. I lingered for a bit, watching as red water swirled around the drain before finally disappearing. I scrubbed my hands and fingers clean, getting dried blood out from under my fingernails.

With the shower done, I got out and toweled off. Slipping into the bedroom, I got into bed, thinking Mel was asleep. But she reached over and grabbed my arm.

"How'd it go?" She asked softly.

"It's done. We'll go back tomorrow to collect the gear so no one else gets their hands on it. There's a lot of military hardware there and it could be bad if the wrong folks got a hold of it."

"Anyone hurt?"

I patted her hand, "No. The bombers did all the work."

She yawned and replied, "Good."

CHAPTER 4

I WOKE UP EARLY THE NEXT morning, knowing the old man would probably want to get started as soon as possible. I slipped out of the bedroom, trying not to wake Mel. I wanted a little time to have a glass of tea and sit and collect my thoughts. I went into the fridge for some ice, what's tea without ice, and found the partial can of Cope there. *What the hell,* I thought and took it out. Cracking the lid, I saw it was almost full. This was the last can I'd ever see and thought I'd share it.

Taking my glass with me, I headed over to Danny's. He was already up, his usual way, and sitting on the porch. He waved when he saw me, and I stepped up onto the porch and dropped into a rocker beside him.

"What's the word?" He asked by way of greeting.

I took a deep breath of the warm moist morning air. It was going to be a hot day. "I guess we'll go back over there today and take all the dangerous shit out."

"How'd that go yesterday?"

"It was nothing. Those bombers really did a number on them. Most of them were too shocked to do anything more than try and run. They just died trying."

"How many were there? Still alive I mean."

Rocking my head from side to side trying to do some

math, I replied, "Little more than two dozen maybe. Lots of wounded though."

Danny looked out across the yard, watching the chickens as they pecked for their breakfast in the pine needles, and he thought for a minute. "Maybe this will be the end of it all."

Reaching into my pocket, I took out the can and opened it. Danny's eyes were immediately on it. I took a pinch and passed the can to him. "Where the hell did this come from?" He asked. Then, feeling the cold still in the can, he added, "How long has this been in your freezer?"

"Since we got back from that trip I guess. I'd forgot about it, found it this morning. I thought you'd like a pinch."

He took a pinch and put it in. "Man, that's good. Damn, I miss this."

I was looking at his hand. He was holding the can in his injured hand. It looked odd, missing the fingers. But he looked like he was adapting to it. "How's the claw?" I asked jokingly.

He held the disfigured hand up and looked at it. "Not bad, actually. It's not quite the handicap I thought it was going to be. Kind of funny really, my hand just adapted to it pretty quickly." He replied as he dropped the can into his shirt pocket.

"That's good; now give me the can back." He laughed and handed it over. "You got anything you can put some of this in?"

"Oh yeah," he said as he got up and headed into the house. He returned with an empty can and handed it to me.

"You saving these for sentimental reasons? Or your hoarding mind just not letting you throw them away?"

As I was splitting the can between the two, he replied, "Both I guess," and laughed.

Capping his can, I handed it back. "That's what I thought," I said with a smile.

We sat on the porch for a while enjoying the buzz from the

nicotine. Not something you experience when you do the crap every day. But a long break like this brings it back. After a bit, I asked, "How are the kids?"

"They're good. They don't ask about their parents anymore. I guess they've accepted it. Of course, Bobby was hard on them. But there's enough people around here and everyone checks on them. They're doing well."

I nodded and asked, "How about you?"

There was a long pause. After a moment, he replied, "It hurt you know, a lot. But there wasn't anything I could do about it and so many people have lost someone. I guess it's just the way of it now."

"We need to change the way. We can't just accept the fact that this is the way things are now. I can't, won't."

Danny nodded. "You're right. I'm really hoping that what you guys did last night changes things for us. Something has to."

"Yes, it does." As I replied, I heard a diesel engine rumble to life. "Sounds like the festivities are about to start. Guess I need to go get my shit together."

"You guys be careful," He said as I got up from the chair.

Going back to the house, I found Mel in the kitchen, preparing breakfast. She was at the Butterfly stove and looked up when I came in. "We're now out of sausage. This is the last of it."

"We have hogs. I'll get with Thad and talk to him about butchering one," I replied.

"We have plenty of eggs. Just no meat."

"Do we have any bacon?" Little Bit asked.

Her sisters laughed, and Taylor said, "Mom just said we didn't have any meat. Bacon is meat."

Little Bit smiled and rocked in her seat. "Bacon's not meat; it's bacon! I wish we had some."

I tussled her hair as I walked past her. "I'll talk to Thad and see if we can make some."

A smile spread across her face and she asked, "You can make it?"

"Maybe," I replied. "We'll try."

"What are you doing today?" Mel asked.

"We're going back to get all the hardware at the auto auction. Those Russians and Cubans had a huge load of stuff and we don't want the wrong people to get their hands on it."

"Is there anyone there?"

"Yeah, a couple of our people stayed there last night. Do you not remember our conversation when I came to bed?"

Still looking at the pan of eggs she was cooking, Mel replied, "Nope. Sure don't."

Laughing, I replied, "Of course not. I was talking and we both know your brain can't detect that particular sound pattern."

Glancing at the girls and seeing them not paying attention, she gave me the finger. I smiled and stepped over and kissed her cheek. "That's my girl."

"You want to eat before you go?"

"Sure! I'm starving."

In honor of the last of the sausage this morning, Mel made tortillas. She prepared me a couple of burritos with fresh tomato. Thank you, Thad. I got my gear together as she fixed them and stopped by the fridge to refill my tea before heading for the door.

"Can we come with you?" Taylor called out as I gripped the door knob.

I had to remove the burrito I was holding in my mouth and looked back. "Sorry, but no. I'll be back later today." She looked deflated but didn't try and argue with me. "Hey," I said, "I've got a project I need your help with later. When I get home, I'll show you what it is. We'll have to go out into the woods for something to help all the injured in town."

Her very unenthusiastic reply was simply, "Ok."

I needed to do something with the girls. They were bored and getting antsy. They weren't little girls anymore and I shouldn't be treating them like they were. It's a hard thing to face, your kids growing up. All those memories of them when they were young are hard to let go of. But there are new memories waiting to be made as they grow. Hopefully, they will get better than some of the ones we've made recently.

Knowing there was a lot of stuff to bring back, I hopped into the Suburban. With a little prayer, I turned the key. The old Cummins rumbled to life and I smiled and took another bite of burrito while I headed towards the gate.

Thad was out in front of his place as I pulled into the drive. He was beside the little red truck and I called out to him. "You taking that today?"

"Yeah. We might need the extra room."

I waved, "Alright. I'll see you at the old man's place."

As I turned onto the road of the old man's place, I was greeted with a fog of blue smoke. The tank sat in the road idling as well as the only remaining two-ton truck and a Hummer. It looked like there were a lot of vehicles headed to town. The problem was drivers. Sarge stood in the road with Jess and Wallner and two other Guardsmen. I assumed these were our drivers.

"Is this all we have?" I asked as I walked up to the old man. He was leaning against the Hummer, drinking coffee.

He looked around and nodded, "I reckon it's all we need."

"Of course, it is. I'm here," Jess said.

Then Doc came out of the house with a pack slung over his shoulder. I smiled and nodded in his direction, "Here comes your boyfriend."

Jess looked back over her shoulder, then back at me and gave me the finger. "Don't be an ass," she added.

I shrugged, "You can deny it all you want."

"Knock it off you two," the old man barked. "We ain't got time for this shit. It's time to get on the road." As he spoke, Thad pulled up. Sarge looked at the little pick-up and my Suburban and asked, "You two planning on driving those?"

I nodded. "Looked to me like there was a load of shit there that needed to be hauled back. I figured the more we had, the better."

Sarge nodded, "Probably a good idea. Let's load up and get on the road. Jess, you drive the Hummer. Wallner, get one of your people in the two-ton and the rest of you in the Stryker with me. Everyone, keep your radios on and pay attention. I've already talked to Teddy, and he said there are no surprises waiting for us. They didn't have any problems last night, so this shouldn't be any trouble. We'll get the shit loaded, blow what we don't take and head back."

Everyone loaded into their respective vehicles and we moved out with me in the lead. The old man didn't want the Stryker at the head of the column and most of the others didn't know where we were going. So, I was at the head of the line of vehicles as we passed through Altoona. The market was bustling this morning. I'd noticed in recent weeks that the markets were getting busier with more and more in the way of offerings.

Food, naturally, was one of the most commonly traded commodities. But other things were showing up as well. Clothes and shoes were becoming a big seller as people wore out the cheap disposable footwear that was so common in the Before. Boots were highly sought after, and a person could just about name their price for a high-quality pair.

But I was also struck by another item on display that was

becoming more common. In each of the markets there was generally a knot of two or three young, and sometimes not so young, women offering their personal services. I wasn't at all happy about seeing this particular activity and thought it was something that would have to be addressed. Or maybe not.

Prostitution is often called the oldest profession in the world; and for the moment, it wasn't a problem. They were consensual encounters between two people. For certain, we would not tolerate anyone being forced into the sex trade. It was something I was torn over. I certainly wouldn't want my daughters doing it. But in some cases, what else would these women do? They're probably trying to feed a family or at least their kids. It was definitely something that needed to be addressed, one way or another.

But that was for another day. There was another task at hand today. I blew the horn on the truck when we passed Baker and her people. They were in Umatilla working on the lines. Baker waved, and I saw Terry look over his shoulder from the bucket. He was cutting a side-line with a pair of ratcheting cutters made just for aerial powerlines. These lines aren't just aluminum as they appear. There's a steel support cable in the center of them to help hold the weight and they will positively destroy conventional cable cutters if used.

Leaving Umatilla behind us, my mood changed. Driving into Eustis wasn't like it used to be. It wasn't something I wanted to do. But we had to pass through town, through what was left of it at least. The column had to slow to navigate the cratered streets and piles of debris. It reminded me of scenes from Middle Eastern cities during the seemingly never-ending wars. Burnt out shells of cars. Shoes, something that always struck me for some reason, lying in the road.

I don't know what it is about seeing a shoe in the road like that; it gets to me. Maybe it's the fact it's usually just *a* shoe. The thought that it had been on someone's foot until it was blasted away. Or they ran out of them in sheer terror as they tried to get away from the hell that was raining down on them. The shoes I saw today weren't on a video from Iraq. They were right here in my town and they only served to worsen the feeling.

Eustis was disturbingly quiet. I only saw a couple of people on our ride through town. Eustis was normally bustling with people. The lakeshore was always crowded with people fishing or working nets, gathering water or tending to other daily tasks. But the worst site was the armory. A pile of blackened twisted metal was all that remained. As I looked at what was left of a building I'd been into many times, all I could see in my mind was Sheffield and Livingston's faces.

A sense of relief washed over me as we made our way out of the downtown area. The rest of the ride was uneventful, relaxing even. As we passed through Zellwood, I saw a number of people. They were friendly, if nervous at the sight of the odd convoy of vehicles. After a short ride to the auto auction, it was time to get to work.

We pulled up to what was left of the auction building. Everyone was gathered up there, except for Dalton and Mike. I imagined Dalton was still out looking for Russian souvenirs, and there's no telling what the hell Mike was up to. The tank rolled to a stop and the old man appeared out the top. Ted walked towards him with a devilish grin on his face.

"I've got something for you," Ted said as he shook the old man's hand.

Sarge looked around, "Yeah? What's that?"

Ted whistled, and Dalton appeared from the ruins of the building. But he wasn't alone. Mike was with him; and between the two of them was another man, his hands bound, and a piece of cloth tied around his head.

As they approached, Ted held his hand out in a welcoming gesture. "I'd like to introduce you to Colonel Aleksei Vodovatov."

"Well no shit?" Sarge growled.

Dalton tore the blindfold off the man's eyes. He blinked and squinted against the early morning sun. Sarge took a couple of steps towards the man, inspecting his uniform. After a moment, he said, "He's not wearing a Colonel's uniform."

"Yeah," Ted replied and held out a small card. "But his ID says he's a Colonel."

Sarge took the ID and inspected it. Then he smiled broadly and said, "So you changed uniforms, huh? Think that was going to help you out? Or were you afraid the actions you ordered against our little town would come to bite you in the ass?" The man didn't reply. He just stared directly back at the old man. "Does he speak English?"

"Oh, he does," Dalton replied. Then he leaned in close to the Colonel and said, "Otvechayte cheloveku, ili ya slomayu vashiyaysta."

The Colonel gave Dalton a sideways glance, obviously considering what he'd just heard. After a moment, he returned his gaze to the old man. His back straightened, and he replied in perfect English with a Russian accent, "Yes," he looked Sarge over for an indication of rank, "Sorry, but I do not see any rank insignia."

"I'm a Colonel too."

The man smiled, "Colonel, then good. I did change my uniform. Most of your people would not know our insignia at all. But when we were hit by the bombers we knew we were dealing with regular military. Not a bunch of civilian rabble."

"Civilian rabble like the ones you killed in your Grad attack?" I asked.

The Colonel looked me up and down. His eyes stopped on the star on my chest and he asked, "And you are, cowboy?"

"I'm the county Sheriff."

The Colonel was confused and looked at Dalton. In reply, Dalton muttered, "Shef politsii."

The Colonel smiled and nodded. "Ah, yes, you are, how you say, police man?" I nodded. "Well then, I will address the Colonel. This is not for local—," he stumbled for the correct word and looked over at Dalton and said something I couldn't hear.

"Bureaucrat," Dalton replied.

"Yes, bureaucrat."

"Sorry, Ivan. But you will have to deal with me," I replied.

He ignored me and looked at Sarge. "Well, Colonel, are you the one in charge of this—" he paused and sought the proper word again, "group?"

"Hey, Ivan." I said. He ignored me, so I repeated it. When he ignored me the second time, I delivered a vicious slap to his face and shouted, "Suka!" I don't know much Russian, nor any other language. But I do know how to start a fight in several languages; call it an interesting hobby. This is Russian for *bitch* and is akin to being called a punk in prison.

The Colonel stared at me. His face was expressionless, though I could imagine just what he was thinking. Sarge interrupted the standoff by stepping between us, "Alright. Enough flirting. We've got work to do. Morgan, you and Thad go over there and check out those Ural trucks. See if they run. We're going to start loading all these weapons and ammo."

Thad gripped my shoulder, "Come on, Morg. Let's go."

As we walked towards a row of trucks, several of which were

charred wrecks, I thought about what we were doing. Kicking an indiscernible hunk of steel lying on the ground, I said, "I sincerely hope this is the last of the bullshit."

"I thought you was going to shoot that Colonel," Thad replied.

Glancing up at him, I replied. "Yet, Thad. Yet."

"I think you should leave him to the old man. We've got plenty of other tasks that need tending."

I nodded. "You're right. Let's get this crap loaded and get the hell out of here."

We found two of the trucks that would run. One of them had the Grad launcher mounted on it. The other was for transporting the rockets. We loaded rockets on it until it wouldn't hold anymore and strapped them down. But there were more, many more rockets. Thad said he was going to look for another truck and I went to find Sarge.

I found him at the two-ton truck. It was mounded up with ammo of all varieties. Rockets, RPGs, ammo for AKs, DShK (the Soviet version of the fifty cal) as well as grenades, both the handheld type and VOGS, like our 203. There was a pile of AKs. PKMs, RPKs and the Soviet sniper rifle, the SVD. There were more weapons here than we'd ever use. But leaving them here, for just anyone to pick up was out of the question.

We loaded every vehicle we could, even managing to find a couple more functioning Russian trucks. Aside from the weapons, there was all the other equipment that a modern military force required. Radios, night vision equipment, rations, medical supplies, batteries, shelters, sleeping bags. Deciding what we'd take and what we'd leave was a monumental process.

We took every bit of the medical gear. It was sorely needed at the gym where all the wounded were being cared for. The food was likewise loaded as a priority. Dalton was piling his personal stash into the Suburban. It included one of just about every variant of rifle and machine gun he found. He even threw an RPG in there and a SPG-9, the Russian recoilless rifle that fired a seventy-three-millimeter projectile. He added in pistols, knives, shelters and pieces of uniforms. He was having a field day.

Everything we couldn't get loaded onto a truck or trailer was piled up. The ammo was going to be blasted in place. Any weapons we couldn't take were laid out on the ground and the Stryker was repeatedly run back and forth over them. We left non-lethal items that folks might be able to use. Things like clothes and boots.

I saw Perez off in the distance patting down a prone corpse. He had a dump pouch on his hip overflowing with packs of Russian cigarettes. I imagine he'd checked every single body looking for them. The particular body he was searching startled me when it raised a hand. Perez didn't flinch however. Instead, he knelt down beside the stricken man.

Curious, I walked over to see exactly what was going on. The soldier was Cuban and mortally wounded. How he'd managed to live this long was a mystery. But Perez knelt beside him and shook a smoke from a pack and lit it. He gently placed the cigarette into the dying man's mouth. In a feeble voice, the man muttered, "gracias."

I took a knee beside the two men. The Cuban looked up at him as he tried to take a drag on the smoke. A fly landed on his face and I waved it away. With the cigarette bouncing, he asked, "agua." I took a canteen from my belt and opened it. Perez took the cigarette and cradled the man's head as I slowly poured water into his mouth. He swallowed with much effort and Perez placed the smoke back between his lips. An expression came over his face, almost like a smile but not quite. Then the cigarette fell from his mouth and he was gone.

Without saying a word, Perez and I wandered off on our own missions. I helped Ian and Jamie load a 120-millimeter mortar onto a truck. Along with crates and crates of ammo for it. We had enough of this commie hardware to start an army. Sadly, a lot of our army was killed in the attack on Eustis. But we have everything we need to build one.

However, an army was something I hoped we'd never need again. I prayed that this action, this final task, would remove the need for further such actions. That we'd finally be safe and be able to start rebuilding. Of course, there would always be individuals that would need to be dealt with. But the thought of facing a large organized force was hopefully a thing of the past now.

It was late evening when everything was finally loaded. Mike had prepared a large pile of munitions with explosives we took from the Russians. We lined all the vehicles up, even more now that we found several Russian trucks that ran, on the far side of the lot closest to the highway. Mike stretched out the det cord and prepared the blasting machine.

"Finally!" Mike shouted, "I get to have some real fun!" He was almost giddy as he finalized the task of getting the blasting machine ready for its job.

"Just hurry up and blow this shit already," Sarge barked. "I want to get home before dark."

"Oh, I'm gonna blow it!" Mike shouted back over his shoulder. Then he looked around and shouted, "Fire in the hole! Fire in the hole! Fire in the hole!" Then he twisted the blasting machine and there was a thunderous, earth-shaking explosion.

The primary explosives set off all the ordinance piled under them, sending debris high into the air which then began to rain down on our heads. After the explosion, Sarge kicked Mike's boot and shouted, "What in the hell? How much demo did you use?"

Mike looked back at the crater in the ground and replied, "Enough I'd say."

"Too damn much, I'd say!" Sarge countered.

"It's done," Ted said. "Let's get the hell out of here."

"A sad day," Dalton lamented.

"How you figure?" Sarge asked.

Dalton nodded towards the crater and said, "Blasting all that fine Russian hardware."

"You like those commie bastards, don't you?" Sarge asked.

"Respect, I have respect for them."

Sarge jerked his chin in the direction of the Colonel. "You got respect for him?"

"I do. He's a soldier. He was doing his job. Just like we were doing our job. We just did ours a little better."

Sarge grunted, "You still going to respect him when he's swinging from a rope?"

"If that's what it comes to, I'll tie the knot."

"You can like them all you want," I said. "They're an occupying force on our land. Fuck 'em all."

"And how many times have we been the occupiers? How many countries did we go into and kill people and take over their lands. Now, we know what it feels like," Dalton replied.

"Enough philosophy," Sarge grumbled. "Let's get the hell out of here. Put the prisoners in Morgan's Suburban and let's head home."

During the course of our search of the place for weapons, we found two other survivors of the airstrike. One was Cuban and the other was a Russian private. Both men were terrified and offered no resistance when found. Sarge said he was going to call Eglin and let them know we had them; they'd probably want them and would send a helicopter to get them. The men were just an annoyance to me because I had to deal with them until we got rid of them.

I led the men to the truck and opened the back door. Looking at the Colonel, I said, "You give me any trouble and I'll shoot you in the fucking face. I don't care if you're ever interrogated or not. Now turn around."

He did as instructed, and I used large heavy tie wraps to bind his hands behind his back. The other two were likewise restrained and all three were piled into the back of the truck. Perez volunteered to ride with me, to keep an eye on the prisoners. He sat in the front seat with his back to the door. Much to the chagrin of our guests, he chain-smoked all the way home. They were obviously dying for a smoke and Perez fucked with them by blowing the smoke at them as he smiled like an ass.

We made it home just as it was getting dark. I drove over to the old man's house to drop off the prisoners. A line of vehicles crowded the road in front of his place as everyone found a spot to park. We eventually cut a section of fence down bordering the pasture across the street from his house and lined all the trucks up there. Perez led the prisoners to the garage where Ted was preparing their accommodations, such as they were. Unlike the previous guests in the garage, these men weren't going to be hung from the rafters.

Since we didn't know how long we'd have to hold onto these guys and there really wasn't anything we needed to know from them, we prepared them for a long stay. Ted drilled a hole in the floor in the middle of the garage and anchored a large eyebolt. He pulled a long chain through it and secured one end around the ankle of one of the men, locking it in place with a pad lock. The other end was likewise secured to another man. The

Colonel, drawing the short straw, was put in the middle of the chain. He wouldn't have nearly as much freedom of movement as the others.

Once the men were secured, Sarge walked in with a bucket and dropped it on the floor. "Here's yer shitter. Now, I know you're thinking about how you're going to get out of here. I don't think you'll be able to, but know if you try and we catch you, it'll hurt. Bad and for a long time. Just hang out here until the decision is made about what to do with you and you'll be fine. Try anything and your time will be much more uncomfortable."

"We understand we are your prisoners," the Russian Colonel said.

"Good," Sarge replied. Then he looked at Mike, "Get one of those Guardsmen in here. We'll keep around-the-clock watch on these assholes."

Mike nodded. "No problem."

"I guess we'll deal with all this shit tomorrow," I said. "I'm going home."

"I think we'll be alright for the night. I'm going down to Danny's for supper myself," Sarge replied.

There was a chorus of hungry approvals at that idea and everyone started to file out. Mike returned with one our Guardsmen who was going to take the first watch and we all headed down the road toward Danny's. I stopped at Thad's truck. The bed was full of Kalashnikovs and I wanted one with the grenade launcher on it. It didn't take long to find one and I even came up with a set of web gear with loaded mags and the shingle the Russians used to carry the grenades.

Sarge stopped in the road and looked back, "What the hell are you doing?" He asked.

"Getting me a commie rifle and grenade launcher. I've always wanted to shoot one of these VOGs."

He studied me for a minute, then said, "Don't be blowing shit up around here."

I pointed to the crowd still walking down the road and said, "You worry about them. I'll take care of myself." The old man snorted and turned to catch up to the group.

I found Little Bit sitting on the front porch with her squirrel. She was feeding it from a small syringe that it was eagerly accepting. Mel was sitting across from her watching. "When he's done, you have to wipe his butt with a wet rag," she said.

"I know," Little Bit answered. "He eats so much! How big is his belly?"

"He's growing," I said with a smile.

Little Bit looked up and grinned at me. "I can't wait for his eyes to open!"

I stepped over to inspect the limb rat. "Shouldn't be too long now."

"I want to be the first person he sees when he opens his eyes!"

I rubbed her head, "I think Ruckus is going to like you just fine."

The syringe was empty and Little Bit announced he was done eating. She was wearing a kid's size Columbia PFG shirt. It'd become her constant wardrobe since the arrival of Ruckus because the pockets were the perfect size for a little squirrel to curl up in. And that's just what happened. She pulled the pocket open and dropped him down inside. The little critter wriggled around for a moment or two before curling up into a ball.

Little Bit stared down into the pocket and looked up with the wonder and amazement only a child can have, and said, "He likes it in my pocket," then scrunching her shoulders, added, "he's so cute!"

Mel got up and came over to me. "So, it's done then?"

I nodded and wrapped my arms around her waist. "It's done. As far as we know, there are no more military forces in the area."

Her reaction was odd. As if I'd just told her I'd rid the yard of a pesky armadillo. "Good. Then that should be the end of that." She stood up and asked, "Are you hungry?"

"Starving."

"We have meatloaf and sweet potato greens."

"That's sounds awesome to me."

She headed for the door. "You want to eat out here or in the house?"

It was a nice evening and the mosquitos weren't out yet. "Out here would be nice."

She disappeared into the house and returned with a plate and a glass of tea for me. I sat on the porch as Little Bit regaled me with tales of the squirrel. I asked where the two big girls were and was told they were inside listening to music on the iPad. As I was finishing my supper, Drake and Meathead showed up and assumed the begging positions. Meathead had drool running out of his mouth and pooling on the deck beneath him. I laughed, and when I was down to the last bite, I cut it in half and gave each of them a piece. Naturally, they swallowed it without a moment of savoring. All that anticipation, and for what?

When I carried my plate into the kitchen, Lee Ann asked if she could show me something. "Sure," I replied and followed her outside.

She walked around the shed in the backyard and pulled back a tarp to reveal Jeff's Harley. "I want to ride this," she said.

It caught me off guard. "Uh, I don't know about that, kiddo."

"I'm not a little kid anymore, dad. I carry a machine gun." To emphasize her point, she held the H&K up.

"I know. But motorcycles are dangerous."

"Not as dangerous as they used to be. There are no other cars on the road. It's not like I'm going to be t-boned in an intersection."

She had me there and I had to admit it. "You're right about that."

She looked at the motorcycle and ran her hand over the tank. "It's just a waste to let it sit here and rust away."

It was indeed a shame what was happening to the beautiful machine. "I tell you what. Tomorrow, we'll pull it out and see if we can get it running."

"It won't start," she replied glumly.

I smiled, "Already tried it, huh?"

With a half-smile, she nodded. "I've been thinking about this for a long time. It's so cool and I want to take it for a ride."

"Your mother is not going to be happy."

Now with a full smile, she said, "You'll just have to convince her it's alright."

"Oh! It's my job? You better start coming up with your case. Convincing her is on you!" I replied with a laugh.

She reached out and gripped the throttle handle for a moment before letting it go and walking back to the house. I could see the youthful infatuation in her eyes. I remembered it from when I was young. I'd had a motorcycle too and it was the ultimate freedom when I got it. It gave me the leeway to go where I wanted, when I wanted. That initial taste of highway liberty was exhilarating, and I understood the tug of it. But selling that to her mom would be another story.

CHAPTER 5

I WOKE FEELING REFRESHED. LIKE I'D just had the best night's sleep in my life. Maybe it was the thought that things would be different now. That our greatest threat was at last vanquished. Or so I hoped anyway. Whatever it was, I felt great. Leaving Mel in the bed, I went to the kitchen with the intention of cooking breakfast. But there were only a couple of eggs in the fridge. No matter, the egg factory was next door.

Since the introduction of the automatic chicken feeder, we'd kept the bucket supplied with one form of leftovers or another. As a result, the coop was a little aromatic at times. But the cloud of flies it drew created plenty of feed for the birds. Between that and them being allowed to free range during the day, they stayed well fed; and as a result, the egg yield was plentiful. We could count on at least a couple dozen eggs a day; and as the flock grew, so would production.

I collected a half-dozen eggs to take home. It was normally the kids' job to check the nesting boxes every day and bring the eggs in. They'd be around later for the rest. Wishing we had sausage, something Thad and I needed to deal with, I scrambled up a large skillet of eggs. Since we had flour, I mixed up a batch of dough and made biscuits as well. Butter was thankfully still available, and when they were done, I brushed the tops with it. A scoop of eggs stuffed inside a buttery biscuit was a pretty damn good breakfast.

Not wanting to wake anyone up, I went out to the porch and enjoyed my breakfast with a glass of tea. Something else I needed to check on, how much tea was left. It would be a sad day when it ran out. But I did have an alternative. It would just mean getting out into the woods to find it. Living in Florida, I'm fortunate to share the woods with the plant that has the highest amount of caffeine. The Seminole Indians used it for ceremonies as well as daily consumption. When the Spaniards first contacted native Florida tribes, they were introduced to it and soon became addicted to the effects of the caffeine. Luckily, I know where to find the yaupon holly.

As I finished my breakfast, the dogs came trotting back up. They looked as though they'd had a long night and didn't even bother sniffing around to see what I had. They simply collapsed on the deck with their tongues lolling from their mouths. With my breakfast done, I went back inside. I wanted to wake everyone up, so they could have a hot breakfast. But I found Mel already up. She was fixing biscuits for the girls when I came in.

"I was just coming to wake you up," I said.

"Why didn't you wake me earlier? I would have made breakfast."

I came up behind her and wrapped my arms around her. "I wanted you to sleep. And I know how to cook too."

"Yes, you do. These biscuits are amazing. Wish we had some gravy to go with them."

"I'm going to get with Thad on that. See what we have for hogs that are ready to butcher. We'll get one done. We need soap as well. So, now's as good a time as any."

Mel carried her plate over to the table and sat down, eyeing me suspiciously. "What?" I asked.

She leaned back in her chair and crossed her legs, the top one bouncing up and down. "So, uh, you talk to Lee Ann?"

I shrugged. "Yeah."

She leaned forward and took a bite of her biscuit. Wiping her mouth with a cloth, she asked, "What'd you talk about?"

I knew where she was going with this. She obviously knew about the motorcycle and there was no sense in pretending otherwise. "She asked about Jeff's Harley. She said she wants to get it running so she can ride it."

Her leg was bouncing again. "And you didn't tell her no?"

"No, I didn't. Whether we like it or not, our girls are growing up. We can't treat them like kids forever."

"But those things are so dangerous."

I smiled. "I don't seem to remember you complaining when you were on the back of mine."

She scowled, "That was different."

"You're right, it was. It was far more dangerous when we were running around on one. There's no traffic now. The likelihood of her being hit by another car is nonexistent. Hell, even the odds of a deer running out in front of her are almost zero."

She wasn't liking my line of reasoning. "I don't care. They're still dangerous."

"Look, they're good kids. Their lives have been altered so profoundly that we can't look back on the way things used to be as a reference for right and wrong. I'm going to get the bike running and I'll teach her how to ride it. She'll be fine."

"I'm just worried about her is all." She pointed an accusatory finger at me. "If she gets hurt, it's on you!"

"She'll be fine. I promise." What I meant was *I hoped.* Shit can go wrong in a hurry on a motorcycle. I'd just have to do my best to teach her how to safely ride it, then hope she listens and doesn't do anything stupid.

"What are you doing today?" She asked, changing the subject.

"I'm going to get with Thad. Plus, we have to figure out where we're going to store all that damn crap we brought back yesterday."

"I'm taking the girls with Jess to town. We're going to work in the gym where the wounded are. They need help and it's the least we can do." That surprised me. I didn't know she was even thinking about such things. But it also made me proud to know they we're all willing to help those that needed it.

"That's really good. I'm glad to hear the girls are willing to step up to the plate like that. We recovered a bunch of medical supplies yesterday. Make sure you get with the old man and load that up for the trip to town. I'm sure they can use everything they can get their hands on."

"Ok, that's good. Because they're already asking for people to bring in old sheets and towels to be cut up and made into bandages. So those will come in real handy."

"When are you guys going up there?" I asked.

"I'm waiting on Jess. She said she'd come down when she was ready. Fred wants to go too but she's dealing with morning sickness. It's hit her pretty hard."

"I think it's great you guys are doing this. You're not taking Little Bit, are you?"

Mel shook her head. "No. She's too young. She's staying here with Danny and Kay."

"I'll be around too."

"I have to get the girls up, so they can eat," Mel said and headed down the hallway.

It wasn't long before I heard them voicing their complaints about being woke up. But it was all good natured and they all came filing out into the kitchen, looking like a sorry lot.

"Well, good morning!" I nearly shouted. "Glad you could join us!"

Taylor rubbed her face and yawned. "You're one to talk. You're usually the last one to wake up."

"That's only because I do more than all of you combined," I replied with a smile. Lee Ann snorted in reply.

Little Bit came plodding down the hall, dragging her bear Peanut Butter behind her. She rubbed her eyes and climbed up into a chair asking, "What's for breakfast?"

"I made biscuits and eggs this morning," I replied.

Her face lit up and she asked, "Can I have honey with mine?"

Mel slid a plate in front of her and set the jar of honey on the table. Little Bit licked her lips as she spun the lid off. First, she dipped her finger into the jar and jabbed it into her mouth. Mel told her to use a spoon to get the honey and she laughed. Sticking a spoon into the golden goo, Little Bit drizzled it all over her biscuit and the plate and a little on the table. I watched her and couldn't help but smile. She was covered in the sticky mess in no time.

It reminded me of a story from when I was little. My dad let me get honey all over my hands and face. Then handed me a cotton ball. From the way he told it, he got a really good laugh out of it. Mom, however, didn't think it was so funny. Looking at Little Bit covered in stickiness made me really want to hand her a cotton ball to wipe it off. But she was a little older than I was when it was it was done to me and probably too smart to fall for it.

"I'm going to get with Thad and see about butchering a hog," I said as I collected my gear by the door.

"Okay," Mel replied. "We're headed over to town in a bit and will be gone all day."

"Dad," Lee Ann called out. I knew what she wanted.

"Yes, kiddo. We'll look at it in a little while." She and Taylor shared a giggle, causing Mel to ask what we were talking about. "Oh, nothing. Just a little project for the girls." But I wasn't fooling her; she knew what was up.

I left the house and went over to Danny's. He was out in the garden doing a little weeding. "Yo," I called out.

He stood up and tossed a handful of weeds over the fence. "Yo. How'd it go yesterday?"

"We got everything we could carry and blew the rest of it up. Those Russians brought a lot of shit with them. They planned on being here a while. We found three alive and brought them back as well."

That got Danny's attention. "Brought them here?"

I nodded. "Yeah. They're at the old man's place. Hey, I'm going to get with Thad about butchering a hog. We're out of pork and we need to make soap again."

"I'll help. I just have something to do first."

"Cool. I knew you would. Let's go up onto the porch. I got something else I want to talk to you about."

We walked up to the porch and took a seat in the rocking chairs. Almost immediately, Miss Kay came out with two Mason jars of iced tea and handed them to us. "It's hot out here and you two look like you could use a cold drink."

Taking the offered glass, I replied, "You're an angel. Thank you."

Taking a sip of his tea, Danny asked, "What's up?"

I rocked for a moment, then said, "I was thinking about Mom and Dad today. With all those Russians and Cubans gone, I was thinking of taking a couple of days and trying to get to their place. Check on them, maybe even bring them back here."

"You want to do it by boat, take the river?"

"I think it'll be the safest way. Probably the quickest too."

"Probably would be. We could probably do it in two days. Three tops," Danny replied.

"That's what I was thinking. Hell, we could probably get there in one day. Barring any trouble on the river. We'll take sufficient hardware so that any trouble we do encounter can be squashed pretty quick."

"I'm in. When do you want to go?"

"In a couple of days. There's a lot to do first. I want to get this hog butchered and make damn sure there are no surprises waiting for us anywhere. Then we'll go."

Danny stood up and drained his glass. "Where you want to butcher the hog?"

I looked over at the shop and said, "Figured we'd set the tub up over there and do it like before. I want to scald this one, get every ounce off it we can."

"Alright. Let me take care of a couple of things and I'll meet you guys over there."

I left Danny to go find Thad. As I was walking down the road, Mel passed me in the Suburban and slowed to wave and say, "I love you." I waved, and they continued on, turning to go to the old man's place. All those Russian medical supplies would come in very handy in town. I knocked on Thad's door, but there was no answer. So, I opened it and called out. The house was quiet, and it was obvious he and Mary were not there.

Leaving his house, I walked to Sarge's place. There were a lot of people there. The gear we captured was still being sorted and they were trying to decide on a place for an armory. Seeing the stuff now, I was shocked at just how much there was. Thad and Mary were there helping, and I got Thad's attention.

"You want to butcher a hog today? We're out of sausage and soap."

He smiled, "Sure. When do you want to do it?"

"The sooner, the better."

As we talked, Mary walked up. "Thad, I'm going to town with Mel and Jess to help at the gym. We're taking the medical supplies there and going to spend the day doing what we can."

"Ok, just be careful."

Mary smiled, "Sarge is sending an escort with us. Ian and Jamie are going as well. Plus, we're all armed." I felt better hearing they were going to have an escort. And it struck me as I thought about it. I'd never seen Mary armed before. I remembered her being so fragile when she came here. This was no longer so. Maybe she was absorbing strength from Thad. Whatever the reason, I was glad to see it.

Leaving Thad and Mary, I found Mel and asked if they had a radio. She held it up and replied, "Yes. Everyone keeps asking. We have a radio."

I smiled and patted her ass, "Just checking, babe."

As we were discussing their trip, Danny walked up. He looked around and headed for the garage. Watching him, I said to Mel, "I'll be right back." And I headed towards the garage. As I stepped through the door, I saw Danny talking to Wallner. The three prisoners were sitting on the floor, paying very little attention to the two as they talked.

Then in a swift motion, Danny drew his pistol and shot one of the men in the top of the head. Wallner jumped and I ran forward and wrapped my arms around Danny. The garage was quickly filled with people as everyone came running to the sound of the shot. Danny didn't struggle and remained quite calm. I took his pistol without resistance.

The old man came running in. "What the hell is going on?" He shouted as he came in. Then seeing the dead man, he said, "Oh for fuck sake!" He looked at me, holding the pistol, and said, "Dammit, Morgan! Would you stop killing all of our prisoners! I told Eglin I had these people and they want them! How the hell am I supposed to explain this?"

"It wasn't me!" I shot back.

"I shot him," Danny replied calmly. "They owed me a life."

Sarge shook his head. "I get it, Danny. I really do. But if you'd been at the auction, you'd see they paid dearly for every person they killed or injured. This is all that's left of them." Sarge looked at the Colonel and asked, "How many men did you have?" But he wouldn't answer. "It doesn't matter now. They're all dead. If you want to stay alive, I suggest you answer the question. Or I'll just let this man have your ass."

"This is how you Americans treat prisoners of war?" The Colonel asked.

"Fuck you, Ivan." I said. "You're an invading force. Besides, you have no ground to talk about how to treat prisoners. Look at what your people did to the Germans after the fall of Stalingrad. You're lucky to be alive, so shut the fuck up."

He smiled at me and replied, "As you wish, bureaucrat."

"Colonel," Sarge said, "you might want to stop fucking with him."

I pointed at the Colonel. "You're going to talk your way into hell. Maybe I should take him to the pig pen for a while."

"No dammit!" Sarge shouted. "I'm turning him over to Eglin!"

"You better do it quick," I replied and turned to leave. Danny followed me out and I handed him his pistol back. As he holstered it, I asked, "You feel better now?"

"Not really. I wanted to set him on fire. But I had to do it, an eye for an eye."

I slapped him on the back. "I know, buddy. We're going to get a hog and we'll be over shortly."

"I'll get the tub set up and a fire going under it."

I glanced sideways at him and asked, "Is this what you said you needed to take care of earlier?"

He nodded. "Yep."

Mel, Jess, Mary and the girls loaded most of the medical supplies into the Suburban before heading out. Jamie and Ian would escort them in a Hummer there and back. Once they were gone, Thad and I headed for the hog pen.

We were leaning on the fence looking at the hogs. Whenever anyone came to the pen, they would come running, anticipating food. Feeding the pigs was just another of the never-ending tasks that needed tending to daily. But they were a valuable resource and certainly worth the effort. Thad kept a close eye on them, and as litters were born, he would cut out some of the boars for butchering later. We were keeping all the sows to breed more, and the system was beginning to pay off in a big way. So much so that we were discussing trading out some of the hogs. We could trade breeding pairs or even single hogs.

"I think we should give a breeding pair to Gina and Dillon," I said.

"That would be a good idea. They've always been there to help us."

"Mario too. I'd like to give him a pair."

Thad pointed to a large boar rooting around in the dirt and said, "Let's take that one. He's been cut and should make some good sausage."

"Alright. You know, I've been thinking. Cecil has that field of corn. And there's far fewer people here now than there was. We can probably use some of that corn to feed these hogs."

"That would be great. They'd taste better and finish off good on corn."

"We'll give Cecil a pair too if he wants them. That'll spread the hogs out some. Give other folks the ability to produce their own pork."

"I'll go get the tractor."

When Thad returned with the tractor, I dumped a bucket of swamp cabbage over the fence, away from the gate. While the hogs were focused on the food, Thad pulled the tractor into the pen. Using a stick, I swatted the hogs on the ass, breaking them up. When the boar we wanted was clear of the others, I shot it behind the ear with my pistol. It dropped and kicked as the other hogs ran from the sound of the shot. Thad set the bucket down and I rolled the pig in. After closing the gate behind the tractor, I stepped up onto the three-point hitch and held onto the roll bar for the trip to Danny's.

Danny had the tub set up and a fire going under it when we got there. Using a chain, we slung the hog under the bucket to make dunking it into the scalding water easier. As we waited for the water to heat, we talked about the job ahead. I said I wanted to keep all the organs to make dog food.

Miss Kay came out with a tray with glasses of tea for us. She inspected the hog and nodded her approval. "That's a fine animal. You're going to get all the fat off it too?"

"Oh yeah," I replied. "We need to make some soap."

"I'd like a little lard too if there's enough."

"I'm sure we can manage that," Thad replied.

"Are you guys going to want lunch now? Or wait until you're done to eat?"

"I'd rather wait," I replied, and Thad and Danny agreed with that.

"Ok then. If you need anything, just let me know."

"Yes ma'am," Thad said with a smile.

Once the water was hot enough, we got to work. It took several dunks and pouring hot water on in a couple of stubborn places to get all the hair scraped off. This was by far my least favorite part of the butchering process. But a necessary one. When we were done, the hog looked like a newborn baby. Pink and smooth.

With the hard part completed, the rest of the job went quickly. Once the pig was gutted, Thad cut the belly off and set it aside for bacon. The loins were cut out and saved, and the rest of the pig was going to be ground into sausage, save one ham. Thad wanted to try making a salt-cured ham. If it worked, it would be a great addition to our food supplies and if it didn't, we'd only loose one ham.

Sausage was popular fare. Everyone had it for breakfast or in the meatloaf Miss Kay made. We used a lot of it and it was work to stay ahead of the demand. Plus, there was the fat on the animal. All of this was saved in a bucket. Some would be used for the sausage, and some would be used for soap. Having the ability to produce our own soap was a blessing beyond words. There was no other supply and it meant being able to keep everything from dishes and clothes to our bodies clean. Something I really noticed when I went to the markets and got around a group of people. There was certainly a deficit of soap in our world.

Thad cut the skin away from the animal with great precision. I noticed he was taking extreme care and asked why. "I want to make cracklins," He replied.

"Oh, that would be good," Danny said.

"Hell, yeah it would!" I added. "Why haven't we made them before?"

Thad shrugged, "I don't know. Just thought about it. Momma used to make them, and I always liked it."

"Damn," I lamented. "Wish we had some pimento cheese, real pimento cheese, to go with them."

"Some what?" Danny asked.

Thad laughed. "You ain't never had pimento cheese with your cracklins?"

"I don't think he's ever had real cracklins," I offered.

"They're just pork rinds," Danny replied.

Thad and I both laughed at that. "Oh no they're not!" I shouted.

Thad reached out and patted Danny's shoulder. "If you like pork rinds, you'll love what I'm gonna make."

"Well, aside from not having pimento cheese to go with it, I'm really looking forward to it," Danny replied with a smile.

"Looks like this is about done. Can you guys handle the grinding?" I asked.

"Miss Kay is going to do it," Thad replied and raised his eyebrows and added, "she insisted."

I laughed at the thought. Kay was an incredible woman and queen of the kitchen. "I bet she did. If you guys can handle this, then I've got another little project I need to get to."

Danny nodded, "We got this."

Mel and the girls arrived at the gym without incident. Jamie and Ian helped them carry the medical supplies inside. The gym was beyond words. It was hot and muggy. The air was still and thick with the odor of putrid flesh, feces and urine. The few staff tending to the wounded looked nearly as bad as their charges. Some of them were also suffering from injuries sustained in the rocket attack. Chris Yates, the medic, came over when he saw the group arrive.

"What's all this?" The weary man asked.

"It's Russian medical supplies. We've got all kinds of stuff here and more in the truck," Ian replied. "We've also got some rations to help feed these people."

"Clean bandages," Chris muttered as he looked over the items. Picking up a small box, he said, "This is morphine! Where did you get all this?"

"We just got it," Ian replied. "Can you get a couple of people to help unload all of it?"

"Absolutely!" Chris replied and waved a couple of people over.

Once all the supplies were inside, Mel told Chris they were there to help for the day and asked what she and the girls could do.

"I'll pair you up with our people. They know what needs to be done and an extra set of hands will be greatly appreciated."

While he went off to get his people together, Mel and the girls looked around the gym. Those that had family members had them at their side, many of them fanning flies away from wounds. There were pans and buckets of what had to be human waste in several places and people could be heard begging for water or painkillers.

Holding her nose, Taylor said, "Mom, this smells awful."

"I know. But we can help for a day. Imagine having to be here all day, every day. Imagine being one of the wounded." She looked at her daughter and added, "we're lucky. We get to go home when we're ready. Where we have running water, hot food and ice. Look at these poor people. Like Dad says, suck it up, buttercup."

Chris came back and paired each of the girls up with one of his people. Using the fresh supplies, they set to work cleaning wounds, changing dressings, and trying to comfort the suffering. Lee Ann was helping a female nurse with the Guard change the dressing on a woman's leg. The entire leg had been burned and was wrapped in pink gauze.

"Here," the nurse said, handing Lee Ann a large plastic bottle with a long nozzle. "Squeeze the water onto the gauze where I'm removing it. It'll make it come off easier."

Lee Ann did as instructed, and the woman cried in pain at having the dressing peeled from her. The wound was horrible looking, with skin hanging in ribbons or coming off with the gauze. The fetid gauze was placed in a bucket as it was unrolled. The nurse looked into it and commented, "At least we don't have to boil those again."

"What do you mean?" Lee Ann asked as she carefully drizzled water onto a stubborn piece of gauze.

"We've been boiling and reusing the gauze. We didn't have anymore. You'll see some wounds are wrapped in bed sheets, or strips we've cut from them, boiled and used as dressings."

Lee Ann looked down into the bucket and asked, "How many times have those been reused?"

"Three," came the flat reply.

Mel worked with Chris. They were at the bed of a small child, no more than seven years old. The little girl's head was wrapped in a puffy bandage that Chris was unwrapping. Tears ran down Mel's face as Chris worked.

"She's already dead, you know. But her heart hasn't got the message yet," Chris said as he removed the bandage to reveal a hole the size of a golf ball in the child's skull.

Mel choked on a breath and covered her mouth. "Oh, no, I, I, can't look at that," she said, before turning away.

"It's ok. You wouldn't be normal if it didn't bother you. It bothers me too, but I've been doing this for a long time and can deal with it. Just take the new bandage out of the wrapper and hand it to me."

Mel did as he asked and waited what she thought was sufficient time for Chris to have the wound covered before turning back to look. She was relieved when she saw the clean white dressing covering the hole. Chris finished dressing the wound and checked the child's pulse.

"There's no hope for her?" Mel asked.

Chris took a small penlight from his pocket and held the child's right eye open. Shinning the light into the eye, he replied, "No. See, the pupil doesn't react at all. She's brain dead and will probably pass today or tomorrow."

"Where are her parents?"

As he stood up, he replied, "No idea. She came in alone. A lot of kids came in alone."

Jess worked with a young man. The two were changing the dressing on a young man's leg. He couldn't have been more than eighteen. His left leg was missing above the knee. Once the bandage was removed, Jess looked at the wound.

The amputation had been closed, but it wasn't a clean job. The sutures looked rough with flaps of skin pulled over in an almost haphazard manner and stitched together. As the EMT worked to clean the wound before applying the new dressing, Jess looked at the young man lying on the canvas cot. He made no complaints, verbal or physical. He just lay there and stared at Jess. She smiled and asked, "What's your name?"

"Robert," he replied without emotion.

Glancing back at the leg, Jess said, "You're going to be fine. Looks like it's going to heal well."

"No, I'm not. I don't have a leg. I had a football scholarship. I was going to go to the NFL." He turned his attention to the rafters of the gym. "Then all this happened. The world ended, and I'll be a cripple for the rest of my life."

"The world hasn't ended," Jess tried to assure him. "Sure,

it's changed. Different from what it once was. But we're all still here and life goes on."

Still staring at the ceiling, he replied, "That's easy for you to say. You still have both legs." Then he turned his face away and didn't speak again.

They finished the job and moved to the next patient. As they walked, Jess asked, "How can you do this every day?"

The young man didn't hesitate in his reply, "Someone has to. And I have the skills to make a difference. Besides, what else would I be doing? I wouldn't be able to sleep at night if I were at home while these people suffered. Here, I can make a difference."

They stepped over to another cot where an aged man sat fanning an equally elderly woman with a piece of cardboard. She had several bandages on various parts of her body. When they approached, the man looked up and asked, "Can you help her?"

The young man looked at the woman, then leaned in close to Jess and whispered, "Take him outside. Get him some water or something."

Looking at the old man, who was still watching them, Jess asked, "Why?"

"His wife is dead."

It was a long, very long, day for them in the gym.

The battery was dead on the Harley. I checked with a meter to confirm and decided to just jump-start it. I pushed it, with much effort, over to the trailer where the solar system was housed. Mel had the Suburban, so I couldn't use that; but the solar setup also had twelve-volt batteries, so it would do the job. After hooking up the jumper cables, I stood for a minute looking at the bike. I remembered when Jeff rode up on it. Thinking of him made me smile.

I opened the saddlebag of the right side and looked in. There were two pieces of Bazooka bubble gum in a plastic bag and it brought me back to the day he choked on that massive wad of gum at the end of the road. The look on his face when I dropped my boot on his chest and the image of that wad of gum shooting up into the air. Then the smile faded as the other image from a later time of his lifeless body lying in the road came to me. I slowly unwrapped both pieces of gum and stuffed them into my mouth.

Turning the key on, I hit the start button and the bike rumbled to life. After removing the cables, I tossed them aside and straddled the bike. I worked the throttle, revving the engine for a few seconds. Then, without thinking about it, I dropped the bike into gear and rode it around the house, down the drive and out to the road. Being careful in the loose dirt, I turned the machine and headed down the road towards the bunker.

When I hit the paved part of the road, I opened the bike up and roared past the bunker to the bewilderment of the two men standing there. As I passed the road to Sarge's place, I saw Mike and Ted walking down the road. Mike shouted something as I raced past them, pushing the beast of a machine even faster, but I didn't respond. I was thinking of Jeff and was taking a ride, for him.

Slowing to navigate the barricades at the end of the road, I turned onto nineteen and really opened the bike up. It was exhilarating to go so fast and feel the rush of the air, the vibration of the machine beneath me; and I pushed it still faster. When the market in Altoona came into view, which only took a minute or two, I looked at the people gathered there as they passed in a blur. Several of them seemed genuinely surprised at the sight of the machine as it roared by. The same thing happened when I passed the market in Umatilla.

Maybe it was just the machine they were looking at. Maybe it was the speed at which I raced by that caught their attention. But it didn't matter, and I was enjoying thrill of it all. I did wave at Baker and Terry as I passed them. Baker had a huge smile on her face as I blew by them and Terry was waving wildly, grinning like an ass eating briars. Scott ran out into the road, waving his arms frantically with a look of excitement on his face. He wanted a ride. But I didn't stop.

But I couldn't bring myself to go into Eustis and instead, I turned onto forty-four and headed east. I hadn't been past the farm on this piece of road and as it passed by on my left, I could see Cecil out there working the tractor. He didn't see me, and I didn't stop for a chat. Instead, I continued down the road. I was seeing places I hadn't been to since all this shit started. Even though I was only a mile or two off a track that I traveled all the time.

It struck me how my world had shrunk. In the Before, I would travel anywhere without a thought. I often went to the beach to surf fish, or to Orlando for something or another. A trip which is now unthinkable was undertaken with no more consideration than turning the key in the truck. Such a trip now would be an expedition on par with those undertaken by those that settled this land. But when you considered most folks had to walk everywhere they went, we were essentially in the same place those early settlers were. Actually, they were ahead of us for the most part. Most people back then had horses or mules and could use them to travel on. Such animals were rare today.

My ride took me over to highway 439 where I turned north. I didn't want to push my luck in going too far. For one, I didn't check the fuel in the Harley before leaving and two, no one knew where I was. That and the fact I didn't bring my rifle with me. This entire thing was a little foolhardy, but I was loving it.

So far, I'd seen a few people, though not many. Most of those I saw were engaged in working some small plot of dirt trying to scratch out a living. Everyone was a farmer of one sort or another today. I cruised down this stretch of road, again seeing only a few people. I was surprised to see a couple of people walking down the road. This was a pretty long walk from town, so I had no idea where they were going. They weren't carrying packs or anything, so they couldn't be going far.

The two men stepped to the side of the road as I approached, moving into the opposite lane to give them plenty of space as I did. One of the men raised his hand as I passed, and I replied in kind. I thought of stopping and having a chat with them. But as I was only armed with my pistol and there were two of them, the numbers didn't add up correctly and I kept going.

At forty-two I turned west and headed back towards Altoona. The first part of this stretch is pretty desolate with no houses on it. I was cruising along at a good clip when something on the side of the road caught my eye. The fence line was covered in wild grape vines and I thought I saw a bunch of hanging fruit, so I turned around and slowly rode back, watching the vines as I did.

As I thought, the vine was hanging heavy with fruit and I stopped the bike and got off, intent to fill the saddlebags with as much fruit as I could fit. This was a great find. While Florida is covered with wild grape vines, only about ten percent of them actually bear fruit. And I'd just found one that did, in abundance.

The fence I was picking fruit on was the northern boundary of a large cattle ranch. Or it had been in the Before. I hadn't thought of the place since the change, and as I filled my hat with clumps of grapes so dark they looked black, I wondered if the place was still in operation. As I pulled grapes from the vine, I looked the land over on the other side of the fence and was struck by something so obvious, I wondered how I hadn't noticed it immediately. The grass on that side of the fence was short. Like mowed short. Like, mowed by cows short.

On the ranch, a short distance from where I was picking fruit, was a large bay head of mixed trees. There were some cypress, cabbage palms and other trees associated with low, wet lands. I was looking at this area when I saw something move. Standing up, I strained my eyes to see, before remembering I had my binoculars in my vest and took them out. Putting them up to my eyes, I immediately made out a large black angus cow.

In shock, I lowered the optic and stared in disbelief. Now that I'd seen the first cow, I immediately made out others. And they were all headed towards me. In a few short minutes, a heard of fifty or sixty big black cows meandered out of the swamp. I stood in sheer amazement at the sight before me. I thought cows were gone, at least from around here. And yet, here before my very eyes was a herd!

Moments after the cows came into view, two men on horseback emerged from the same swamp. They were the stereotypical cowboys, broad brimmed hats, jeans and boots. They were busy talking, leaned back in their saddles in apparent ease. After a couple minutes of them not noticing me, I called out to them.

The sound of my voice startled the men and they looked for the source as they each drew a rifle from a scabbard on the saddle. While the men took a moment to find me, the horses looked directly at me with their ears perked. I waved to make sure they could see me and stood in the open with my hands clearly visible. Once they finally saw me, the two men talked for a moment before nudging their horses in my direction.

They approached closer but stayed a fair distance from me. I waved again as they drew near. "Damn," I shouted. "I didn't think there was a cow anywhere around here now."

One of them, wearing a white hat, nodded and replied, "We've got a few."

I looked over at the herd again and said, "I haven't been out this way since the Day. I was just out riding and saw all these grapes here and stopped to pick some."

His partner was wearing a very wide brimmed black hat. He nudged his horse and rode even closer to me. Cocking his head to the side, he asked, "You the one calling yourself the Sheriff?"

I looked down at the badge and replied, "It wasn't my idea. Not something I wanted to do. But the job was hung on me and I guess I accepted it." The man in the white hat came closer as well and took a handheld radio from his belt and spoke into it.

Nodding towards the cows, I said, "You guys have any trouble with folks trying to steal your cows? That used to be a hanging offense."

The man in the black hat reached behind himself and pulled out a coiled manila rope. Holding it out, he replied, "Still is. Around here anyway."

"Good. I'm glad to hear you're taking care of yourselves."

As I replied, two side by sides came running up. Each had two occupants and when they came to stop, the two men in one of the machines quickly hopped out. They were both armed with rifles and looked at me uneasily. The other machine had carried an older man and a woman.

The older man wore an immaculately clean straw hat, pressed jeans and what looked like a freshly starched shirt. He had the look of man that no longer worked cows. But everything about him said he had for most of his life. The woman with him was probably in her thirties and beautiful. She had long auburn hair and was dressed like the others in jeans, a checked shirt and a cowboy hat. She also wore a nicely tooled leather gun belt around her waist and carried herself with an air of confidence.

The older man walked towards me and I moved down the fence line to a clear spot where we could talk. The woman came with him, not following, but beside him as an equal. When he got to the fence, the man held his hand out and said, "Dave McFarland's the name. This is my daughter Janet."

I shook his hand, "Nice to meet you Dave. I'm Morgan."

A sly smile cut his face and he said, "Oh, I know who you are, Morgan Carter."

His comment caught me off guard. "How do you know my name?"

"Everyone knows who the Sheriff is," Janet replied.

I looked at her, "Well, I hope it's for a good reason. Nice to meet you as well, Janet."

She tipped her hat and replied, "Pleasure."

"I have to admit, I was shocked when I saw the cows. I really didn't think there were any left."

Dave looked back at the small herd. "That's only a little piece of them. We have over three hundred head."

I was dumbfounded, "What?" Was all I could muster.

He smiled. "Used to have a lot more. But we've pretty well taken care of the cattle rustlers in these parts."

"Your man there showed me the rope. I hope you didn't lose many."

"So, the Sheriff ain't got no problem with me hanging rustlers?"

I shook my head. "Hell no. Serves 'em right. Besides, saves me from having to deal with it had you been so inclined to involve me. I believe folks can and should take care of themselves. The days of the nanny state are over."

Dave chewed on those words for a minute before looking at his daughter and saying, "You were right."

Curious, I asked, "In what regard?"

Dave took his hat off and mopped at his bald head with a handkerchief. "That you weren't some busybody do-gooder out to get into people's business. Into their lives."

"No. Me and the deputies with me are here to help people. You need us, we'll be there. Otherwise, I like a nice quiet life."

"Hasn't been much quiet," Janet chimed in. "We saw what happened to town and heard what you did about it."

"That wasn't so much me as it was my military counterparts. They organized that little deal. They handle the military stuff and I try to deal with the civilian stuff."

"That's the way it ought to be," Dave replied. "These military folks, whose side are they on?"

"What do you mean?" I asked.

"Do they still answer to the President?"

I laughed. "No. If you knew these men, you'd know better than that. They answer to the DOD. And me," I added as an afterthought.

"You?" Janet asked.

"Yeah, their superiors consider me the local civilian authority, and as such, they have to answer to me. But these men are my friends and I leave them to do what needs to be done. If they need my help, I help them. If I need theirs, they stand ready as well."

"This is sounding better all the time," Dave said. "But I have one question, who made you the local civilian authority?"

I scratched my head, "Well, there's the funny part. The military did. It was actually the local commander of the National

Guard unit in Eustis that did it. Then the folks higher up the chain of command accepted it as fact. I was never consulted about it. I just stepped in and did what needed doing."

"Morgan, we've stayed out of things to this point. Not really sure who was who or what was what. But now that we've talked, and I see you're not some jackleg looking to be king, we'd like to help out a bit. What can we do to assist with all the wounded folks in town?"

That surprised me. "Well, a beef donated to the folks would be real nice. Food, as you know, is pretty scarce for a lot folks."

Dave nodded. "Done. Anything else?"

"I can't really think of anything right now. But I do have a question."

"What's that?"

"You selling any cows?"

"This is a cattle ranch. But money is an uncertain issue at the moment. What are you offering? I'd take silver or gold."

Nodding, I replied, "We have that. But would you be interested in trading for some hogs?"

"Hogs?" Dave asked with surprise.

"Yeah. I've got a bunch of hogs. Plus, I've got something else you could probably use."

The haggler in Dave was coming out and he looked down his nose at me and asked, "Oh yeah? What's that?"

"Well, I would imagine this place has a tractor or two and probably a couple of trucks that still run. I've got diesel fuel."

While he was interested in the hogs, the mention of the fuel visibly excited him. He slowly started to nod his head. "I think we can make a deal." Looking at Janet, he asked, "How many heifers we got carrying calves right now?"

"About seventy-five."

Dave pointed at me in the way a man willing to make a

deal will do. "Tell you what, Morgan. I'll give you two pregnant heifers that'll calve soon. That gives you four head, for five hundred gallons of diesel and four hogs."

I rubbed the back of my neck as I made a visible play of thinking it over. "Five hundred gallons is a lot of fuel. How about three hundred and I'll give you a pregnant sow. That'll give you a litter. I'll also make sure you have a good boar in the mix to keep you in hogs."

"Some pork would be real nice," Janet said. "Don't get me wrong, I love beef. But when it's all you have, a little variety is real appealing."

"I totally agree," I replied. Then I looked at Dave and asked, "We got a deal?"

He held his hand out and replied, "Deal. You want me to deliver the cows? Or do you have a stock trailer?"

"If you'd deliver them, that would be a big help. I'm assuming you've got a tank around here for the fuel. Bring it and the cows. We'll unload the cows and put the hogs in the trailer. Then we'll get your fuel." I was already starting to like Dave and thought I'd add a little sweetener to the deal, though I didn't have to. "Tell you what, I'll also throw in a fifty-pound sack of flour."

Dave's eyes got wide and he looked at Janet. She smiled and said, "Yes, Dad. I'll make biscuits and gravy."

"Morgan, that really says something about you. You didn't need to do that. But the fact you did really speaks volumes about your character. I see us becoming very good friends," he said with a smile. "I tell you what I'll do. Let's have us a cookout. Bring your folks over here and I'll put on a feed. We'll grill up a bunch of steaks for everyone."

"Now that sounds awesome. But make some burgers too.

I've got some youngins as well. We'll make buns for them. I'll also bring some sausages."

Laughing, Dave replied, "You're just full of surprises! How many folks you got?"

"Figure about twenty-five, give or take."

"You got that many folks you've been feeding all this time? How the hell have you done it?"

"Ain't been easy. But we've managed. They're all really good people. Salt of the earth and I trust them with my life, literally."

"Give me a couple of days and we'll bring the beeves over. Then we'll have us a hell of a cookout."

"You need any security for the delivery? I can provide that if you need."

Dave smiled. "Naw. My boys can handle that. Janet will take care of everything."

I told Janet how to get to our place and we shook hands again before I dumped the hat full of grapes I'd been holding the whole time into the saddlebag and mounted the Harley. It started right up fortunately and as the loud pipes rumbled, Dave laughed. I waved and headed home. This was an amazing development and I wanted to let the old man know about it.

As I approached the market in Altoona, I thought about stopping for some butter. But decided not to. Looking at the market as I passed it, I saw two off-road Endura-style bikes there. They stuck out because I hadn't seen anything like it in a long time, that and I just happened to be riding a motorcycle as well.

Making it back to the neighborhood, I rolled to a stop at the bunker. One of the Guardsmen, Stinness, was waving me down. I rolled to a stop and he asked, "What is this? National ride your motorcycle day?"

I glanced down at the Harley and replied, "Just taking it out to blow the dust and cobwebs off it."

"You're not the only one. Saw a couple others a little while ago," Stinness replied. Then he pointed towards the country road and said, "See, there they are."

I looked back over my shoulder to see the two bikes I'd seen at the market sitting in the road. The riders looked as though they were discussing something, then they sped away to the north.

"That's weird," I replied. "I haven't seen anything moving in a long time and today there just happens to be three motorcycles out on the road."

"I thought it was odd too. Even more so because they stopped down there and looked in."

"Yeah, we need to keep a careful eye out for a while. That just seems odd."

I said goodbye and rode over to the old man's place. I shut the bike down in the driveway of his house. And walked to the one next door where all the weapons we'd looted from the Russian's were being carried in.

"All that going to fit in there?" I asked.

Sarge looked up from a clipboard he was making notes on and replied, "Yeah, it's gonna fit. But it's gonna be crowded."

"At least we won't have to worry about weapons or ammo. For like, ever."

"Naw. We should be pretty well set. If you don't mind using commie guns," Sarge replied and looked over at the bike. "What in the hell are you doing out riding around on that thing?"

"I just took it out to blow the carbon out of it. No sense in just letting it sit there and rot away."

"About as useless as a piece of shit. You can't carry a damn thing on it."

Pointing at the bike, I replied, "Actually, those saddlebags are full of grapes. I found a vine that was heavy with fruit and picked a load of them. We'll turn them into juice for jelly and whatnot. I'm sure Miss Kay will have a use for them."

"There's no doubt she'll find something to do with them."

"A couple other things. First, I saw two bikes at the market in Altoona. Stinness told me he saw them ride by earlier and while we were talking, they stopped at the end of the road down there. And I don't think they were admiring the Harley."

Sarge thought about it for a minute, then asked, "Who do you think they are?"

"Same ones you're thinking of. Some guys with a deuce and a half and bunch of motorcycles."

"Yeah, that's what I was thinking. We need to set up an OP out there closer to the road."

"I don't think they'll just ride up to the entry there and come down in here. Needs to be someplace where they can see down the road."

The old man snorted, "Leave the army shit to me. I'm going to put a couple of guys in one of the burned-out trucks over there. They'll be able to see all the way down the road and give us a heads up if they head this way and dip off into the woods."

"Ok, good. Next thing, in a day or so, a truck is coming here to deliver two pregnant cows."

Sarge's eyes nearly bulged out of his head. "What? Cows? How in the hell did you pull that off? Who the hell has cows?"

I told him the story of how I found the cows and about meeting Dave and his daughter. I explained the deal I'd worked out and about the cookout we were invited to. When I finished, he stood there and pondered it all for a moment, which I found fascinating. The old man was usually quick with a comeback, but sometimes he'd a take a minute to work up the proper response.

"Well shit. Sounds like a hell of deal to me. We've got several thousand gallons of diesel still, so that's no problem. And from what I've seen in that pig pen, trading four shouldn't be an issue either. Plus, I'd like to meet Dave. Who knows what else we might be able to work together on."

"Exactly! He was a little standoffish when I first started talking to him. But he warmed up pretty quick. I think his daughter Janet pretty much runs the show now. She's the one bringing the cows over."

"Alright. I'll let the guys at the bunker know to keep an eye out for a truck pulling a stock trailer. Some beef would be good."

I laughed, "We ain't butchering these cows. Both of them will need to drop a calf and get it weened."

"I know that, dipshit! But after they've both calved, then we can butcher one of them."

"Yeah; or keep milking her for as long as possible."

He poked a crooked finger at me, "That too. Then butcher her. I want a steak!"

"You remember that black cow we found on the road out there?"

A smile cut the old man's face. "You thinking it was one of his?"

"Has to be. I doubt many folks around here happen to have enough black angus that one can get away and they don't come looking for it."

"Probably right," Sarge replied. Then he cut me a conspiratorial smile and said, "We won't mention that cow to him."

"No, we won't. I figure it was stolen from him anyway." I replied with the same smile.

Mike and Ted came out of the house and stopped in front of us. Mike was looking back and forth between me and the old man. Lowering his sunglasses, he said, "Looks to me like you two are up to something. You about to kiss?"

"Don't worry about it, shithead! And you can kiss my ass!" Sarge barked back and pointed at the truck sitting in the road, "Get that shit unloaded!"

Ted gave Mike a shove and they headed for the truck. "Come on, Mikey, he doesn't want to play right now."

"He never wants to play!" Mike grumbled.

"You're damn right!" Sarge shouted back.

Turning and having to walk backwards because Ted was pushing him, Mike shouted, "You're a shitty father figure!"

"I'd cut my nut sack off if I was your daddy!" Sarge barked back.

As all this was going on, Dalton and Aric came out of the house as well. I waved Dalton over as they were heading for the truck and asked, "You know how to build a still?"

"Do I!"

"I want to start on one."

Dalton looked at Sarge and said, "We'll be back in a minute."

"I ain't got time for grab-ass games! This shit ain't gonna unload itself!"

"Yeah," Dalton replied. Then he put a finger to his chin like he was thinking and said, "If only there were another person to help." He looked at Sarge and asked, "You know anyone doing something utterly useless, like making a fucking list when there's real work to do?"

Sarge's right leg flew out in an attempt to kick Dalton in the ass. But the big man is surprisingly limber and easily dodged it, shouting, "I didn't think so!"

We left Sarge in a flurry of cussing, kicking and stammering as Dalton led the way. "Where are we going?" I asked.

"I want to show you something."

I looked at Aric for an answer. But he just shrugged. Dalton led us to the house where he has his forge set up. He walked under the little cabana he'd built and turned around.

"You brought that copper sheeting back and said you wanted to build a still."

I nodded, "Yeah."

"But you never did anything with it."

"Doesn't change the fact I got it to build a still."

Dalton turned and grabbed a tarp covering something behind him and pulled it off. "So, I did!"

Under the tarp was a beautiful round kettle still. "Holy shit," Aric said.

"Yeah, holy shit," I repeated. Then asked, "When did you do this?"

"I've been working on it for a while now. It takes a lot time to hammer out sheet material into this shape. I had to make some of the tools too," Dalton replied and picked up a hammer with a broad curved face. "Just have to sit here and tap, tap, tap, until it starts to take on the form."

"That's just awesome. What did you solder it with?" I asked.

"Another challenge. I searched every garage around here for lead-free solder and finally managed to get enough."

I ran my hand over the smooth exterior. "Amazing work, man. Really."

Dalton patted the side of the vessel and replied, "It's been a labor of love." Then he looked at me with a serious tone. "Now for the important question. Just what are we going to distill?"

"As soon as that corn's dried, we're going to make some liquor."

Dalton hopped around on one foot, shouting. "Hot damn!"

"Calm down there, Jack Daniels. We're aren't going into

the wholesale liquor business. It'd just be good to have a little around. For medicinal purposes and such."

Dalton nodded eagerly. "Oh yeah, yeah, I totally agree. Medicinal, yeah."

I shook my head and rubbed my face with my hands. "Let me guess. You want to do the distilling."

Dalton cocked his head to the side and patted the still. "Well, I mean, unless you've got a still somewhere."

"What?" I asked, unsure if I was catching exactly what he was insinuating.

"I have a still and you'll have corn. Looks like a match made in heaven to me."

Aric started to laugh and said, "Oh man, that's priceless."

"No, that's horse shit. But whatever. You can do it. Better come up with a souring tank too."

"Don't worry. I've already got a fermenter."

Aric laughed, "You're already to go, aren't you? I don't think it would hurt to have a little hooch around."

"Tis proof God loves us!" Dalton shouted with a flourish.

"That's beer, bonehead," I replied.

Shrugging it off, Dalton replied, "Potato, tomato; it's the same thing."

"Ah, you don't know how that saying works, do you?"

"Sod off!" Dalton shouted and picked up his little hammer, "I've work to do!"

Jabbing a thumb over my shoulder, I said, "Yeah, back over there at that house. Your boss man is probably already looking for you."

Dalton laid the hammer back down and leaned in close to the still. Patting it, he whispered, "I'll be back soon, sweetie; don't worry."

As we walked back towards the old man's place, I told

Dalton and Aric about the two bikes we saw. As soon as I mentioned them, Dalton said, "You think it's the same crew we had a run – in with down the road?"

I nodded. "I think they're out looking for that fuel tanker."

"We need to set up another OP and catch them sneaking around."

"The old man wants to put a couple of guys in one of the burned-out vehicles out there at the end of the road. They'll be able to see all the way down the road to the north, where they'll have to come from."

"I say we go pay them a visit in the middle of the night. We know where they are."

"We could take boats up the creek. They probably wouldn't be expecting that," Aric said.

"Maybe. But I'd prefer to deal with them when and where we choose. Not go kicking their door in and trying to slug it out," I replied.

Dalton nodded. "We need to catch them away from their AO for sure. If we take a couple out, they may send others to look for them. If they don't come home as well, they'll either call the game because they can't take the losses, or they'll come in force. Either way, we'll be able to take care of them. No way they have the kind of resources we do."

"Maybe, but I do not want another fight here. I've had enough of that shit."

"Me neither. Not with Fred being pregnant," Aric added.

"Fugetaboutit!" Dalton shouted. "We'll take care of them."

As we walked up to the house, the old man looked at his watch. Shaking his head, he replied, "About damn time you cheesedicks got back here!"

"Come on, Top," Dalton replied. "We were on important legal business."

Sarge stared down his finger at Dalton and shouted, "You best unfuck yourself and fast! I ain't got time for your grab ass games."

Dalton stopped and thought for a minute. "Top, you know what Army stands for?"

"Don't press your luck, asshole!"

"Ain't ready to be a Marine yet."

"You ain't even a Marine!" Sarge shouted, adding, "you fucking window-licking retard!"

"I am!" Ian called from the driveway as he and Jamie carried a crate inside.

Sarge looked back at him and shouted, "Marine my ass! About as useful as the maître fucking d' on the fucking Titanic! You halfwits get your asses to work!"

"On that note, I'm leaving," I said as I mounted the Harley.

Sarge turned and shouted, "Damn right! Get to steppin'; you're about useless too!"

I started the Harley and held my hand to my ear, "Huh? What'd you say? I can't hear you."

When the old man went to shout something at me, I revved the big bike. It infuriated him and got everyone else to laughing, which of course only made it worse. But I was smart and dropped it into gear and got the hell out of the blast zone before he could get a hand around my neck. I rode back to the house and pulled the bike up front. Going in, I grabbed a big cloth bag and brought it back out and loaded the grapes into it.

Mel and the girls weren't back yet, so I was going to use the time to process the grapes. Since a large part of the job was smashing them, I carried the bag over to Danny's. The kids were in the back yard playing in the sprinkler. No doubt, they'd get a kick out of mashing the fruit. Danny brought out a bucket and when I asked for something to pound them with, he disappeared and returned with what looked like a table leg. It was raw wood and unfinished and would do the job perfectly.

We set the bucket on the porch and dropped the leg in. Then I called the kids up to the porch. They all came running, dripping water all over the porch. I showed them what I wanted them to do and Little Bit quickly grabbed the leg and went to work. The kids were all giggles as they smashed the grapes, taking turns in a not-so-round robin. I instructed the kids to not pound too hard, but to pick the masher up and drop it.

"Why?" Danny asked.

"You don't want to crush the seeds. It'll make it really bitter."

As the kids were working and we were talking, Miss Kay came out of the house with a couple glasses of ice tea.

"You boys look hot. Brought you some tea to cool you off," she said and looked down at the bucket, "what's this?"

Taking the offered glass, I thanked her and said, "I found some grapes today. Thought we would process them down into juice for you."

"Grapes?" Kay asked as she leaned over the bucket. "Oh my, that looks amazing. I can make jelly out of that for sure!"

"We have to get the juice ready first. This isn't like commercial grapes."

"What do you have to do other than smash and strain them?"

"Once we've strained it through a cheesecloth or something, the juice needs to sit in the fridge for a couple of days. Wild grapes have tartrate. It forms gritty little crystals that will really irritate your throat. It'll even burn your hands if you handle it too long."

"The juice will?" Danny asked.

"We can't do anything with that," Kay said.

"Sure, you can. Once it settles, you just pour the juice off and leave the gray sludge behind. It makes up a lot of the juice, but we have enough to make jelly for sure."

"Ok, Morgan, if you say so," Kay replied.

"Trust me on this one," I replied with a smile and took a sip of the tea.

"Kay, Morgan's been eating weeds as long as I've known him. He's taught me some things too. I trust him," Danny added.

Kay smiled, "Oh, I trust him. Just having a little fun." She turned and looked at me, asking, "Are the girls back yet?"

"They weren't when I came over here. Soon as we strain this juice, I'll go home and wait on them."

"Then I'll get you a cloth too," Kay said as she disappeared into the house.

She returned with a cheesecloth and large bowl. We dismissed the kids to go back to the sprinkler and I held the cloth over the bowl while Danny poured the juice through it. Once the bucket was empty, I twisted up the cloth and started to wring it out.

"I thought you said it would burn your hands," Danny said.

"Only if you don't rinse your hands soon after handling the juice. Or if you're working with the juice for a long time. Then it will burn you. This will only take a minute." With the juice squeezed from the cloth, I went out the door into the yard.

"Where are you going?" Danny asked.

"To spread these seeds around the pond. Maybe we'll get a bearing vine to grow here!" I called back.

I walked around the pond and spread the seeds and skins in large handfuls. Naturally, the kids followed me and ended up splashing around in the pond, chasing minnows and tadpoles. Edie fell forward into the tea-colored water and I had to fish her out. But she was laughing; and before I knew it, all the kids were in the pond. I managed to fish them all out and herded them to the back to the sprinkler.

As we walked back, Little Bit grabbed my hand, "Daddy, daddy! We need to feed Ruckus!"

"I'll do it, baby. I'm about to head to the house anyway."

"Can I come and feed him?"

I patted her head, "You stay here and play with your friends. I'll take care of it."

She smiled in the way a child can go from one thing to another in the blink of an eye; and then she ran back to the swirling kids running through the spraying water. I went back into the kitchen to see what Kay was doing with the juice. Thad was there when I came in, working on some of the pork and getting ready to make some sausage.

I slapped him on the back and asked how it was going. He smiled and looked over his shoulder, "Now the work starts."

"Well, we got more work coming."

Thad's brow furrowed, and he asked, with a hint of suspicion, "What'd you do now?"

"Well, I bought a couple of cows. Heifers that are going to calve."

His eyes went wide, but before he could reply, Kay asked, "Cows? Where did you ever come up with cows?"

I told them the story of seeing the cows while I was picking the grapes and seeing the ranch hands watching over them.

"So, in a day or so, they're bringing two cows out and then we'll have four."

"What'd they cost?" Thad asked.

"I said we'd give them a pregnant sow and three other hogs. That and three hundred gallons of diesel."

"They gonna trade two cows for that?" Thad asked.

I nodded, "Yep."

"That's going to be amazing!" Kay shouted. "We'll be able to milk them for a long time."

"That's a lot of work," Thad replied.

"But it'll be worth it," I replied. "We'll have all the butter we need, not to mention milk and anything else we can think of."

"You said they're bringing them here? Gonna deliver them?" Thad asked.

"Yeah. They're bringing them in a stock trailer."

"Where you planning on putting them?" Thad asked.

"I was thinking in the field across the road there. What do you think?"

"In the graveyard?"

"I don't think anyone over there will mind."

"Oh, Morgan, that's just awful," Kay snapped.

Shrugging, I replied, "Am I wrong?"

"No," Thad said, "you ain't wrong. How you planning on watering them?"

"Same way we do the pigs. With the tanker. Just pull the trailer over there and fill a stock tank."

Thad nodded as he chopped the pork. "I think that'll work. But if they're going to be here in a couple of days, we need to get a tank set up over there for them."

"We do. I'll see if I can find one."

"I know where one is. I'll get it with the tractor and fill it up."

"You're my hero," I replied. "When I grow up, I want to be just like you."

Thad laughed and shook his head. Kay laughed too, adding, "Morgan, I don't think you'll ever grow up that big."

I looked Thad up and down and said, "What? He ain't that big."

Thad cut his eyes to the side and said, "What'er you talking about little man?"

It got all of us to laughing. "On that note, I'm out of here. I have a mouse to go feed."

"How is that little squirrel doing?" Kay asked.

"Just fine. I think his eyes will open in a few days."

"When they do, bring him over. I want to see him."

As I was heading for the door, I said, "Will do, Miss Kay."

Ruckus was in his shoebox sound asleep. But as soon as I picked him up and put the dropper to his mouth, he was wide awake. Baby squirrels are funny. They push against what they're feeding from. I guess it stimulates milk in the mother. So, he was pushing against the dropper as hard as he could. You don't have to squeeze the milk out, they'll get it! And you have to be careful not to let them take so much they aspirate it. Not only will they choke, they could develop pneumonia.

So, when Ruckus started coughing up milk, I took the dropper away and let him get it up. Wiped his little face and finished feeding him. Then I dampened a cloth with warm water and wiped his butt. They gotta poop and I ain't about to lick it like his momma. With the mouse fed, I put him back in the box and closed it up.

Mel still wasn't back, and I had free time, so I checked on the vinegar. It was certainly vinegary and tasted about ready to me. I got the crock through the plywood door, only thing I had to repair it with, and onto the back deck. Going to the shed, I grabbed an empty bucket and looked for something to strain it with. I found a little pool net, the sort of thing you dip leaves from your pool with and set it on top of the bucket and slowly poured the contents of the crock through it.

I had to stop a couple of times to clean the net; there were a lot of fruit skins and they quickly filled the shallow net. Once it was all filtered into the bucket, I tasted it again. Definitely vinegar, and I estimated there was a little over two gallons. Satisfied with the product, I set it in a corner and poured myself a glass of tea and headed for the porch to wait for Mel and the girls.

I was on my second glass of tea before the Suburban rolled into the yard. As soon as they got out, I could tell it was a hard day for them. They looked hollow, spent. I stood up and stepped down off the porch. Taylor walked towards the house with her shoulders slumped. As though every step took considerable effort.

As she approached, I said, "Hey, kiddo. How'd it go?"

Without looking up, she replied, "It was terrible. I'm really tired and want to go to bed."

"You don't want supper?"

"No. I'm not hungry."

"You alright?"

"I'm fine," she muttered as she opened the door and went into the house.

As Lee Ann walked up, she asked, "What's for supper? I'm starving."

"Miss Kay is working on something over there."

Adjusting the H&K slung over her shoulder, she replied, "I'm going over there now. I haven't eaten all day." Mary was standing behind her and said she'd go with her.

As they trotted off towards Danny's house, Mel walked up and stopped in front of me. Her head was hanging, and I leaned out and wrapped my arms around her. "How bad was it?" I asked.

Her head rocked against my chest and she said, "It was terrible. The children, the women; it was horrible." She stepped back and wiped a tear from her eye.

"Well, you don't have to go back if you don't want to."

She shook her head. "No. It wasn't easy, but I'll go back. We all need to do our part."

Stepping beside her, I put an arm around her. "You hungry? You want to go get something to eat?"

"I'm tired and all I want to do is go to bed, but I do need to eat something first."

"Ok, let's go see what Kay's cooked up."

She rubbed her face and said, "I need to go feed the Ruckus."

"I already did. Let's get you something to eat."

She patted my chest, "Thank you, baby."

We found a loud gathering on the back porch. The kids were sitting together, eagerly eating from their bowls. Aric and Fred were sitting with Jess and Doc. Mike, Ted, Dalton and Wallner were all sitting together. Kay and Sarge were sitting together, and when she saw us, Kay got up, saying, "You two sit down and I'll get you something to eat."

Mary poked her head out of the kitchen window and said, "Just stay there, Kay. I'll bring it out."

Mary came out of the kitchen and Mel and I sat down at a table with Lee Ann. Mary set bowls in front of us and she and Mel talked for a minute about the trip to town. As they were talking, I looked into the bowl and asked Kay, "What is this?"

Acting apologetic, Kay replied, "Oh, it's a goulash of sorts. I'm sorry, it's not very good."

"Nonsense!" Sarge barked. "It's fantastic!"

I sampled the concoction. "Damn!" I shouted, and Kay looked over. "I don't know what you're talking about, Kay. This is really good!"

"Well, thank you, Morgan. I'm happy you like it."

We finished dinner and collected Little Bit, said our goodbyes and left for home. I checked with Lee Ann, but she said she wanted to stay and wasn't ready to go. Mel was tired and not very chatty during dinner. I could tell she just wanted to go to bed. It was uncomfortably warm for this time of evening. It felt as though a low-pressure system had moved in and pushed a lot of humid air with it. It was going to be a hard night to sleep.

"Daddy, did you feed Ruckus?" Little Bit asked. She was holding my hand as we walked to the house.

"I did," I replied with a smile. "But he probably needs to be fed again. You want to feed him before bed?"

"I do, I do!"

"Can you help her?" Mel asked.

Squeezing her hand, I replied, "No problem, babe. I know you're tired."

When we went inside, Mel kissed Little Bit goodnight and headed into the bedroom. I told Little Bit to sit at the table and I went into our room to get the shoebox. Mel was getting undressed and I grabbed the box and left the room without bothering her. I gave Little Bit the box, much to her delight, and went into the kitchen and mixed up a little formula and filled the dropper.

"Here, baby." I said as I handed her the dropper. "Be careful. Don't squeeze it, just let him suck it out."

"I won't," she replied with a large smile as she cradled Ruckus and cooed baby words at him.

I left her to feed the mouse and went into the kitchen and brewed a pot of tea. My jug was nearly empty and running out of tea was a cardinal sin as I saw it. As I was mixing sugar into the tea, Little Bit announced Ruckus was done. I told her to put him in the box, which she protested, but finally did as she was told, and I sent her off to bed.

"You going to tuck me in?"

Rubbing a hand through her hair, I replied, "Of course. Go brush your teeth and get in bed and I'll come see you."

While she brushed her teeth, I went in to see Taylor. She was wrapped up in her blanket, despite the heat in the house, which was nearly unbearable to me. I sat on the edge of her bed and patted her leg. "How you doing, kiddo?"

Without rolling over, she replied, "I'm fine."

"I know today was a rough day. But I'm glad you went. As weird as it sounds, it was good for you."

"It didn't feel good to me. But, I get what you mean. I learned a lot about where we are. How good we have it. It was horrible though."

"I'm sorry you had to see it. But, I'm happy you don't have to live it. Know what I'm saying?"

She was quiet for a long minute. Then she replied, "I do, dad. And I'm thankful." She rolled over and sat up. "It's easy to forget, you know, that as bad as things are, they could be worse."

"Things aren't that bad."

"Really, dad? It's like a million degrees in here."

I lifted the blanket and dropped it, "Get out from under this rug."

"You know what I mean."

"Sure, we don't have AC. But if you think about it, that's about all that's missing."

She laughed, "Are you out of your mind? That's all that's missing?"

"Ok, maybe that's all that I'm missing," I said. "Think about it. What is life about? Is it spending most of your life working your ass off to make someone else a bunch of money? Or is it doing whatever you want, to pursue your personal desires?"

"There isn't much we can pursue though. I'd gladly go to work at McDonalds for minimum wage."

I smiled. "I guess I can see your point of view. You're young and not yet disillusioned. Or should I say, haven't had the opportunity to become disillusioned yet. You know, I worked for many, many years trying to take care of you, your sisters and your mom. Where'd it get me?"

"I remember you spent a lot of time away from home. You were gone a lot."

"See, that's what I'm talking about," I replied, pointing at her. "I spent all that time away from home. All those years, I could have been doing something else. It's a dichotomy I guess."

"What's a dichotomy?"

"It's a comparison of two things that are opposite of one another."

"Oh, like today compared to how things used to be."

"Exactly," I replied.

"Well, that's certainly a dichotomy."

"I'm in bed, Daddy!" Little Bit called from her bedroom.

I laughed and patted Taylor's leg. "Get some sleep, kiddo. I'll see you tomorrow."

"Goodnight," Taylor replied.

I exited her room, leaving the door open to help circulate some air. It was miserable in the house. Little Bit was in her bed with the sheet pulled up to her chin. It made me smile and I leaned over and kissed her forehead. "Goodnight, kiddo."

"Eskimo noses!" She shouted.

She was such a bright spot in a world short on light. I leaned in and rubbed noses with her. She giggled and pulled the sheet up over her head. I tickled her and she giggled and squirmed. "Goodnight, baby girl. Love you."

"I love you too," she replied between giggles.

"Get some sleep. I'll see you in the morning."

I turned the light off as I left and grabbed a quick cold

shower to help cool off before going to bed. As I was toweling off, I heard Lee Ann come in and I threw my robe on and stuck my head out. She smiled and gave me a little wave. I whispered *goodnight*. She disappeared into her room and I went to bed.

CHAPTER 6

THE GUYS IN THE BURNED-OUT MRAP called on the radio to say they saw a large truck pulling a trailer coming down the road. Sarge had put two-man teams into the scorched hull on rotating watches of four hours. We hadn't seen anything more out of the motorcycles, but the old man was very particular when it came to security. Hearing the call on the radio, I hopped on a four-wheeler and headed towards the bunker.

The truck was parked when I got there. Wallner and another Guardsmen were talking to Janet and one of her ranch hands. Getting off the ATV, I offered Janet my hand, which she took with a firm grip. "How are you doing?" I asked.

With a bright smile, she replied, "Great. It's hotter than hell. But I'm good."

Sarge pulled up in a Hummer with the three muskie queers. He got out of the truck and walked up with a smile and said, "You must be Janet."

Holding her hand out, Janet replied, "I am. Good to meet you."

Sarge took her hand and shook it. "I hear you have a couple beeves for us."

Janet looked surprised. "Most people don't know what that word is. I'm impressed."

"Well, when you been around as long as I have, you pick up on a couple of things."

Mike came strolling up with a cheesy grin on his face. Looking at Janet, he asked, "Well, to what do you owe the pleasure of meeting me?" He lowered his glasses and made a show of looking her up and down.

Janet laughed. "Nice try, Sport. But high school was a long time ago."

"Not for you. Couldn't have been. Last year, tops." Mike replied with a big smile.

"Teddy!" Sarge barked. "Get his ass out of here. The grownups are talking."

Ted grabbed Mike by the back of his shirt. "Come on, Mikey. We got shit to do."

"Alright, I'll see you later," Mike replied with a wink.

Janet looked past him to Ted and said, "Thank you."

Ted shrugged, "No big deal. Every animal needs a handler." He tugged on Mike's shirt again and said, "Come on, Milo."

Janet laughed, and Mike looked over his shoulder, "Who's Milo?"

"Planet of the Apes, sweetie," Janet replied.

"What?" Mike asked.

Ted pulled him away, saying, "Come on, let's get you a banana."

Mike's mind switched quickly, "You got a banana?"

"Now that the wildlife is gone," Sarge said, "let's get down to business. You got a couple of heifers in there for us?"

Janet folded her arms and replied, "You got some hogs and diesel for me?"

Sarge turned and pointed down the road at the tanker. "There's the diesel. The hogs are in a pen not far from here."

She clapped her hands, "Great! Where do you want the beeves?"

Thad rode up on a four-wheeler and Sarge pointed at him, "There's your man. He'll lead you to the pasture where you can unload them."

"Alright, let's go."

We rode down the road to the pasture where Thad opened the gate and the truck pulled through. While they were getting the cows unloaded, I took a minute to ride the fence. It hadn't been checked and I didn't want our new livestock getting away from us. Which made me think about someone stealing them, or worse, shooting one and taking only what they could carry and leaving the rest to rot. We'd have to keep an eye on them.

I didn't find any breaks in the fence and by the time I got back, the cows were out and already mowing the lawn. Thad smiled when I pulled up, "Find any breaks in the fence?"

"No. Looks good."

"Neither did I."

I laughed, "Should have known you would have already done it."

We left the cows to graze and headed back down the road to get the diesel. One of Janet's hands got in the trailer and Thad passed the hose through to him. As the tank filled, we talked with Janet.

"Why don't you all come over tomorrow afternoon," Janet said. "We've got a swimming hole at the house if anyone wants to cool off. And there will be plenty of beef."

"Kay is going to make buns for the burgers," I offered.

"That sounds just fine," Sarge replied. "I'm looking forward to meeting your daddy."

Janet smiled, "You'll like him, I think. You two should get

along just fine. He's been the force that held us all together during all this. But it's taken a toll on him."

"It's taken a toll on all of us," Sarge replied.

"Indeed," I added.

Her mood brightening, Janet said, "All the more reason to get together. I'll take any chance to smile now. We've been pretty isolated since things changed. We were basically self-sufficient and didn't need to go to town."

"Did you ever go?" I asked.

She shook her head. "I didn't. But a couple of the hands went in from time to time just to see what was going on."

"Tank's full," Thad said as he hung up the hose. I introduced Thad to Janet as he walked over.

"It's nice to meet you," she replied as she shook his hand.

"Good to meet you. You ready to go load some hogs?"

"Oh yes. I'm really looking forward to some breakfast sausage and a nice fat porkchop!"

Sarge laughed, "Sounds like you want some pig meat as bad as I want some beef!"

"You always miss what you don't have," she replied.

"Ain't that the truth," Thad added.

Thad and I walked over to the pig pen as one of Janet's men drove the truck over. Seeing people, the pigs came running. Thad had already prepared some feed for them, more swamp cabbage and scraps from the kitchen. Using a couple of fence panels, we sectioned off the small gate the trailer backed up to. Getting in, Thad and I worked together to get the pigs sorted, so only the ones we wanted to load were inside the new makeshift pen. It required a lot of kicking, prodding and pushing, but we finally got it done. Of course, there was a lot of advice from those gathered around and watching.

By the time they were loaded, we were both breathing hard

and laughing, as were all those gathered to watch. Once we had only the ones we wanted in the little pen, Thad walked into the stock trailer and dumped out the feed he'd prepared. I threw open the gate and the hogs rushed into the trailer. Thad swung the door shut and they were in.

"Hell, that was easy," Sarge said when the gate banged shut.

I wiped the sweat running down my nose with the back of my hand and replied, "It is easy when all you're doing is holding down that fence post."

"I got my job and you got yours," the old man replied.

Janet laughed and pointed at the hand that drove the truck, "You all sound like these guys."

He shrugged, "Just the way it is, I reckon."

I held my hand out, "I'm Morgan."

"Travis," he replied as he shook it.

"We're going to head back," Janet said. "I want to get these pigs home and into their pen before anything happens to them."

"I hope you have good fences," Thad said with a big smile. "We had to put in a hot wire to keep them in."

"Oh, we have a pen," Travis replied. "Been working on it since Morgan here made the deal."

They said their goodbyes, with Janet adding we should come over any time after noon tomorrow. We promised we'd be there and waved as they climbed into the truck and headed down the road.

After they left, I told Sarge I wanted to go to town to talk to Cecil. I wanted him to go with us to this little cookout. "That's a fine idea. I'll take that ride to town with you," Sarge replied.

I went home to tell Mel we were going into town. She replied she wanted to go too. Lee Ann said she wanted to as well. Since they were going, I asked Taylor if she wanted to go.

"No. I'll stay here. Ashley wants to go see the cows. I'll take her over there."

"And then we're going to play in the pool too!" Little Bit shouted.

Taylor smiled at her little sister, "Yes, then I'll play in the pool with you."

"Alright," I replied. "We'll be back later."

I pulled my armor on and picked up my rifle. Lee Ann came out with her H&K slung over her shoulder. Mel came out of the bedroom and I looked at her. "You going to put your pistol on?"

She looked at me and cocked her head to the side. "Aren't we just going to town?"

I nodded. "Yeah, so put your pistol on." While she went to get her pistol, I went to the kitchen and poured myself a thermos of tea and filled an insulated mug with ice and tea. This was one luxury we had, ice, and I was thankful for it!

She went back into the bedroom and came out, lacing a belt into her jeans and threading the holster on. "Let's go over and get some pork to take to Gina," I said.

"That's a great idea," Mel replied.

We walked over to Danny's. He was in the shed, messing with something and waved as we passed. Thad, Mary and Miss Kay were in the kitchen working on the pork. I asked for some to take to Gina.

"That's a fine idea," Kay replied. She took out a loaf pan and laid a couple of thick pork chops into it and packed the rest of the pan with some of the sausage that they were busy grinding. "You think that's enough?" She asked.

"I'm sure it is," I replied.

"They'll be happy with it," Mel added.

"You going to town?" Thad asked.

"Yeah, I want to go talk to Cecil. I'd like him to come with us tomorrow."

"Oh, that's nice, Morgan," Kay said. "You're always thinking of others." She made me smile. Kay was such a gentle soul. The epitome of an iconic grandmother.

"It's just what we have to do," I replied with a smile. We left the house headed towards the old man's place.

"Man, it's hot," Mel said as we made our way down the road.

"Tell me about it. I really, really miss air conditioning," I replied.

"Me too," Lee Ann added.

Sarge was sitting in the Hummer at the end of his street. Seeing us, he shouted, "You brought back up!" As we were getting in the truck, he said, "Mornin', Mel, Lee Ann. Glad to see you two getting out."

As Mel settled into her seat, she said, "It's about time I started doing more. This is life now. The old one isn't coming back."

When I got in, Sarge looked at me with raised eyebrows. I shrugged, and he smiled and dropped the truck in gear and we headed out.

"Stop by Gina's place. We have some pork to give them," I said. He nodded as we pulled out onto the county road.

Gina and Dylan were sitting on the porch when we pulled up. They both got up and walked out to meet us as everyone got out. "What a surprise!" Gina said when she saw Mel.

"We brought you some pork," Mel said, holding the pan out.

Gina took it and lifted the little towel covering the meat. "Oh, Batman is going to love this!"

"What is it?" Dylan asked as he shook Sarge's hand, then mine.

Gina tilted the pan, so he could see in it, "Pork chops and sausage!"

Dylan clapped his hands, "Hot damn!" He shouted.

"Come inside, Mel. I'll find something to put this in, so you can take the pan back," Gina said as they headed towards the house.

"What are you up to today?" Dylan asked.

"We're headed into town," I replied. "How are things here? How's Gina doing?"

"Oh, we're fine. Gina is good. She hasn't had an episode in a couple of weeks."

"That's good to hear," Sarge replied. "You know, if you ever need anything, we're just across the road."

"We know, we know; and we appreciate it too."

Mel and Gina came out of the house. They were laughing about something. "What are you two up to?" I asked with suspicion.

"Don't you worry about it, Sheriff!" Gina shouted.

Folding my arms, I replied, "Gina, I've been married long enough to know when women are up to something. And you two are definitely up to something."

Mel walked past me and smiled, "It's nothing you need to worry about."

Sarge looked at her, then at Gina. Then at Dylan. "Yep. They're up to something."

"Ya think?" Dylan asked with a laugh.

"Alright. We're outta here before these two get into trouble," Sarge replied.

"Indeed," I added. "Say, tomorrow we're going to a little get together with some folks we met. They're putting on a cookout. Would you like to come?"

"Cookout?" Dylan asked. "What are they cooking?"

"Steak."

"Steak?" Gina asked in surprise.

"They have cattle," Sarge added.

"Well, we wouldn't want to intrude," Dylan replied, looking at Gina.

"You wouldn't be. You're more than welcome," I said.

Dylan looked at Gina, "It sure would be nice to get away. Not to mention eating some steak."

Gina looked at me, "We'd love to come. If it's no trouble."

"We'll swing by and pick you up on our way," Sarge said.

We waved goodbye and got on the road towards Eustis. But we didn't go far. When we came to the market in Altoona, there was a crowd gathered and it was obvious from the road something was up.

"Better go check on this," I said to Sarge. Even though he was already turning into the market.

A throng of people was gathered into a tight knot. There were shouts and objects being thrown. I looked over at Mario, who was in his usual spot and he smiled and nodded at the crowd. We got out and Sarge and I waded into the crowd, pushing people out of the way. When we got to the center of the mass of people, two men were on the ground. They were both bloodied and bruised from the hail of kicks and punches raining down on them.

Sarge and I tried to pull the people back, shoving, cussing and in a couple of cases, having to punch them in the face. But we just couldn't get the crowd off the two men. Just when I was thinking of drawing my pistol, a shot rang out. The crowd froze. I looked at Sarge, expecting to see a pistol in his hand. But he had some long-haired bearded man in a headlock and was looking at me. Then two more shots rang out and the crowd began to flee.

I looked back to see Mel holding her pistol above her head. "That's about enough of that shit!" She shouted. Lee Ann was standing beside her, the H&K at her shoulder as she eyed the crowd with a look that said, *make my day.* I was stunned.

Sarge's voice brought me back around. "What in the hell is going on here?" He demanded.

The man he had in the headlock pointed to the two men now cowering on the ground. He managed to choke out, "Them sons of bitches are stealing!"

"From who?" I asked.

"From everybody!" A voice called out as the crowd began to close in again.

I looked at the people, then back at Mel and Lee Ann and said, "You better keep your distance unless you want those ladies to smoke your ass."

Many of the people in the crowd made a gesture of half raising their hands in submission. Sarge released the man he had ahold of and asked, "Now, just what in the hell is going on here?"

We were finally able to work out what was happening. The two men worked together to shoplift, for lack of a better term. It was an old tactic. One would distract the trader and the other would pocket the goods.

"They been doing it for a long time," one of the traders shouted. "But we caught their asses today!" Several trade goods were held out as evidence of the crime.

I looked down at them and asked, "Is that true? You two stealing from these folks?"

One of the men sat up. "We only take a little bit. What else are we supposed to do? We need to eat as well."

"You don't steal, asshole!" Sarge shouted and the crowd joined in with shouts of approval.

I kicked one in the ass, "Get on your feet." Then I told Sarge to keep an eye on them.

"Where the hell you going?" He asked,

"To talk to Mario."

I walked over to Mario, who was laughing as I came up. "Glad you enjoyed the show."

"That's the best thing I've seen in a long time!"

"Yeah, yeah. So, were they stealing?"

"Yeah they were," Shelly answered. "They were busted red-handed."

I looked back at the two men and Mario asked, "What are you going to go with them?"

"I don't know. We don't have a jail now. I'll have to figure something out."

I walked back over to Sarge. "I don't know what to do with them. We don't have a jail."

"You're the Sheriff, so you say!" Someone shouted. "You need to do something!"

"And we will!" I shouted back. Looking at Lee Ann, I asked, "You mind hanging around here for a while?"

"Sure."

"Alright. Let's take them over there. I've got some cuffs. We'll secure them for now. We'll run to town and get Mitch and bring him out here to settle this today."

"Good call," Sarge said. "Law and order."

"I'll stay here too," Mel said.

"You sure." I asked.

"Why not? That way, nothing happens to them. Plus, I can talk to Shelly, I haven't seen her in a long time."

"Sounds like this is settled," Sarge said. Then he added, "Leave them your radio, Morgan."

"Good idea. But just to make sure there isn't any trouble," I keyed the mic on my radio. "Hey, Jamie."

Go ahead.

"I need some people at the market in Altoona for security."

We're on our way.

I handed the radio to Mel. "Here. You've got some help coming too. Don't let these people try anything. We'll be back later."

"We don't need the help," Mel replied, insulted.

"Babe, you always need the help. Just like I needed it from you earlier."

"Always stack the odds in your favor, Mel," Sarge added. "You want it to be as unfair, on your side, as you can get it."

She nodded, "I see your point."

I leaned in and kissed her, "We'll be back as soon as we can."

"We got this," Lee Ann offered.

Sarge and I secured the two men to a U-shaped bollard at the gas pumps with two sets of cuffs, chaining the two men together. As I clicked the cuffs closed, I whispered to them, "Now, if you guys are thinking of fucking with those two, understand that they will kill you where you stand, understand? They're here to protect you from them," I said and nodded at the still fuming traders discussing what they would like to do to the two men.

Sarge and I left the market and headed towards town. As he pulled out of the parking lot, he looked over and asked, "What the hell happened to your bride? That's not the same Mel I know."

"I have no idea," I answered honestly. "I think the day she spent working at the gym with the wounded from the attack really hit her hard."

"I knew something was up earlier when she made that

statement about having to do more. I knew something had clicked in her."

"Yeah, I could tell something was different," I replied and looked over, "in a good way."

Slapping the steering wheel, Sarge shouted, "In a damn good way!"

"Yeah, I kinda like it."

Sarge glanced over at me. "You better watch yourself now. It's looking to me like Mel is getting ready to kick some ass."

I laughed. "Yeah, but you're on deck. She still ain't got over you showing your ass in the front yard."

The old man's face soured. "Now why you gotta go being an asshole? Here we were having a perfectly good conversation and you had to go and fuck it all up!"

Shrugging, I replied, "I wasn't the one dropping my trou..."

"Kiss my ass!"

Now, I laughed. "Pick a spot, old man."

We found Cecil at the first place we stopped to look, the cornfield. Cecil seemed to like spending time there. Maybe because it was so far away no one would walk out there, and he could be left alone. Maybe he just liked to watch the corn grow. Either way, he was sitting in the shade of the oak tree when we rolled up.

"What kind of trouble are you two up to?" He asked as we got out.

"Come looking for you," Sarge replied.

I was carrying my thermos of tea with me and sat down beside Cecil on an old wire reel. I held it out and asked, "Want some?"

He waved it off, "It's too damn hot for coffee."

Sarge snorted, "Nonsense! It's never too hot for coffee. That's like saying it's too hot for air!"

Cecil sipped water from a plastic cup and replied, "It is too hot for air today."

"This is ice tea. Some of us ain't bat shit crazy," I said.

Cecil pitched the water out of his cup and held it out. "Now, that I'll take." I poured his cup full and after taking a long drink of the cold tea, he asked, "What do you want with me?"

"We're going to a little get-together tomorrow with some folks Morgan found. Wanted you to come along," Sarge replied.

Cecil looked at me, "Where'd you find 'em?"

"In a cow pasture."

The old man laughed, showing his long teeth. "You mean a pasture, ain't no more cows."

"That's the thing, Cecil. They got cows too. Lots of them. They're going to give one to the town to help with the injured at the gym. And we also traded for two cows. Tomorrow, they're putting on a feed, all the steak you can eat."

Cecil's eyes went wide. "Steak?" He nearly shouted. "Say no more! I'm definitely in!"

"Thought you might want to come," Sarge said.

"Where are these folks?"

"Out off of forty-two."

Cecil nodded, "That big ranch there by four fifty. I know where you're talking about. Didn't know there was anyone out there."

Taking a sip of my own tea, I said, "They've been laying low. Unsure of just what was going on. Sounds like they've got a few people out there."

"Boy," Cecil said and wiped his chin, "I ain't had any beef since you all gave me some. That sure would be good."

"Well, tomorrow you can eat till your belly busts," Sarge replied.

"What time?"

"They said after noon. We'll come up and get you and carry you home afterwards," I answered.

"That sure will be fine. Just come here and get me. I'll be up here waiting on you."

We looked out at the stand of corn. It was starting to turn brown, the stalks dying and beginning to wither. I asked, "How much longer till it's ready?"

"Not much longer. But it's going to be tough to get enough people out here to pick it all. I'm fearing we're going to lose a bunch. So many folks are gone now. We're going to be short of hands."

"We'll get it picked," Sarge replied. "If it takes all of us working day and night. We can't let any of it go to waste."

"We'll be up here tomorrow to get you, Cecil. We have to go find Mitch to take care of some other business now," I said.

"Alright, fellers. I'll see you tomorrow."

We left Cecil in the shade of the tree and headed into Eustis. As Sarge pulled out onto nineteen, a sense of loss came over me. I used to bitch about having to go to Eustis to see Sheffield and Livingston. But today, I wish they were there to visit. We rode through what was left of the town. The blackened and charred remains still littered the streets and impacts where rockets had blasted away the road, sidewalks and curbs were still very evident. The place was a ghost town. The once busy lakeside park was empty, save the shattered trees and playground equipment littering the grounds. The tables the traders used were also destroyed and not a soul ventured there. Even the gallows so much work had been put into were burned to the ground. We turned east on forty-four and headed towards Mitch's place.

With so much of the town destroyed and so many to be buried, we'd selected a spot on the edge of town as the cemetery.

Lake Gracie was just a few blocks east of downtown and I suggested we ride over there and see how it was going.

"Might as well," Sarge replied as he turned onto Prescott Street.

Shane and Shawn were heading up the burial detail. They managed to find a small excavator and with the help of Scott and Terry, got it running. The deceased residents of Eustis were being interred in mass graves. It was awful work, but it needed to be done.

"Must be close," I said as I wrinkled my nose. You could smell the location long before you could see it.

"I recognize the smell," Sarge replied.

We stopped a short distance from where the excavator was working. Shawn sat in the seat, a bandana tied around his face as he dug the long ditch. It took a long time to dig them as they had to be wide enough for the bodies to be laid in and deep enough. The machine was seriously undersized for such a project, but it was all we had.

Shane was at the other end of the trench with a group of men who were loading the bodies on a small wagon connected to an ATV that would carry them over to the trench where other men would place them into their final resting place. The bodies looked like something out of Civil War photographs. They were bloated and swollen. Blackened from lying exposed as space was made for them. Fluids ran from every opening and each body was torn apart to varying degrees. Many were in pieces and care was taken to try and keep the bodies together. Flies filled the air and the stench assaulted the nostrils under the brutal Florida heat. It really was a terrible scene.

As I walked towards Shane, I choked on the smell. It hung thick in the air, a presence unto itself that couldn't be ignored. Or so I thought until I looked over at Sarge. He appeared to take no notice of the assault on the senses and strolled along as though he were walking through the park.

"How can you stand this?" I asked as I shook my bandana out and covered my nose.

"Seen it all before," was all he said.

Shane looked worn out. He was soaked in sweat and filthy from the task he managed. He pulled the cloth down that was covering his face as we approached.

"This the last one?" Sarge asked, looking at the trench.

He nodded, "Yeah. Thank God. This is it."

I looked over at the line of at least thirty corpses lying in the sun. My eyes didn't linger though. I didn't want to see the maggots that were certainly there. They were of all ages. Men, women, kids. Teenagers and elderly. "You guys need anything?" I asked.

He shook his head. "No. We'll finish this today. I wish we could do something for the men that worked on this though. It wasn't easy."

"We'll do something for all of you," Sarge replied.

"What was the total?" I asked.

Shane looked down the long scar in the dirt where previous trenches had been filled. "It was three-hundred and seventy-three."

"That's a hell of a lot of people," I replied.

"And we're still finding them. People come and tell us where a body is, and we go collect it. It's not too hard to find them now, depending on which way the wind is blowing."

I shook my head. "It's awful that these people managed to survive the aftermath of the EMP, eking out a living in all this shit, and then this happened to them."

"It's the way the world works, Morgan," Sarge replied. He still looked totally unphased by all of this.

"Let's hope there's a little change to the way things are," I said.

"I sure as hell hope so. I don't ever want to have to do this again," Shane said.

"We'll leave you to it," Sarge said. "We have things to tend to." I gave Shane a nod, he returned it grimly and we left them to complete their morbid task.

We found Mitch at his house. He came out to meet us when we pulled up. Smiling, he waved as we got out. "What brings you guys out here?"

"Well, we got some business for you, your honor," Sarge said.

Mitch never did like the formal address and it showed on his face. "What kind of business?"

"We have a couple of people that were stealing from some of the traders in Altoona. There isn't a jail anymore and I don't know what to do with them," I replied.

Mitch scratched his head. "I don't really know either."

"What has to happen," Sarge said, "is you have to go out there. Hold court there and pass sentence. In front of everyone."

"What kind of sentence can we pass? Town is destroyed. We can't jail them or anything. There isn't a farm to put them to work on. There aren't really any people there anymore."

"Corporal punishment," Sarge replied.

"What?" Both Mitch and I asked.

"Just that. Corporal punishment. It's all we have left," Sarge replied.

"And who the hell is going to do that?" I asked.

Sarge pointed at me, "You're the Sheriff. It's up to you. I can't do it." He pointed at Mitch, "he's the judge; he can't do it. You're the law enforcement; it's your job."

"He's got a point," Mitch said.

"I don't want to do that shit!"

Sarge took a deep breath and looked at me, "I'm sure you can find someone in your crew to take the job."

I started to ask just who in the hell would want such a job, then I realized who he was talking about. I nodded. "Alright. Let's ride out there. While you two hold court, I'll go get him. But we need to figure out just what sort of punishment we're going to mete out."

"We'll discuss that on the way back."

Looking at Sarge, I asked, "You going to bring him back tonight? Or do you expect him to walk?"

"Mitch," Sarge said, "Why don't you and Michelle come out and stay the night with us tonight. We're going to a little shindig tomorrow and you should probably be there as well."

"What sort of a shindig?"

"A bar-b-que," I said. "Steaks."

"Like, beef?" He nearly shouted.

"Not like beef; it is beef!" Sarge exclaimed.

Mitch held up a finger and disappeared into the house. He returned shortly with Michelle and a small bag. Sarge laughed and asked, "I assume then, it's a yes?"

"Mitch said we were going to have steaks?" Michelle asked.

"Tomorrow," I nodded.

"What are we waiting for then?" Mitch asked.

On the ride back to Altoona, we discussed what sort of corporal punishments would be appropriate for such things as theft. Sarge naturally was a little heavy handed in his ideas and Mitch and I had to shoot down several of them; one was even to bring back the wooden horse. This was a medieval punishment where one straddled a square post, set so one of the corners faced up and weights were hung around the legs. Just the idea of it made me woozy.

In the end, it was Michelle that settled it. "Caning," she

said. "Remember years ago, the story of the kid in Singapore that was caught vandalizing cars or something. They did it to him."

"Yeah," Mitch said as he recalled the incident. "It's not permanent and will certainly get the point across."

"But, who's going to do it?" Michelle asked.

"I have the man," I replied.

Once we got back to the market, I got out and checked on Mel. She and Shelly were sitting in the shade talking when we pulled up. I told her I had to run back to the house and I'd be back. She said she'd stay there and asked why I was going back.

"To get Dalton," I said.

I found Dalton with Mike and Ted and some of the Guardsmen. They were hanging out in the shade of a tree, trying to avoid the heat. When I got out of the Hummer, Mike looked at me and asked, "How bad is it?"

"What?" I asked.

"Whatever happened to have you driving the old man's Hummer around."

"I need Dalton," I said.

He was sitting on a bucket sharpening his kukri and looked up. "What's up?"

"We have a situation. We've got some guys that were caught stealing. There is no jail now. But there have to be consequences. We can't let people think they can do whatever they want."

Dalton nodded, "Going old school? What's it to be?"

"Caning," I replied.

He nodded again. "And you want me to do it?"

"If you will."

"I'll do it!" Mike shouted as he jumped up.

"No, you can't."

"Why the hell not?" He asked.

"First, you're still part of the Army. So, we can't have you going around beating people. Second, you want to."

"Thank you," Ted said with a nod.

"Oh, that's bullshit. Did the old man say that?" Mike asked.

"No, I did. This is my job. But as the Sheriff, I shouldn't do it either. It needs to be a third party to keep it right."

Dalton rose to his feet. "I'll do it. Give me a minute."

"Well, can we at least come watch?" Mike asked.

"I don't care. Maybe you should take notes," I said.

Ted laughed, "Yeah, so when it's your turn to be caned, you'll know what to expect."

"Shit, ain't nobody beating me with a cane."

"Tell that to Dalton," I said with a laugh.

"You'd just have to shoot that big bastard," Mike replied. "You ain't got to shoot every bastard, but you would have to shoot him."

Dalton returned with a long cane pole. He studied it for a minute then cut the really flexible thin end off several feet from the tip. Then he held it up and swung it a couple of times. He then took about a foot off the other end and tested it again. After one more modification, he judged it suitable.

"The point here isn't to break the skin," Dalton said. "Though, depending on the number of licks, it could happen. This is just to get the point across to them."

"We've done it before. It looks about right to me," I said.

"How many licks they getting?" Ted asked.

"I don't know. Mitch is there now holding court. Let's get over there and get this done. You guys drive this and I'll take the Suburban. We've got a few people to bring back."

By the time we made it back to town, the issue was settled. The two men were surely guilty, and many people had testified against them. While it wasn't the crime of the century, the men had been stealing from their neighbors. And the stealing of food was one of the highest crimes you could commit in our current situation.

"So, what's the word?" I asked.

"Guilty, both of them," Mitch replied. There were plenty of witnesses to testify. They've been doing it for a long time.

"Sentence?"

Mitch hesitated for a moment. Letting out a loud breath, he replied, "Five lashes; that's five each."

Looking at the two men, I announced for all to hear, "You've been tried and found guilty of stealing food from your neighbors. Your sentence is five lashes each from a cane. To be carried out immediately." Neither of them protested. They were either in disbelief or shock.

The men were moved over to the gas island. As we were preparing to cuff their hands around one of the supports for the canopy, Dalton said to remove their shirts. "It'll probably cut their shirts. No sense ruining them."

He was right, clothing, good clothing, was hard to come by. So, the shirts the men were wearing were removed. They naturally complained during all this.

"You can't do this! This is cruel and unusual punishment! We have rights!" One of them shouted.

As his hands were forced around the column, I said, "Your neighbors have rights too. You violated those rights. You did this to yourself. You've no one to blame but yourself."

Once both men were secured, I turned to face the crowd. "Let this be a lesson to you all! This is how crime will be dealt with now. Our jail is destroyed, justice will be administered on the street, at the time and place of the crime. No long appeals. No courtroom shenanigans. If you're found guilty, you will be punished." I looked at Dalton and gave him a nod.

Dalton squared up to the first man and checked the distance by holding out the cane. He brought it back and delivered what I thought a forceful, yet measured strike to the man's back, just below his shoulder blades. The man's knees went weak and he cried out in a shriek of pain. But it didn't deter Dalton and he delivered four more. By the last strike, the man no longer complained. He was slumped on his knees, his back covered in thick red welts with blood running from a couple of the deeper impacts.

The crowd, which up to this point was jeering and cat calling, had fallen silent when the punishment began. Not a sound could be heard, save the cane cutting through the air, then cutting into the flesh. These people wanted retribution. They wanted vengeance, but as is the case most of the time, imagining it and seeing it are two different things. Their enthusiasm quickly faded.

Dalton left the first man in a sobbing heap and stepped over to the next. He was wild with fear, pulling against the cuffs trying to free himself. He shouted in near hysteria, his eyes wide and spittle hanging from his mouth and chin as he looked back over his shoulder. He was firmly in the grip of abject fear.

As Dalton stepped up behind him, he turned his head to see the big man and began shouting, "You don't have to do this! No, no, no, no, no…." His pleas were cut short when the first blow landed. His groveling stopped as his mouth hung open in a silent scream. It appeared his eyes rolled back and for a moment, his body went rigid. Then he was able to take a breath and let out a blood curdling scream.

Dalton completed the sentence in a very mechanical fashion. The blows were delivered evenly and with an even gap between them. When the last lash landed, Dalton turned and walked away. The men's restraints were removed and both of them collapsed to the ground. The crowd that so eagerly wanted their blood earlier, gave them a wide birth. Most trying hard to not make eye contact.

I followed Dalton over to the truck where he tossed the cane into the back. "You alright with this?" I asked.

He shrugged, "I didn't enjoy it. I didn't not enjoy it. It's just a task that needs to be done. We can't have people running around here thinking they can do as they please. It drives home a serious message. If people know that justice will be handed out immediately, they are far less tempted to try and steal, rob or commit other crimes the rest of the community has agreed cannot be allowed. It is what it is."

"Just wanted to make sure you were good with it. You sure that it didn't bother you?"

Dalton laughed. "No, this doesn't bother me. Hell, in my youth I once beat a man with a car antenna. I told him to go away. But he wouldn't listen. So, as I'm unscrewing the antenna from his car he kept asking, *what the hell you gonna do with that?* Once I got it off, I showed him. I beat him like a slave. A good beating delivers a lasting message that one is not apt to forget. I think this is the best way to deal with such things and I have no problem being *that guy.*"

As we were loading up to head home, Mario walked over. "Damn, Morgan. You're going all medieval."

"What else are we supposed to do? Can't just let people rob and steal from others."

"I'm with you. I think it will have a profound effect on the folks around here. Them standing there and watching those two take that beating will leave an impression."

"That's the point. You need anything before we leave? You still having trouble with people trying to poach your honey?"

He shook his head. "No, we're good. We deal with them as we catch them."

With a sideways look, I asked, "Do I need to ask how?"

Mario looked off in the direction of the gas canopy, "I'd say you'd approve."

"Fair enough. You need anything, just give me a holler."

As we shook hands, Mario replied, "Will do. And same goes for me."

I walked over to where Mel, Lee Ann and Jess were talking. They seemed unphased by what they'd just witnessed and were chatting as if it were a normal day. "You guys ready to go home?" I asked.

Lee Ann rubbed her stomach and said, "I'm hungry."

"Let's head home then."

Sarge echoed my statement when he announced, "Supper will be ready soon! Let's get on the road to the house!"

We spent the evening at Danny's house. Mitch and Michelle were given the spare upstairs bedroom for the night. But, as was our custom, we all hung out on the back porch where we had dinner and just enjoyed the company. Aric brought Fred down on an ATV. She said she wanted to get out of the house, needed a change of scenery. She sat with Mel, Jess and Mary. Miss Kay busied herself in the kitchen. She was baking the buns we were taking to the cookout tomorrow as well as serving food to people as they arrived.

I sat on the porch with Sarge, looking out at the pond. The kids were down there wading around in the water trying to catch minnows or tadpoles. Glancing over at Sarge, I asked, "How's Ivan doing?"

"Bitching. He never stops bitching." He looked over at me and with a laugh and said, "Ivan really hates you."

"The feeling's mutual, I assure you. I'd like to spend some quality time alone with him. Maybe bring Dalton along."

"Don't take it personal, Morgan. He's just a soldier doing what he's told. No different than our guys that were over in Iraq or Afghanistan."

"That may be true from his perspective. But from mine, I don't see it that way. To willingly fire artillery into a civilian area is a war crime. But beyond that, it's just wrong."

The old man shrugged and took his pocket knife out. As he dug under his fingernails, he said, "Again, it's about perspective. At the time, they thought they had us licked. Ole Ivan thought that was the final nail in the coffin. So, there wouldn't be any consequences. It's the old, would you rob a bank if you knew you wouldn't get caught? It's a moral test."

"Yeah, well he fucking failed that test."

"His only mistake was getting caught."

I leaned back and stretched. "How much longer are we going to have to deal with his ass? I thought Eglin wanted him."

"They do," Sarge replied with a nod. "But there isn't exactly an overabundance of aircraft right now. And coming down here just to scoop up one little commie Colonel isn't at the top of the list."

"Miss Kay fixing them food?" I asked.

"Yeah. I have to carry it down there in a bit."

Getting up, I said, "I'll do it. I'd like to have a word with Ivan."

"Now Morgan, don't go killing the man. We need him."

"I'm not going to kill him," I snapped back. "I just want to talk to the man. He's no threat to us now."

Going inside, I asked Kay for the food for the prisoners. She gave me a large bag, telling me there were also meals for the guards. Taking the bag and a large jug of tea, I left the house and walked down to the old man's place. It was warm, nearly hot and terribly muggy. It wasn't a comfortable evening out for a walk.

I found Wallner in the garage with Ivan and his buddy. He was sitting in a chair next to the workbench, casually watching the two men watch him. Seeing me come through the door, his mood brightened.

"Hey, Morgan! You bring us supper?" Wallner asked.

I held the bag out and replied, "I did. You hungry?"

"Starving," Wallner replied.

Hearing there was food, Ivan and his fellow prisoner sat up and took notice. Both of the men had a look of hunger on their faces and it was obvious they were ready to eat. I placed the bag on the bench and Wallner immediately dove into it. I looked at Ivan and asked, "These two giving you any trouble?"

"Naw," Wallner replied. "They can't do anything."

I took a covered container out and lifted the lid. Steam rose out of it and I made a show of sniffing it. Looking at Ivan, I said, "Man, that smells good." He glared back at me but said nothing. I walked over to him and held the dish out to him. As he reached for it, I held it just out of his grasp. "I have to wonder," I said. "Would you take such good care of your prisoners?"

"We are much alike. Though you may not like to hear that. You Americans think you're so good, so, what's the word, wholesome. Above reproach, I think is another way to say it. But you've committed more crimes against the world than any other nation."

I handed him the dish and replied, "Maybe. You Russians only kill your own as I recall."

"By the millions," Wallner added with a mouthful of food.

"And you have killed millions of your own as well," Ivan replied as he scooped at the food with his fingers. We didn't give them a fork.

I laughed. "But you're far ahead of us in the body count. Not to mention, most of your mass murder was state sponsored."

Ivan looked up at me, "Was your Civil War not state-sponsored mass murder?"

"I can see the argument. But when our Civil War ended, the North didn't go out and try to erase the South."

Ivan shrugged, "History is written by the victors. Dead men cannot argue."

"Well, it looks like Russia won't be writing the history of America this time either."

"Perhaps not. But you will never achieve the level of success you've enjoyed for so many decades. America is now a third world country," Ivan replied and laughed. "Even Mexico doesn't want your people. No one does. Not that you can go anywhere. There are no ships or planes to carry you away. You are stuck here in your dead country."

"As are you," I reminded him. "Only, it is my country and you're just an invader. So, I like my chances better than yours."

"I am a prisoner of war. You Americans will recognize my rights, as you always have. No harm will come to me and in the end, I will go home, to Russia." He pointed at me, "While you are stuck here to live the rest of your life toiling for your daily bread."

I laughed. "You still buy into the propaganda, huh? We may have been knocked back, but we're far from down."

"Anyone could defeat you now. Your country is weak," he sneered.

"Anyone, huh? Anyone but you. You got your ass handed

to you and lost all your men in the process. If you did make it home, I don't think the Russian Army would be quite so happy to see you. You failed against us. It wasn't even a real fight. You played your hand and we played ours. You lost."

"Yes, I lost because of your bombers. That was unexpected. If it hadn't been for them, we wouldn't be having this conversation right now."

"And why is that?" I asked.

He looked up at me and said, "Because you'd either be dead or in chains."

"Well, I'm not dead and you're the one in chains."

Finishing his meal, Ivan looked around and asked, "How much longer will I be kept here like an animal? When will I be transferred to a more suitable location?"

I shrugged. "As much as you may think of yourself, you're not high on the priority list. The DOD knows we have you. Hell, they might just leave you here for all I know. And if that happens, then you're going to have to start earning your keep. No one eats for free around here."

Ivan scoffed, "Earn my keep? What do you expect me to do? Wash dishes?"

"Whatever you're told. And I know you're thinking you won't. But I promise you, we can be very persuasive."

"We shall see, bureaucrat."

I winked at him and said, "Count on it, Ivan. Count on it."

"He doesn't talk much to me," Wallner said as I collected the supper dishes. "You come over and he's a chatty Kathy."

I looked back at Ivan sitting on the floor watching us. "That's because he's afraid. I know he won't admit it, but he is. Aren't you, Ivan?"

The man snorted and lay back on the bare floor, covering his eyes with his hands. "I fear you like a tiger does an antelope."

"Told you," I said to Wallner.

I carried the dishes back to Danny's house. Everyone was winding down and Mel was ready to go home. We rounded up Little Bit and told the girls we were leaving. They were sitting with Jess and Fred talking and wanted to stay a while longer.

As we walked home, Little Bit said she wanted to feed Ruckus before going to bed. Mel said that was fine; he needed to eat. Mel fixed the formula while Little Bit ran and got the little rodent. He was still so small, and she asked when his eyes would open.

"I don't know. Shouldn't be too much longer. He's starting to get fur on his tail. I bet it's soon," I replied.

She sat on the couch talking to him in a baby voice, then said, "I want to be the first person he sees! I want to be his mom."

I rubbed her head, "You'll make a good squirrel mom."

Mel brought her the dropper and we sat on the sofa with her as she fed the little guy. He was hungry and took to the dropper eagerly, finishing it quickly. Mel refilled it two more times. By the time he was done eating, his belly looked as though he'd swallowed a ping pong ball. With a full belly, the little guy started to drift off to sleep.

"Don't go to sleep Ruckus, I want to play with you!" Little Bit shouted.

"He's just a baby, honey. All he does is eat and sleep," I said. "But don't worry. He'll be full of play soon."

"Yes, he will," Mel added. "He'll have more play in him than you'll know what to do with."

Little Bit had the little critter cupped in her hands and held it up to her face, "I can't wait till you're big enough to play with."

"Alright," Mel said. "Put him back in the box. Time for bed."

Little Bit laid him into the shoebox and covered him with one of the rags we had lined it with. Gently rubbing his head, she said goodnight and ran off to get ready for bed herself. Picking up the box, I said, "I'll put him away and then grab a shower."

"Soon as I get her to bed, I'll be there," Mel replied.

CHAPTER 7

I STOOD ON THE BACK PORCH of Dave's house looking out over a small lake. It was an odd sensation, smelling the grilling meat, seeing the kids playing in the water and hearing so many voices engaged in conversation around me. It wasn't the sort of thing I'd experienced in quite some time, a genuine cookout. Walking over to the edge of the porch, I sat down in a well-worn rocker beside Sarge. He and Dave were in deep conversation.

"This is an impressive spread you have here," I said.

Dave looked down towards the lake. "It's home."

"I can see why you folks didn't venture out. No need to. You've got everything you need here."

"We were blessed is all I can say. Family came together, and we made some good friends. We were fortunate. Much like you, from what Linus here tells me."

"We got lucky too," I agreed.

"Lucky hell," Sarge snorted. "It's been a hell of a lot of hard work to get where we are. And it ain't over by a stretch."

As we talked, a tall young blonde woman came out of the house. She was wearing a sheer wrap, the sort of thing you'd see at the beach. Dropping her sunglasses down over her eyes, she started to walk towards the lake. The wrap blew open to reveal the bikini she was wearing underneath.

"Now there's something you don't see every day," I said in surprise.

"That's Crystal. She's one of my granddaughters."

Sarge looked at Dave, "I bet that's been hell to keep on the ranch."

He laughed, "You have no idea. But Janet keeps a close eye on her. Crystal is her niece. Janet's sister lives up north." His voice changed when he added, "we don't know what happened to her."

"There's a lot of that these days," I replied.

I was watching the girl as she headed for the lake and laughed when Mikey saw her. He and Ted were down at the lake's edge fishing and having considerable success. Mike lifted a bass from the water that had to weight four pounds. When he turned to show it to those of us on the porch, he spotted Crystal. He dropped the fish and lowered his sunglasses, doing a double-take. When he was sure he was seeing what he thought he was seeing, he held the rod out in Ted's direction and dropped it as well. Ted rolled his eyes as Mike started towards her.

"This is going to be good," I said.

"What's that?" Sarge asked.

I pointed at Mike and said, "Mike just saw Crystal. This should be entertaining."

"For the love of God," Sarge grumbled. Leaning close to Dave, he said, "I'm really sorry, Dave. He's a good kid, but if I had my way, I'd drown him."

Dave just smiled and rocked in his chair. "It's good to see young people find someone. Besides, I ain't worried about Crystal." He leaned back in his chair and with a broad smile, he added, "He's got to get past Janet."

I laughed at the image of Mike meeting Janet. "And they're such good friends."

"Good," Sarge replied. "But I'm warning you now, he'll give her a run for her money."

"Maybe it'll distract her," Dave said. "She hasn't been happy here. There's no one around her age. I mean, there's a couple of hands here, but I made it pretty clear to them what would happen to them if they started sniffing around."

Sarge pointed down at the lake and said, "That one doesn't take a hint. It takes something a little less subtle to get him to take notice…like a two-by-four."

"Look at it this way," I said, turning toward Sarge. "Maybe it'll get him out of your hair some. Give him something else to focus on."

"Focus? He couldn't find focus on a telescope!" Sarge barked back, then pointed towards the lake. "And any focus he may have had just went out the window."

"A young woman will do that to you," Dave said with a smile.

"Maybe we'll get lucky and she won't like him. Tell his sorry ass to kick rocks."

The two were standing together. While we couldn't hear what was being said, it was pretty obvious that Mike was running a game on her. When she laughed and reached out and touched his arm, I laughed. "Don't count on it from the looks of things down there."

"Whatever you do, don't feed him, Dave. You'll never get rid of him," Sarge added.

Dave smiled, "I don't think it's his belly he's thinking with at the moment."

I left Sarge and Dave to contemplate the consequences of Mikey moving in on Crystal. Which surprisingly enough, Dave wasn't all that against the idea of. Not that I was either. For as much shit as we give Mike, he's a solid guy and I love him like a brother.

I found my way over to the grill, following my nose and the sound of fat spitting on a fire. There was quite a crowd there. Thad and Mary were there. As well as Dalton, Cecil and Perez with a couple of the ranch hands. They were grilling meat over an enormous built-in stone grill. This wasn't the sort of thing you bought at Home Depot. This was built onsite from some sort of stone and was six-foot square. A support system overhead allowed the entire grilling surface to be raised or lowered and it was covered in beef. There were steaks, brisket and burgers. It was more meat than I'd seen in more than a year and it looked and smelled delicious.

"Holy hell," I said as I walked up. "That's some grill."

Travis was tending the meat. "Pretty nice isn't it?"

"I don't think I'd ever be able to come up with enough meat to fill that thing," I replied.

"We did today," Thad replied with a big grin.

"I can see that."

"We only burn oak in this. Sometimes hickory if we're cooking pork," Travis said. "But, there's a separate smoker for that. This is just for good old grilling."

Perez was sitting in a lawn chair at eye level with the top of the grill. Naturally, there was a cigarette hanging from his lips. I pulled a chair up beside him and sat down. "Looks like you got the best seat in the house."

He nodded, "Just waiting. It'll come."

"And it'll be glorious!" Dalton shouted.

The smell coming from the meat was enough to drive you mad. I hadn't smelled anything like it in a long time. It wasn't just the meat. It was the wood, the smoke, the fat burning off. It reminded me of every cookout I had ever attended, not that they were noteworthy at the time. But now, each was a very fond memory.

"If only we had some beers," Perez lamented.

"That would make for a perfect day," I replied.

Thad pointed at the searing meat with a long fork, "I'll make do with this here."

"Me too," I replied, "I'll suffer through it." My comment got a laugh from them.

Travis shook his head, "It ain't easy. But some one's got to do it."

A petite woman walked up with a huge platter. "Here, Travis," she said as she slid it onto a small table beside the grill.

"Thanks, babe." he replied. Then he introduced her. "This is my wife Erin. This is everybody."

She smiled. "Hi, everybody." We all took a minute to introduce ourselves and she disappeared as quickly as she had arrived.

I saw Mel and Janet talking and could see Janet glancing over in our direction. It was so noticeable that I started watching her, to see what it was she was interested in. It didn't take long to discover though. She guided Mel in our direction and stopped in front of Perez. She looked at him anxiously and when he looked up, she flashed him a smile and asked, "Where did you find cigarettes?"

Perez took the butt from his lips and looked at it. "I have my sources. A man has to be resourceful today."

She fidgeted for a moment, then asked, "Can I have one, please? I was never a big smoker, just one every now and then. And I haven't even thought about a cigarette in a long time. But I just caught the smell of yours and now I can't stand it."

Squinting against the sun, Perez replied, "I don't know. I'd hate for you to start a bad habit."

"Quit being an ass and give the lady a cigarette," I said.

Signaling defeat, Perez shook one out of a pack he produced from his shirt. When he leaned forward to offer her the smoke, I grabbed the pack and tossed it to Janet. "Just keep it. He's got plenty more of those commie smokes. He looted the bodies of all the Russians we killed. While we were collecting weapons and ammo, he was busy taking their smokes."

Janet quickly took a cigarette from the pack and held it up, asking, "Do you mind?"

As he fished into his pocket, Perez asked, "You don't have a lighter either?" Finding his lighter, he lit her cigarette. Janet took a long drag and held it before letting it out.

With her eyes closed, she said, "That. That's what I miss. That little rush." She looked at the pack, then at Perez, "Thank you for the gift."

He pulled another unopened pack from his pocket and waved her off, "No problem."

Looking at Mel, I asked, "What have you two been up to?"

"Nothing. Just girl talk. You wouldn't be interested."

I looked at her, then at Janet. "Yeah, I've been married long enough to know when I hear bullshit. And I'm hearing bullshit."

Janet started to laugh. "You're right. You two have been married too long."

"It only feels like forever," I replied. "Right, babe?"

Mel gave me a snarky smile and gave Janet a gentle push, "Come on. I'll introduce you to Ted."

"What?" I asked quickly. "Introduce you to Ted? You already met Ted."

Mel shook her head. "You have been married too long."

Then it hit me, "Oh, *introduce* him. I get it. Good for you. He's a good guy. Just remember, he comes with an annoying pet."

Janet looked down towards the lake. "I think his dog has a new chew toy and won't be a bother."

I looked down at Mike and Crystal; they were obviously getting along pretty well. But I was curious about something. "I've got to ask. Why is everyone so casual about her hooking up with someone you don't even know? I mean, I've known these guys for a while and I don't want them hooking up with my daughters."

"That's because they're your girls," Mel replied.

"Crystal is a grown woman. She's been stuck on the ranch since the Day. We all have. So, seeing new faces is nice. That and we always worried what would happen to her. Whether or not she would be able to find a man when the time was right." She looked off into the distance and added, "And it's like Daddy says. After all we've been through, we need to grab a hold of happiness whenever and wherever we find it."

"That I agree with," Mel said.

"I'll leave you two up to your shenanigans," I said as I walked off. I found Danny where I'd expect to find him, out near one of the large barns.

The place was scattered with old, broke-down and discarded farm equipment of all kinds. Danny was looking at an old row planter when I came up behind him. "You seen any corn harvesters?" I asked.

"Not yet," he replied as he stood up.

"It would be a life saver if we found one."

He pointed to another larger barn a short distance off. "Let's go look over there."

We walked around the big metal building for a while marveling at the vast variety of equipment quietly rusting under the sun. When we walked around to the back of it, we saw something interesting.

"I think this is a corn harvester," Danny said as he ran his hand over one of the large cone-shaped pieces on the front.

I knelt down and looked into the machine. "I don't know anything about corn pickers, but it looks like it could only harvest two rows at a time."

"That's twice as many as we can pick by hand."

"Looks like you pull it with a tractor."

Danny walked around to the rear of the machine and said, "Here's the belt where the finished corn comes out."

"I think you're right. Let's go up to the house and talk to Dave about it. If we could use this, it would save us so much time. Even if it only does two rows at a time."

We walked back up to the house. Dave and Sarge were still sitting beside one another in the rocking chairs. It made me smile to think of the old show, *The Odd Couple*. Because if ever there was such, they were it.

"Hey, Dave." I said as we walked up. "Out there behind that big barn is what I think is a corn picker. Am I right?"

"Oh yeah. That's a New Idea 2540. It'll pick two rows at a time. But ain't nobody got no corn now, so I don't think it'll ever run again."

"What if someone did have some corn? Say, about fifty acres of it?"

He looked up and asked, "You folks have a cornfield?"

"We do. We found some feed corn and planted it. It did well and is about ready to harvest. That machine would make the job a lot easier."

Dave got up from his chair. "That thing's been sitting for years. It probably doesn't work now. But we can damn sure fix that!"

"Morgan, go over and get Cecil," Sarge said, giving voice to what I was already thinking.

I returned with Cecil and introduced him to Dave. Shaking the man's hand, Cecil said, "Good to meet you. Thank you for having us over today."

"Morgan here tells me you got a field of corn about ready to pick."

Cecil nodded. "I do. And it's going to take everyone we know to get it done."

"What if you had a New Idea two-row picker?"

"I ain't seen one of those in years!" Cecil announced. "It sure would save the corn crop."

"Well, it just so happens that I have one."

Cecil looked surprised, "You pullin' my leg?"

"No, we saw it," I replied. "You want to walk over and look at it?"

"Yes, I do!" Cecil nearly shouted.

We all walked back over to the barn. After pulling weeds up from around it and scraping out all manner of rat nests and who knows what, we got a look at the machine.

"She's going to need a lot of work," Sarge said.

"It does," Dave replied. "But these were made to be used on small family farms. They were simple machines that anyone could work on. Not to mention, they were built like a tank. We'll get this thing pulled out and back into shape in a couple of days."

Pointing at the contraption, Cecil asked, "You mean I can have this?"

Dave laughed, "You're the only man I know of with a cornfield. Hell yes, you can have it! If it'll help bring in that corn, you can damn sure have it."

"That sure will make it easier. Say, you don't mind if I come over and help put it back together? I like to know how to work on the equipment I use."

"Feel free, we could use the help."

Just then, a loud clanging erupted from the direction of the house. I looked up to see Janet ringing a very large triangle hanging from a post in the backyard and announcing, "Supper's ready!"

"Gentlemen, this thing isn't going anywhere, and I've been smelling that cooking meat all day. What do you say we go up and get us a plate?" Cecil said.

"That's a fine idea," Dave said. With a sweep of his arm, he added, "Come on, boys. Let's eat."

The spread of food was rather impressive. Of course, there was plenty of beef. But there were to my amazement also French fries. They were a huge hit with everyone as it had been so long since anyone had had a fry. The buns Kay made went over well too. She even made a pretty decent ketchup that really dressed up the burgers and went well with the fries.

"Kay, this ketchup is really good. I have missed ketchup so much," Mel said.

I laughed, "That's putting it really mildly," I said. "You ate fries as a vehicle for ketchup."

Mel dipped a potato into the sauce and replied, "You're right and this is really good."

"But it's not Heinz."

"Heinz hasn't got a thing on this stuff."

"Thank you, Mel." Kay said. "It's alright. Better than nothing."

She was shouted down with cat calls and praise for her variation. It was just nice to have something like it, something different. I looked across the table at Dave and asked, "How big a tater field do you guys have?"

"We grow a few acres of them," he replied as he stabbed one with his fork. "This variety does well down here and is really prolific. We dehydrate a lot of them and use as many fresh as we can. We can give you some for seed if you want."

"That would be great," Thad quickly said.

Nodding in Thad's direction, I said, "Thad is our resident farmer. He's the primary one that takes care of our garden."

"Be sure and take some of the seed spuds with you. We've got plenty of them."

"Things are looking up," Sarge announced. "We've got beef, taters and corn. Things are starting to change!"

"Amen," I said.

I ate two hamburgers and a steak. Not to mention a pile of fries. The kids stuffed themselves on the potatoes. It probably helped that they were fried in beef fat in a big pot over the fire. That fat added something to them that was hard to describe. A heart surgeon's nightmare, but damn good. Besides, we could afford to eat like this every now and then. There just weren't many opportunities to indulge in foods that were less than healthy.

The kids all ran for the lake as soon as they finished their food. Well, almost finished. I saw Edie running for the water with half a burger in her hand. There were other kids here as well and when Travis walked past me, I asked about them.

He pointed to two little towheaded kids. "Those two are ours."

The kids were splashing and playing at the edge of the lake with Jace and Edie. "How are you related to Dave?" I asked.

"We're not. I just knew the family and when things went south, we eventually found our way here. I work for them and in turn, they took us in. Treat us like family. Dave and his family are good people."

"That's good. It'd be hard to be on your own now."

"Yeah, it was tough. Erin is a nurse, so they really like

having her around. I can work on about anything, so it's a good deal for all of us."

"I've got something in the truck for Dave, I almost forgot," I said as I headed for the front of the house.

Slinging the sack of flour over my shoulder, I walked it back to the house and set it on the floor in the kitchen. Going out to the porch, I told Dave.

"You didn't have to do that. But we really appreciate it."

"I told you I'd give it to you and I want to keep my word."

"We'll surely put it to use. I can already taste the biscuits and gravy."

I looked at Travis and asked, "You get those hogs into a pen?"

"Oh yeah. We fixed up a pen for them. They're not getting out of it either."

"Well, fellers, I think I'm going to go for a swim," I announced and headed for the lake.

The lake was nice, with a white sandy beach and all the weeds cleaned out from the swimming area. The water was cool and clear. When I asked about gators, Dave laughed and said he was waiting on another one to move in. He was out of gator meat. Naturally, this gave him and Sarge something else to talk about. He also told me the lake was spring fed, so it never heated up like smaller bodies of water will do in Florida.

Seeing me coming, Little Bit got excited and started calling for me to get in the water. I took off my shirt and shoes and waded into the water where I was immediately attacked by a throng of kids. I fought back by picking little bodies up and tossing them through the air to splash down in the water. The kids loved it and I spent the next several minutes hurling small bodies and splashing around.

But they wore me out and I squatted down in the water.

Little Bit climbed up on my back and I swam around with her. Then, I had to give all the other kids a ride as well. They wore me out! My intention to relax in the water had not played out as planned, but that was ok. So, after giving the last little one a quick ride, I said I was getting out and started for the bank.

"Come on, Daddy! Don't get out!" Little Bit cried as I tried to walk out of the water. She was wrapped around my leg, making it slightly difficult.

Reaching down and tickling her, I replied, "You've worn me out, kiddo! I need to go sit down and relax now." She wouldn't let go, so I wrenched her from my leg, held her up over my head and waded back out to a little deeper water and tossed her in. It gave me the chance I needed to get away.

I took a seat in a chair in the field between the house and lake where I could watch the kids and dry in the sun. Mike and Crystal were still together, sitting on a small dock in the center of the lake. As people finished their meal, they made their way to the lake's edge. Some went for a swim and others just sat in the water. Dave and Sarge moved chairs down to the water's edge and sat with Kay.

The oppressive heat of the day was starting to release its grip and it was cooling off a bit. Being close to the water helped too. Thad and Mary pulled chairs up beside me and sat down. I looked over and asked, "You aren't going swimming?"

"No. I'm good. My belly is full, all I want to do is sit for a minute."

I leaned forward so I could see Mary and said, "You should get him in the water."

She smiled. "I know. I tried. But he wasn't having it."

"The water feels great. You should go for a swim even if he doesn't want to."

"I think you're right." She stood up and stripped off her

t-shirt to reveal the bathing suit beneath. "I think I will go for a swim." She leaned over and kissed Thad before running into the water. Of course, she was swarmed by the kids who were excited to see any adult get in.

Fred and Aric walked by holding hands and waded out into the water. The kids wanted to play with them as well, but Fred said she couldn't play, leaving Aric to deal with them on his own. He managed to shoo them away and wrapped his arms around Fred as they moved around in the shallow water. Gina and Dylan were sitting in the shallow water at the edge of the lake. Dylan had a steak in his hand that he was ripping large chunks from and chewing on.

"Those were some damn good steaks," I said.

"The burgers were good too," Thad replied.

"And those fries," I said.

"Fried in fat like that; damn they were good."

"Make sure you get the seed potatoes before leaving."

He grinned, "Already in the truck."

"Good man."

Mel came up and held out her hand, "Come on. Let's get in the water."

I was surprised. Mel never wanted to swim. "You want to swim?"

"Yeah, come on."

"Looks like you're going swimming," Thad said as I got up.

We walked down to the lake and sat down in the shallows beside Ted and Janet. They seemed to be getting along pretty well. I found it kind of funny. To be invited over and Mike and Ted both manage to hook up. I hoped it didn't look bad though.

Taking Mel's hand, I said, "Babe, I'm thinking about going to go see if I can find Mom and Dad. Hopefully bring them back here."

"You think they're alright?"

"I hope so. Being on the river, I'm sure they've managed to get by. I'm just worried about other people that may have showed up there."

"You're going to take a boat up the river?"

"I think it will be a lot safer than trying to drive."

"I'm not trying to ease drop," Janet said, "but where are you taking a boat?"

"My parents live on the river over in Debary. I want to go check on them. Now that things are kind of calmed down, I can do it."

"Do you have a boat?"

"We have a bass boat."

"You should take ours. It's a big aluminum thing. Dad used it for duck hunting. It's got the camo skirt and all on it." Janet pointed towards a large pole barn. "It's over there if you want to go look at it."

"How many people can it hold?" I asked.

Thinking about the reply, she answered, "Ten. It's a pretty big boat."

Ted stood up and said, "Come on, Morgan. Let's go look at it."

I patted Mel's leg. "I'll be right back."

"Take your time. We can talk girl-talk."

Ted and I walked over to the pole barn. Janet was right, it was a big boat. Eighteen feet as a matter of fact, and it had a mud motor mounted to the transom. Mud motors are a great little invention that allows a boat to be operated in shallow weed-choked waterways. The motor will cut through the vegetation and also allow the boat to run in mere inches of water.

"This would be a lot better than that bass boat," Ted said.

"Yeah it would. We could take more people, more security."

"And have room for your parents on the way out."

"Yeah. If they'll let me borrow it, I'll take it."

We walked back to the lake where a rousing game of chicken was going on in the water. Jess was up on Doc's shoulders. Erin was on Travis and Danny had all three kids on his shoulders. All of them were splashing in the water. Mike and Crystal were swimming towards the mass of bodies and swirling water to get in on the fun.

I dropped back down beside Mel and asked, "You want to get on my shoulders out there?"

"No. You'd just drop me."

"Good, I don't think my back could take it," I replied as I rubbed my lower back, feigning pain.

Mel slugged me in the shoulder, "I'll show you pain!"

"What'd you think of the boat?" Janet asked.

"If you'll let me use it, I'll gladly accept. It's much larger than the boat we have, and that mud motor will ensure I can get down the river."

"The bottom is slick-coated as well. It's pretty fast on the water. You're welcome to it, especially if it will help with getting to your mom and dad."

We hung out on the lake until the sun started to dip towards the horizon and the skeeters came out. They were the real reason we left the water. Because when they showed up, they did so in force! It wasn't long before people were running towards the house, arms flailing at the tiny pests.

I backed the Suburban up to the boat and connected it before pulling back around in front of the house. Dave was out front with Sarge when I got out.

"That's a fine boat, Morgan. She's pretty fast too," Dave said.

"I appreciate you letting me use it. It'll make what I have to do a lot easier."

Dave shook his head. "I don't envy you the task. But anything we can do to help, we'll do it."

"What about the beef for the folks in town?"

"They're going to deliver it tomorrow," Sarge replied.

"We're going to section up two beeves tomorrow and carry them up there. They'll have to either cook it or start smoking it right away," Dave added.

"I'll take care of that," Cecil said. "I have a big smoker and can easily fit one in it. I'll put a slow cold smoke on it. It'll just take some time to get it all cut up." Thad and Mary had joined us, and Thad offered to help. "That'd be fine. I could use the help."

Sarge held his hand out to Dave, "Thank you very much for the hospitality, Dave. You know where we are now, so if you need anything, don't hesitate to ask."

Shaking Sarge's hand, Dave replied, "It's been truly great to meet you all. It's good to know there are people out there trying to get things put back together. And we're here to help in any way we can."

"Dave," Cecil said, "it was a pleasure to meet you. Since you're bringing that beef to town tomorrow, how about we come out in a few days to work on that picker? It sure would make harvesting that corn a hell of a lot easier."

"That'll be fine. I'll get the boys started on it. I don't think it will take much to get it going."

Janet made sure we had plenty of leftovers to take home with us. She knew we had some people that couldn't make it out because they were on security. As we were all loading up, I saw Mike and Crystal holding hands as they walked towards the Hummer. Sarge was already standing at the passenger door and shouted at Mike.

"Get her number! It's time to go!"

"Ignore him," Mike said. "When can I see you again?"

Crystal shrugged, "Whenever you come over. I don't leave the ranch. They wouldn't let me go anywhere alone and I'm not going to ask someone to come and hold my hand."

"I'll hold your hand," Mike said with a smile. "I'll be back soon. I promise."

"Saddle up!" Sarge barked again. Then he looked at Ted, who was still talking to Janet. "You too, lover boy!"

Ted gave her hand a squeeze. "I'll see you in a couple of days."

"Ok, take care of Milo there too. I think Crystal likes him."

Ted rubbed his head. "Yeah. I really thought she would be smarter than that."

Janet folded her arms over her chest, "Same could be said about me."

"Not hardly," Ted laughed. "I'm nothing like Milo there."

"We'll see."

CHAPTER 8

FTER MUCH DISCUSSION AND DELIBERATION, it was decided that Danny and the old man would go with me to Mom and Dad's. I didn't think we needed three of us to go, but Sarge insisted. I think his real motivation was to just get away for a few days. We planned for the trip to last three days, but with the understanding that no one should worry about us for five days. We had radios and would be able to stay in contact, we hoped. As a precaution, we were taking some extra antennas that could be thrown up into a tree to get a better signal.

Of course, we went heavy on weapons. For this trip, I added to the boat one of the new Kalashnikovs we'd taken from the Russians. It had a grenade launcher on it and there were piles of the VOGs to go with it. We also brought a couple of disposable rocket launchers, you know, for just in case. Enough food was added to see all of us through, both some fresh stuff and a couple cases of MREs.

Everyone assembled their own gear to be able to support themselves for however long we'd be on the river. I added a spare NVG to my pack and made sure I had plenty of charged batteries. As an afterthought, I tossed two light spinning rods into the boat as well. Might as well try a little fishing should the opportunity arise.

We were set to leave at daylight the next day. Thad was off in town; he'd taken Mitch and Michelle back when he went to help Cecil with the beef that Dave's people delivered. Everyone else was around the neighborhood someplace. Sarge left standing orders that no one travel alone while we were gone. He knew the guys would want to go see their new lady friends and there was no way he could stop them. So, he made it clear that everyone should at least travel in pairs.

I talked with Dalton, Jess, Aric, Mel and the girls. I told them now that the major threats to us were gone, we needed to start focusing on the community. Or what was left of it. And that meant doing routine patrols. We planned it out so that the two markets would be visited every day, at least once. And there would also be a patrol all the way to Eustis to check in with Shane.

"We need to start showing more of a presence. Give people a sense that there is some kind of law," I said.

"What do we do if we catch someone up to no good?" Jess asked.

"You go get Mitch. He will hold court right there. Any sentence he passes will be carried out by Dalton."

"Don't worry. We can handle this." Dalton said. "You just worry about yourself and getting back here."

"Yes," Mel replied, "that's all you need to be concerned with."

"We'll be fine. I doubt there will be any trouble on the water and we'll have an escort to the boat ramp. There shouldn't be any issues."

We went home and spent a quiet evening there. Mel fixed a light supper at the house and we hung out, lounging around the living-room and watching a movie on the TV. I'd found a blue ray player in a house still in the box, and it worked; so, we could watch some of the DVDs we had. It had been part of our preps, to buy lots of movies as a distraction should this very thing we're living through happen. And now, with a working player, we were watching movies.

It's funny the sort of thing you want to watch when you've been living such a different life than what you were used to. The first movie we watched was *The Wizard of Oz*. We moved on from there to *Super Troopers* when Little Bit was in bed. Comedies are what everyone wanted to see, and *Caddy Shack* was on deck.

Hearing the laughter from Mel and the girls was like music. Sure, there was the occasional reason to laugh. But having everyone in the room all laughing hysterically was amazing. And we kept it going until late into the night. Little Bit fell asleep, as did Taylor. Once they were asleep, Lee Ann said she wanted to watch something else. I tossed her the remote to the player and told her she could watch whatever she wanted as I was going to bed.

I picked Little Bit up and carried her to her bed and Mel woke Taylor up and got her headed to bed as well. Once we were in bed, Mel asked how long I really thought it would take to go to Mom and Dad's.

"Looking at the map, it appears to be about twenty river miles. I figure it'll take five or six hours to cover that distance, depending on what the river is like. It could happen quicker, but I'm planning on there being problems."

"What kind of problems?"

"The river being blocked and having to stop and chainsaw out blowdowns, that sort of thing. I'm sure there will be people on the river. Hopefully they're just trying to scratch out a living and won't be interested in us. But if they're looking for a fight, we'll have plenty of shit with us for that too."

"Danny is going with you?"

"Yeah, him and the old man. I wanted to spend some time with Danny and I think Sarge just wants to go on a *Hobbit* adventure. Can't say I blame him."

Mel rolled over onto her back and stared at the ceiling. "I think it's good to get Danny out. He's been really withdrawn lately. You two spending some time together, away, will be good for him."

"That's what I was thinking. I could use a little break too."

"What are you going to do if they're not there?"

I thought about that for a minute. It's something I'd considered as a worst case. "I don't know. I don't where they would go. I just hope they're still at the house. I want to bring them here."

"It would be good to have them around. I know the girls would like it."

"And I can stop worrying about them."

Mel reached out and squeezed my arm. "Get some sleep. You have to get up early and you have a few long days ahead of you."

"What are you guys going to do while I'm gone?"

"The girls and I are going to keep an eye on the kids for Danny. And I'm going to try and ride on the patrols to town. I think we really need to do more of that. Get out there where people can see us, so they know we're around."

I patted her thigh. "I'm really glad to hear you're getting more involved in this."

"You're not worried about me and the girls going out and doing patrols?"

I laughed. "No. I think you gals can handle yourselves. I know Lee Ann can."

"I'll probably spend some time with Janet too. I like her.

Not having Bobbie to talk to has been rough and Janet kind of fills that void. She's easy to talk to and we have a lot in common."

"That's great. I think you should talk to Erin too, Travis's wife. She's a nurse and they seemed like a great couple. I really liked Travis. He seems to be one of those guys that can do anything."

"Like Dalton," Mel replied.

With a chuckle, I replied, "Yeah, like Dalton. But not nearly as dangerous. Which reminds me. On your patrols, take him with you. Not that I don't think you can do it, but he's been doing it longer and he's wicked good at it. Remember what we said, you want the deck stacked in your favor. And Dalton is an entire deck of aces."

"If he'll listen to me, I'll take him along."

"Just tell him you're going. He'll go along. I'd feel better about it."

Mel leaned over and kissed my cheek, "Get some sleep and make sure you get your ass back home to us. We need you."

"And I need you guys. Love you, babe."

"Love you too, goodnight."

I was up long before sunrise navigating the house by the glow of a red headlamp. I didn't want to wake anyone up, so I moved quietly. Since I already had everything packed, the only thing I really needed to add was my thermos of tea. After filling it, I grabbed the gear by the door and slung it over my shoulder before gently closing it.

I was walking up the driveway when I saw another light heading my way. It was Danny, wearing a headlamp. I waited for him and we walked out the gate together.

"Feels like we're going hunting this morning," I said.

"Yeah. Hunting doesn't feel the same now. You know, it used to be fun. Something you did to get out in the woods on the weekend. To get away." He looked around and added, "That's every day now."

"I feel you. But this is still a little exciting. For me anyway. I'm really hoping Mom and Dad are there and we can find them."

"I hope so too. It's been a while since I've seen them."

"As long as we don't run into any problems on the river, this should be a pretty easy trip. Just go up river and pick them up and bring them back."

"Let's hope it's boring."

The Hummer was waiting at the bunker for us. The boat was connected to it and one of the MRAPs sat idling behind it. It would be our escort and provide fire support should someone get a little frisky.

As we walked up, Sarge asked, "You put that chainsaw in the boat?"

"Yep," I replied. "And a gallon of mixed gas and a spare chain."

"Good. Let's hope we don't need it. But better to have it with us."

"I agree. Let's get this show on the road," I said as Danny and I got in the truck.

We left the neighborhood and went south to forty-two. We were going to take it east until it connected with forty-four, then take that road to Crows Bluff and launch the boat there. We'd discussed putting the boat into Blackwater Creek, but Danny and I decided against it. Even during good times, that little waterway was very prone to being blocked by fallen trees and it could take forever to get out of there. There was far less chance of the river being blocked along its main channel, so we opted for Crows Bluff. Here, we'd put directly into the river proper and should have clear sailing.

The MRAP led the way with Jamie driving and Ian manning

the thermal weapons sight mounted to the turret on top. He could sit in relative safety inside the truck and still offer fire support. Mike and Ted were there as well to drive the Hummer back. It felt strange to be driving down this road. I hadn't been on it since getting back home, at least, not this section.

We were passing through Paisley and I wasn't seeing any sign of life anywhere. Paisley was a small community in the best of times, and now it seemed deserted. It reminded me of the many trips I'd made down this very road on my way to the county transfer station, getting rid of trash and junk around the house.

I had to look at the little store, Paisley Discount Beverage, that I had often stopped at for a cold drink or maybe a can of Cope. It didn't look so good now. The front doors were broken out and there was trash all over the small parking lot. Even the two old gas pumps out front had been torn open in someone's determination to get some fuel. It reminded me of just how desperate people were....or are.

Leaving Paisley, there was nothing else to see for quite a while. Lake Kathryn was the next small neighborhood we'd come to. It was a small neighborhood of several dozen homes. It's pretty far out and there isn't really anything around it. I always found it to be an odd place. While it was out in the middle of nowhere, it was also a conventional neighborhood which would preclude you from doing many of the things that living in the sticks gives you the freedom to do. But to each, his own.

As we passed the houses that lined the side of forty-two, I looked for lights or any sign of life. There was none. No lights, no people seen anywhere. Just another place where people once lived and were now gone. And it made me wonder, as I often did seeing these little abandoned hamlets, where did they go?

Where are these people now? How many bodies were lying in houses out there? All of these are just sadly the signs of the times now.

Aside from my ponderings on the whereabouts of the locals, there was no issue on our ride and before I knew it, we were turning onto forty-four. It was less than half a mile to the bridge over the river. A bridge we'd need to cross because the boat ramp was on the eastern shore. The bridge was an old drawbridge that I had rarely ever seen in action.

After crossing the bridge without incident, we pulled into the parking lot of the ramp. There were a couple of people there fishing from the seawall. They looked up very curiously at the sight of the two armored vehicles pulling up in front of them. They continued their pursuit of dinner as we got out to get the boat ready.

Sarge lined the truck up on the ramp and Danny and I got out and released the straps securing the boat to the trailer. I climbed in and prepped the boat as the old man backed it into the river. I'd checked the motor last night. It started right up then, and I expected it to now. I had been surprised when it did start last night. I figured after sitting for so many months, the battery would be dead. It made me think about what else Dave had going on over there if he had the ability to keep the battery charged on something he had no real use for.

As the boat floated from the trailer, I hit the starter and backed off. Having reverse on this motor was a huge plus. Many of these mud motors didn't have it and that made it difficult at times to run the boat. I nosed the boat up to dock where Danny was waiting. He grabbed the bow and held it while the old man talked to the guys. When Sarge was done giving his final instructions, he grabbed his thermos and walked down the small dock.

Jamie and the guys stood on the ramp and waved as I backed the boat away from the ramp and turned it up river and opened the throttle. We settled down for the nearly twenty-mile trip down to Mom and Dad's. Sarge sat in the front of the boat with his Minimi between his legs and a cup of coffee in his hand.

It was a great feeling being on the river, the wind rushing by, the smell of the water as it sprayed past. Seeing the birds and other wildlife was also a treat. Herons, egrets, coots and cormorants were easily spotted and seemed to be everywhere. Not to mention the gators. I was surprised at the number of them we saw. I figured they would have been hunted out by now. But maybe people found it wasn't quite as easy as the TV show portrayed it.

The St Johns river can be confusing to navigate. There are numerous drainages that empty into it and many of them are wide and can be very easily confused for the actual river channel. But I'd fished this river for years and while I wasn't intimately familiar with it, I knew where the major traps were. When we came to Hontoon Landing, I took the cut to Lake Beresford, leaving the main channel as I headed towards the lake.

Seeing a channel marker pass him, Sarge asked, "What are you doing?"

"We're going to go into the lake and take a channel out of the south end," I shouted. "It runs straighter than the river proper and will save miles. There are a lot of blind curves on the main channel."

Sarge nodded, "Good idea. I don't like blind corners."

As we passed Hontoon Island, I remembered a lazy day of fishing with my dad. We were anchored across the river from the landing, using fishing as the excuse to get out of the house. Mostly what we were doing was talking shit and generally having a good time hanging out. There was quite a bit of boat traffic that day and the landing was crowded with boats launching and coming back in. As well as people just dropping into the store.

So, there was nothing special about the Gheenoe coming down the river towards us. We were anchored parallel to the river and as the small boat came abreast of us, it suddenly started to buck, rock and convulse in the water. Now, this all happened in seconds, but it was like it took place in slow motion.

When the boat started its acrobatics, the woman sitting in the front of the boat with her feet up, relaxing in the sun, gripped the gunnels and started to scream at the man in the back of the boat, "knock that shit off!"

Well, the poor bastard sitting in the stern of the boat had his hands full, literally, with the small Mercury outboard, that had until that very moment been attached to the stern. It was now free of the boat and the only thing keeping it from sinking to the bottom of the river was the fact that he had ahold of it, by the throttle. And it was twisted wide-ass open. It was like he had a giant weed-eater stuck in the water as it splashed and threw up geysers of water.

As the boat started to buck and rock, his lady friend began to scream at him as she held on for dear life. The struggle with the motor only lasted a few seconds though. After it made a couple of revolutions, coming completely out of the water in doing so, and assaulting our ears with the exhaust that was no longer muffled, everything went silent.

Now, up to this point I'd sat in complete shock at what I was witnessing. But when everything fell silent, the poor bastard stood there looking at the rising bubbles where his outboard had disappeared. His brand new outboard. Because, while the sound of the motor and the thrashing were gone, his lady friend's complaints were not.

Finally, he shouted, "Bitch! Shut the fuck up!" Which,

upon reflection was a little harsh. But at the moment, caused me to erupt into laughter, which he surely heard as we were only yards apart. Then he looked back at the bubbles and said, "It's gone! It's fucking gone! It's brand fucking new!"

Of course, this only added to the laughter I was already experiencing, and I felt bad about it. Not bad enough to stop laughing, but bad enough to try and hide in the bottom of the boat. With his boat out of power, he made his lady friend move to the rear and he went to the bow where he dropped the trolling motor in. The current was sufficient enough that all it did was hold him in place, neither allowing him to go forward or to drift back against the current.

Now, I was still laughing. I mean, uncontrollable hysterical laughing as I lay rolling in the bottom of the boat. My dad called out to the man, "You need a hand?"

The man looked around for a second before replying, "Well dammit, I guess I need something!"

So, I had to get up and try and get my laughter under control, so I could look the man in the eye and offer some help. We pulled our anchors and moved out to where his stricken craft sat lazily in the current. Dad tossed him a line that he tied off and we pulled him across the river to Hontoon Landing. After wishing him luck, we went back across the channel and assumed our previous position. Where we could still watch the show of course.

I can remember that day like it was yesterday. And as I steered us into the cut past Hontoon that led to Lake Beresford, I realized I was smiling. I hadn't thought much about Mom and Dad. There was just so much that always needed tending to. It seemed everyday there was a new crisis that demanded all available focus. But that was all gone now, I hoped. And it was time for me to do what I should have done long ago. Go find them and bring them home with me.

We saw a few people fishing or tending nets from the seawall that lined the little community along the river here. They waved, in the way everyone on the water does in acknowledgement of an unspoken kinship. Like bikers always do. It's always struck me as interesting that this only occurs in a few places. Naturally, bikers always do it. But, so do people driving on country roads. I've been all over this land and people in Wyoming and Utah do it just like people here in Lake County. And of course, people on the water. I think if more people did it, we'd be better off for it.

We were only on the lake for a few minutes and were entering the channel leaving the lake when Sarge called for me to slow down. I instinctively started scanning the not too distant shore but didn't see anything. When I looked back to him to ask what was up, he was unscrewing the top of his thermos.

"Really? You're stopping us so you can pour a cup of coffee?" I asked.

He waited until his cup was full and the lid back on the insulated bottle to answer. Holding the cup out, he said, "You have any idea how valuable this cup of coffee is here, in this place? There isn't another cup for thousands of miles I'd guess. So, you're damn straight I made you slow down so I didn't spill any!"

"You done now? Can we continue?"

He stretched back out in his seat and replied, "If you're waiting on me, you're backing up. If you'd close that face hole, we'd be moving already."

I shook my head and gunned the throttle. About the time he was adjusted to the G force of the acceleration, I immediately let off, causing him to rock forward. Then I gunned it again. I smiled when some of his precious coffee sloshed from the cup onto his hand. He looked back, glaring at me. I shrugged and said, "Weeds in the prop."

Licking the coffee from his hand, he replied, "Better not be no more fucking weeds!"

Once I had us moving again, Danny looked back with a huge smile on his face and gave me the thumbs up. I grinned and nodded my reply. The ride down the channel leaving the lake was on smooth water. The sun was coming up and it made for a beautiful scene. This part of the river was totally uninhabited, and it was like stepping back in time. The river here looked just as it would have to native tribes that lived along its banks centuries ago. And we were approaching an area where they were known to have once lived.

Blue Springs State Park was just ahead. Its crystal-clear waters dumped into the tannin-stained waters of the river to make its way up to Jacksonville and into the Atlantic. The St Johns is one of only a couple of rivers in the world that flow from south to north as it slowly courses its way up the Florida peninsula.

Ordinarily, you couldn't take your boat up to the spring. But these weren't ordinary times. As Blue Springs Run came up, I asked, "You guys want to ride up into Blue Springs?"

Danny gave an enthusiastic nod. The old man just shrugged and sipped his coffee. I decided we'd go up and check out the spring and steered the boat into the small run. The water went from the dark brown the river was known for to crystal clear at a near perfect line. I slowed the boat and we cruised lazily up the narrow waterway.

The park was still there and there was plenty of evidence of people having been there since the Day. There was a campground and I wondered if anyone was living back there. We made it to the spring, as close as we could get anyway, without seeing a soul. Letting the boat idle, I reached down and scooped up a handful of water. It was cold, and I splashed it on my neck.

"Man, I'd love to go for a swim," Danny said.

"It'd be nice," I replied.

"We ain't got time for that shit. This ain't no pleasure cruise," Sarge barked back.

"Keep your Depends on. No one said we were going for a swim, just that it would be nice," I shot back.

"Get this damn thing turned around. We've done enough sightseeing."

Danny looked over his shoulder and asked, "Tell me again; why did we bring him?"

"Because I said so!" The old man hollered.

"I have no idea," I replied to Danny.

But I turned the boat around and we headed back down the run towards the river. As we motored slowly along, I said, "Damn, it would be nice to live here. To have this to yourself."

"Yeah it would. I'd never be inside. I'd spend all day lying in that spring," Danny said.

"I wonder if anyone is living in the Thursby house," I said, giving voice to my thoughts.

"It'd be a good place. They still have the wood cookstove in the kitchen. It was built to live in without electricity," Danny replied.

The house, a three-story wood-frame structure, was built in the late 1800s and added to in the early 1900s. It was the site of one of the first steamboat landings on the river. It would be the perfect place to live now. Located here at the spring, you'd have everything one could need.

"I'm betting someone is," I said.

As the small bluff the house occupied came into view, I saw a man standing in the trees, looking out at us.

"Contact on the left!" I shouted.

Sarge immediately turned to the left as he picked up the Minimi. I waved to the man, but he didn't wave back. Instead, he raised his rifle. Panic filled me as we were just idling along. I cried out, "Shit!" As I gunned the throttle. Sarge must have seen the man too, because at that same moment, he opened up with the machine gun and was thrown off balance by the sudden acceleration. Fountains of water erupted where bullets cut into it, then they were ripping limbs and leaves from the trees on the shore. But he got himself steadied and continued to pour fire into the trees on the side of the run as we made our escape.

We were almost into the river again, when I heard the very distinct sound of the Russian grenade launch pop. Danny had picked it up and fired a grenade, which landed in the trees out of sight. He quickly pushed another into the small tube and adjusted his fire and launched it. This one hit at the river's edge, sending water and mud flying into the air.

"Stop shooting!" Sarge shouted as I turned out into the river. "They ain't shooting back and we're too far away now."

"Did that asshole ever get a shot off?" I asked.

Sarge nodded, "Yeah, one I think," he replied with a laugh. "I don't think he was expecting the Minimi."

"Or the grenades," Danny added.

"I bet that woke his ass up," I replied.

Sarge was laughing. "Wish I could have heard what was going through his mind!"

"He probably shit himself," Danny added.

The idea got me to laughing, "Yeah, he probably said it, then did it."

Sarge acted it out from his seat up front. Miming raising

a weapon, then ducking while shouting, *Shit!* Then getting a disgusted look on his face as he patted the seat of his pants. "Ma!" He shouted. "I did it again!" It had all of us laughing by the time he finished the charade.

We quickly passed Goat Island and Flowers Island. As we approached Guava Island, I shouted, "Fort Florida is coming up on the left. Keep an eye out."

Up to this point we hadn't seen any other boats. But the sun was fully up now, and we were entering a section of the river that was more populated. At Guava Island, we passed the Wekiva River where it emptied into the St Johns after flowing for many miles from its spring near Apopka. As a kid, I spent a lot of time in that spring. Diving into the spring and swimming against the incredible current to get to the bottom to scoop up sand was a common pastime there.

The sand would be brought up and searched through for shark's teeth. And in nearly every scoop that came up, there would be teeth in it. It was amazing to think about how they got down there that deep. The power of the spring was forever pushing more up. It was also a great place to look for money! And as a kid, I always took a swim mask with me for just this purpose. Wallets were also not uncommon finds in the swimming area, as were shoes and other swim masks. It was a great place to be a kid in the summer and Mom had taken me there often.

As we rounded a bend, the small community of Fort Florida came into view. Here, there were houses on the river's edge and nearly all of them had a small dock of one sort or another. But what caught our eye were the small boats out in the river. Several small boats, Jon boats and canoes, were out in the middle of the river working a large gill net. As soon as we rounded the bend, the sound of the motor got everyone's attention and they were looking at us.

The old man raised the Minimi and Danny shouldered the AK with the launcher. But the people in the boats just stared in apparent amazement as we drew nearer. I'd slowed the boat, in case we needed to beat a hasty retreat. All of the men working the nets were shirtless and in shorts. Their skin was dark, and it was obvious they spent a lot time on the water.

I slowed further as we approached them. Their net was strung all the way across the river. Not seeing any weapons on any of them, Sarge waved and called out, "How's the fishing?"

A man in a Jon boat had the net laid on the deck as a younger man pulled the catch from it. They were pulling themselves along it, bringing it up over the boat as they worked down its length. Others were doing the same on different sections. The man waved back and said, "Pretty good," and looked around before asking, "Who the hell are you?"

I eased the boat towards him and Sarge replied, "Nobody. Just out to find some folks."

The man looked suspiciously at the machine gun Sarge held. "I'm glad you're not looking for me. Where did you get hardware like that? You in the Army or something?"

"Something like that. Can we slide over the top of this thing? I don't want to damage your net."

The man pointed at a section of the net lying in the water with only the small foam floats visible. "You can come over it there. Just raise that motor when you get to it." Then, as though the realization just came to him, he asked, "Where the hell did you get gas?"

"Like I said, we're something like the Army," Sarge replied.

Then the man pointed at me and asked, "You a deputy sheriff?"

I looked down at the star before replying, "Something like that."

"Something like that?" The man asked rhetorically. "Is that all you guys have to say? Is there help coming or something?"

"Not any time soon," Sarge replied. "You folks look like you're doing alright."

The man looked down at the deck of the small boat and the fish lying there. "I guess." Then he looked back at Sarge, "But I'm getting damn tired of eating fish."

"Maybe so. But if you didn't have them, you'd be thankful to get them. There are still a lot of people out there starving."

"I reckon so," the man replied. "Where are you guys from?"

"Altoona," I replied.

"Altoona! How the hell did you get here?"

Thad was loading some gear into the little red truck to head to town when some of the guys walked up.

"You going to go help with that beef for town?" Perez asked.

"Yeah. I'm gonna meet Cecil."

"I'll come help."

"What the hell does a Mezcan know about butchering cattle?" Mike asked with a laugh.

"I'm not Mexican, blanquito gusano."

Mike looked at Ted, "Means little white worm," Ted said.

Mike nodded, "Whatever. I forgot the PR was the Caribbean cattle capital."

"Actually, Puerto Rico has a lot of cattle. It's a major producer of dairy and beef. My dad owned a butcher shop when I was a kid and I learned how to cut working for him."

"We could really use your help then," Thad said. "We've got two cows to cut up and get smoked. Gonna be a lot of work."

"No problem. Let's go."

"What about us?" Mike asked.

"What about you?" Perez replied.

"You need our help?"

Ted slapped Mike's arm. "We can't. We have something else to do."

With genuine curiosity, Mike asked, "What?"

Ted shook his head and wiped his face. "Come on. I'll fill you in."

"I don't remember anything. What do we have to do?"

Frustrated, Ted pulled Mike over and whispered in his ear. A smile spread over Mike's face and he blurted out, "Hell yeah!" Then he looked at Perez and said, "I forgot about this. Sorry, you boys are on your own."

Thad eyed the two suspiciously. "What have you two got to do that's so important?"

As Mike and Ted turned to leave, Mike waved the question off. "Nothing you need to worry about. We'll take care of it."

As they walked away, Perez said, "They've got shit to do. Those fuckers are up to no good."

Thad laughed. "Probably, but I'd rather not be around it when it happens."

Perez lit a cigarette and pointed at Thad with it, "Good point, amigo."

Perez tossed his gear into the bed of the truck and the two got in and headed for town. As they were driving towards the county road, they passed Jess and Doc. Jess waved and Thad stopped. Leaning on the top of the door, Jess asked, "What are you two up to?"

"Going to town to help with the beef Dave is giving them," Thad replied.

"Hey," Doc said, "can we come with you? I can go check in at the clinic and help out for a while."

"Sure, hop in."

Jess and Doc walked around to the back of the truck and climbed up into the bed. As they were sitting down, Jess said, "I'm not going back in there. I'll help with the beef."

Doc smiled as the truck started to move. "No problem. You help them with the beef."

She nodded, "I don't mind seeing animals cut up. How do you get used to seeing people in that condition?"

"You just get used to it. It's a problem and I approach it like one. What do I have to do to keep this person alive? Wounds are just defects that give me an idea of what's going on inside. You just address the issues in order and work your way down."

Jess shivered, "I still don't like it."

"Inside of a person is like the inside of any other animal. We're all made from the same shit for the most part."

"Yeah, well maybe. But I don't eat people."

Doc laughed, "Not yet."

Jess slapped his arm, "Not ever!"

They found Cecil at the school. The center of activity in Eustis had moved away from the lake and downtown out to the school. That's where the wounded were and that's where most people moved to after the rocket attack. No one wanted to be near downtown where the reminders of that day were everywhere.

Cecil had a large smoker hooked to the tractor and was trying to position it under a covered walkway. Getting out of the truck, Thad walked over to help guide it into position. Doc gave Jess a kiss and told her he'd be in the gym if she needed anything and he left. Once the smoker was in position, Cecil shut the tractor down and climbed off.

"Some shade will make this more bearable," he said.

"I agree," Thad said. Then he pointed at Perez and Jess and added, "I brought help."

Smiling, Cecil replied. "Good. We're going to need it!"

He walked over to a pallet sitting in the shade of the walkway and pulled back a piece of heavy canvas. "Cause we've got lots of work to do!"

Perez looked around. "We need some tables."

Pointing at a door, Cecil replied. "They're in there. Already thought about it."

They worked together to set up the tables, then the three of them wrestled a side of beef up onto one, then another. Cecil went back in the building and came out with a large water keg and set it on the end of the table as well. "Water, so we can clean up."

"Good idea. I was wondering about it." Thad said. Looking at the smoker, he added, "I'll get a fire lit."

Cecil looked at Perez and asked, "You ever butcher a cow before?"

Perez slapped the piece of meat and replied, "Many times. But most of the hard work's already done. All we have to do it section it out."

Cecil nodded. "Yep. So, let's get to cutting."

"What are we going to do with the bones?" Jess asked.

"I don't know, why?" Cecil asked.

"We should crack them open and make bone broth. Kay makes it for Fred when she has morning sickness. She says it's super good for you, something about it being easy to digest. We should make broth out of it for the wounded people inside. Some of them can't eat solid food."

"That's a fine idea," Cecil said. "I've got a big kettle at the house. Let me run get it and I'll bring it back. If you want to tend it, we can be making the broth and smoking meat at the same time."

"Sure, I'll do it," Jess replied.

Cecil rode the tractor back to his house and returned with a kettle an Army mess cook would appreciate. Jess went to work looking for firewood while the guys went to work cutting up the beef. But firewood isn't very plentiful on a school campus.

"Thad, I'm going to take the truck so I can find some wood; there's none around here."

"Miss Jess, I've got wood here. You don't need to go look for any," Cecil replied.

"I figured that was for the smoker. Keeping a fire going to make the broth will take a lot of wood. You think you have enough?"

Cecil looked at the pile of seasoned oak he'd brought to the school. "I think we've got enough and if we don't, I have plenty more at the house."

"Are you sure?"

"I am, now take what you need."

Jess found her a spot in the shade of a large tree to start her fire. Cecil had all the makings for one and it wasn't long before she had a good blaze going. Realizing she needed something to set the huge kettle on, Jess left her fire to burn down a bit and went hunting for a stand of some kind.

She found what she was looking for in what had been the shop class. There were several old metal stools there. You know the kind that look like they were from WW II, painted some form of indescribable governmental color. They had a wood insert in the seat and she figured that it would just burn away and leave her a stand. Once the stool was sitting over the fire, she waited for the wood to burn away and went looking for water.

Water had been provided to the school in any container

that would hold it. People would boil water at home and bring it to help with their loved ones. The school also had a firepit and large kettles they used to boil water in as well, and there never seemed to be enough. She carried two five-gallon jugs back over to the area where they were working and poured all of one and part of the other into the kettle. And there was still room for the bones!

"Cecil, where in the world did you get this thing from?" Jess asked.

"I've had that for years. It came off a Navy ship. Thing's big enough to cook a person in!"

Jess wiped the hair out of her face and replied, "Two, if they're small."

Thad was hard at work cutting the beef. He and Perez both worked with the precision of a skilled butcher and the meat was quickly piling up. Each of them was working on a leg, removing every scrap of meat they could. Perez finished the one he was working on first and looked up at Thad with a smile of satisfaction.

"I beat you!" He announced.

Thad smiled, "Good, get started on the next one."

"Hey, Jess!" Perez shouted. "Come get these bones!"

Jess walked over and looked at the leg bone that was still whole, connected by the ligaments. "What in the world am I supposed to do with that?"

Perez nodded to the kettle that was starting to steam. "Put it in the pot, Chica."

"I can't get all that in there!"

Thad reached over to where Cecil had his wood stacked and gripped an axe. He laid it on the table. "Here, break it up with this."

Jess rolled her eyes as she grabbed the axe and slid it off the table. She looked around for a place to cut the bones up, and seeing no better alternative, she laid the large section of bone out on top of the wood pile. Holding it with one hand, she raised the axe with the other and brought it down with little force, using gravity to do the work.

The axe hit the bone and bounced off, doing nothing more than chipping it. "Damn, that's hard."

"Swing it like you mean it, Chica!" Perez shouted.

Jess looked at him, glaring as she blew a strand of hair out of her face. Gripping the axe tighter, she brought it up again. This time, she put everything she had into it. The head of the axe slammed into the bone, sending chips of the shattered femur into the air, but the bone separated.

Jess smiled, "I got it that time!"

"Be sure and break all those large bones," Thad said. "You'll want that marrow to cook out."

Jess looked at him with a smile and said, "You do your job; I got this."

Thad held the knife he was using up in surrender, "Okay, Okay. I was jus' sayin'."

Jess smiled at him and raised the axe again. "And I was jus' sayin'," she brought the axe down with force again, "that I got this!" The bone snapped, and she collected the large pieces and headed towards the kettle with them.

"Come on!" Mike pleaded.

"Nope," Ted replied. "I ain't riding bitch."

"Whatever, you can drive!"

Ted leaned in, "The answer is no. Get it through your fucking head. If you want to go see Crystal, get in the fucking wagon."

Mike walked around the other side of the war wagon, saying, "Whatever, man. It would just be so cool to ride up on that Harley."

"Yeah, yeah. I think it'll be pretty cool to just go see the girls."

Mike sat in the passenger seat and agreed. "You're right. Let's go see them."

Ted drove out of the neighborhood, waving at Wallner who was sitting on the top of the bunker with no shirt as they passed. As they came to the market, Ted wheeled into it.

"We going shopping?" Mike asked.

"Nah, just flying the flag. Making sure they know we're around."

The people at the market all watched as the war wagon pulled through. Seeing Mario, Ted waved, and he returned the gesture. Leaving out the other side of the market, Ted opened the wagon up and they sped down highway forty-two, leaving swirling leaves and debris in their wake.

Ted pulled up to the gate into the property and stopped. Mike hopped out and ran over to it. Looking back, he shouted, "It's locked! How are we going to get in?"

Ted was thinking when he looked across the pasture. Nodding in the direction he was looking, he said, "Let's ask him."

Mike looked up to see a rider on a horse heading towards them. He wasn't in a hurry, allowing the horse to walk. Mike lowered his sunglasses and looked at the rider, then back at Ted. Ted shrugged and sat back in his seat. Mike put a foot up on the gate and leaned over on it as he watched the rider slowly approach.

"He should get off and push it," Mike complained.

"We aren't in a hurry. Relax."

The rider finally made it to them and stopped the horse. The horse was more interested in the long grass around the fence. The rider sat looking at the two men. Mike held his hands out in a *what the fuck* gesture. After a moment, the rider asked, "Can I help you?"

"Yeah, open the gate," Mike replied.

"No one told me anyone was coming today."

"We didn't call ahead for a reservation," Ted said.

Annoyed, Mike said, "Look dude, we need to talk to Dave. You know who we are. Just open the damn gate."

The rider pulled the horse away from his pursuit of a meal and nudged him towards the gate. He tossed Mike a key and he unlocked the gate. As he was doing so, the rider said, "You know, some people here aren't real happy about you talking to our women folk."

Pulling the chain through the gate, Mike looked up and with a squint and asked, "Yeah? Like who, you?"

The rider held his hand out. Mike thought about tossing the key so that he couldn't catch it but decided against it and tossed the key up to him. Ted pulled through the gate and Mike pushed it closed. As he was getting into the wagon, the rider said, "You watch yourself."

Mike smiled and replied, "Oh, I'll be fine there, Sport."

The rider scowled back without replying as Ted headed for the house. When they arrived at the house, Janet and Crystal were standing out front. While Crystal was visibly excited, Janet had more of an air of suspicion. As soon as Mike was out of the wagon, Crystal ran to him and they hugged. Holding hands, they quickly disappeared around the side of the house.

Watching them as they disappeared, Janet asked, "He's not going to get in trouble, is he?"

Ted snorted, "No promises on that. I've been trying for years."

"And you, what about you?"

"Oh, me? I can go either way," Ted replied, offering an evil grin.

The air of suspicion faded into a faint smile. "That's good to know."

"Who's the guy at the gate?"

"That's Jim, Jim Gifford. Why?"

"He wasn't real keen about letting us in. Said people here didn't like us *messing with the women folk* as he put it."

Janet laughed and looked towards the corner of the house where Mike and Crystal disappeared. "Yeah. Jim has a thing for Crystal. Nothing is ever going to come from it; Crystal can't stand him."

Ted nodded, "Ah. So, if he can't have her, no one can."

"You recognize the attitude?"

Ted scratched his head, "I've, uh, yeah. I recognize it."

"So, what are you two doing here?"

"We had some down time and decided to come by for a short visit. You know, just to hang out."

"Well then, you want something to drink? We have lemonade."

Ted smiled, "Lemonade would be great."

They went into the house together. Heading towards the kitchen, they passed Dave's office. Seeing Ted, he stood up and took off his reading glasses. "Ted," he said as he rounded the desk. "Great to see you again."

Ted shook his hand. "Nice to see you, Dave."

Dave was smiling and looking back and forth between Janet and Ted. "What brings you here?"

"We were in the area."

"That's good. Glad you dropped in."

"We're going to the kitchen for some lemonade, Dad. You want some?"

"No, no. You two go ahead." He motioned at his desk and added, "I'm busy here. Good to see you again, Ted."

"You too, Dave." Dave went back to his office and Janet and Ted continued on their way to the kitchen. As Janet dropped ice cubes into a couple of glasses, Ted commented, "Your dad seemed rather happy to see me."

"Dad likes to see new faces. I think he was getting sick of looking at us every day."

Ted smiled, "Yeah, that was the vibe I was getting too." Then he switched the subject. "Ice, huh?"

As she poured the lemonade, Janet replied, "Thanks to some fuel we traded for recently, we can run the generator a couple of hours a day." She held the glass out to him and replied, "So yes, ice."

Taking the glass, Ted replied, "Thank you."

Janet held her glass up, "You're welcome." And they touched glasses.

Mike and Crystal were walking towards the dock on the lake, holding hands as they went. "Who's your buddy up at the gate?"

"That's just Jim. He's harmless."

"He seemed a little irritated at seeing us."

"He kinda has a thing for me." She turned and looked closely at Mike. "But I don't have a thing for him."

Mike smiled, "That's good."

With a bit of a carefree attitude, Crystal replied, "Well, I hope to find a good guy someday."

"I know how you feel. I've about given up on the idea of finding a good woman."

Crystal cut him a devilish smile, "I have a feeling the last thing you want is a *good woman.*"

Mike walked for a minute, then looked sideways at her. "I want a woman that's good at being a little bad."

Crystal stepped in front of him, taking both of his hands in hers. She leaned in and said, "Funny. That's just what I'm good at." Then she leaned in and kissed him.

Mike smiled, put his arm around her and they continued towards the dock.

CHAPTER 9

As we rounded Alexander Island, I started to look with anticipation for mom and dad's neighborhood. We finally came to the little cut leading to their marina and I turned the boat into it. As the dock and marina came into view, we saw a man with a rifle standing on the shore. Sarge stood up and waved at the man, who was very visibly shaken by our sudden appearance.

The man looked at us nervously as we slowly glided towards him. Sarge called out to the man as we drew nearer. We were doing our best to look nonthreatening. But it didn't work. After another moment's nervous hesitation, he bolted away. Running as fast as his legs would carry him.

"That's not good," Danny said.

"No. I imagine he's going to get help," Sarge added.

"Looks that way," I replied. "Let's just get out of the boat and wait for them. If we go wandering around, it'll only look more suspicious. If we're just hanging out here, we look less threatening."

Sarge agreed and we all climbed out of the boat. We took a moment to stretch out legs and grab a drink. Sarge was filling his cup with coffee when a group of people began appearing. There was a main group, coming straight down the road towards the boat ramp and two smaller ones flanking them on either side. They were being cautious, not that I blame them.

As the group advanced, I took a couple of steps toward them. I'd decided to leave the rifle in the boat, so as to appear less threatening. I hoped the shooting didn't start. But the old man was standing beside the Minimi, so there was that.

The group stopped at a distance of maybe thirty yards. They looked scared and all of them were armed in some fashion or another. One had an AR, the rest was a collection of shotguns, pistols, revolvers and lever and bolt-action guns. One old timer even had an M1 Garand. They looked ragged. Their clothes hung from their shrunken frames.

One of their fellows stepped forward tentatively and called out. "What do you want?"

"I'm looking for my dad, Butch! Butch Carter!" I called back.

The man turned and looked back at the crowd behind him. Then I saw a thin man break away from the group on the right side and start walking towards the ramp. It was Dad, but it didn't look like him. I started to walk towards him and as I did, the leader of the group in front shouted for me to stop.

"Knock that shit off!" Dad called out, "That's my son!" And I knew it was him and started to jog towards him.

When I got to him, I wrapped him up in a hug. He was much thinner than I remember, almost frail. I could feel his ribs when I embraced him. After a long minute, we finally let go enough to look at one another. There were tears in his eyes, just like the ones in mine. Then we started to laugh. Then, we hugged again, with tears streaming down our faces.

"I didn't think I'd ever see you again," Dad said.

"Sorry it took so long to get here," I replied, feeling the weight of how long it took me to make it here.

He pulled away from me. "Are you crazy? None of that

matters. What matters is you're here now. Your mom is going to be surprised to say the least."

"Where is she?"

"She's at home right now."

"Let me introduce you to someone. I think you know the other guy," I said, pointing to Danny and Sarge who were still standing by the boat.

Dad looked towards the boat and saw Danny. A broad smile spread across his face. "You brought Danny with you?"

I put my arm around him and we started towards the boat. As we walked, one of the men from the group called out, "Butch, where are you goin?"

Dad looked back, "I'm alright. You guys can go on. We're good here."

Danny walked up and offered his hand. Dad shook it and asked how he was. Danny held up the injured hand and replied, "Not bad, all things considered."

"What the hell happened?"

"We've been through a lot." Danny replied.

Dad looked at me. "They're all fine. We're all ok."

A look of relief washed over him. "Good, good."

"I want to introduce you to someone," I said. When Sarge walked up, I introduced the two.

"Good to meet you, Butch. Morgan has been wanting to come here for a long time. But things have been preventing it," Sarge replied.

"It's alright. You're all here now."

"Let's go see mom," I said.

"Good idea," Dad replied and we all started towards his house.

"What are you carrying there?" Sarge asked.

Dad looked at the little carbine tucked under his arm. "It's the Circuit Judge, a .410 and .45 long Colt."

Sarge laughed. "That's a hell of a combo!"

"Yeah. You ain't always got the gun you want. You gotta use the one you brought. And this is what I had."

"Ain't that the damn truth!"

Dad looked over at Sarge, "You in the 101st?"

The old man nodded, "Retired. You?"

"I arrived in Vietnam right after Tet. Spent most of my time up in the A Sầu Valley at Camp Eagle."

"That was an ugly place. What was your MOS?"

"Crew chief and door gunner on a LOACH."

Sarge reached out and slapped Dad on the back, "I knew I liked you! That was a hell of a job. How many of those have you had shot out from under you?"

"Three."

"And made it out alive. That's a hell of an accomplishment."

"How did you two meet?" Dad asked as we turned onto his street.

I laughed, "That's a long story. Way more than we could cover on this short walk."

"Like hell!" Sarge barked. "I saved his ass! And it's all I've been doing since then!"

"I forgot to tell you something," I said. "Don't believe a word he says. He's so full of shit he doesn't even see reality."

Sarge put his arm around Dad's shoulders. "I don't know how you did it. But it must have been a hell of a job to turn him into what he is today. I can't imagine what it was like trying to raise his ignorant ass."

"Say what you want, old man. You wouldn't have a place to live if it weren't for me," I said.

Before Sarge could explode, Dad reached over and tapped the star on my chest. "What's this?"

"Another long story," I said.

Sarge jabbed a thumb at me and said, "He's the Sheriff of the north half of Lake county."

"How the hell did you pull that off?"

"Wasn't my idea," I replied. "We'll have plenty of time to talk about all this shit. It's been a hell of a ride since the Day."

Turning up Dad's driveway, I said, "Let me go up there and just walk in."

"No, no. Your mom isn't the same as she used to be. She's got a gun and won't hesitate to use it. And she's not going to recognize you with that beard."

I nodded. "Yeah, guess I should let you go first."

We waited under the carport to get out of the sun as Dad opened the door and called Mom, telling her to come outside. Then he stepped back and stood beside me. The door opened, and Mom looked out. Surprised, she stood there for a minute looking at everyone.

Her eyes worked across everyone's face. Then her eyes landed on me and she asked, "Morgan?"

I stepped towards her and replied, "Yeah."

She rushed out and wrapped me up in a strong hug. She cried hard as she held me tight. And it made me cry as well. She held me for a long time before finally letting go enough that I could look at her. Her eyes were full of tears and she looked smaller than I remembered.

Shakily, I managed to say, "Sorry it took so long for me to get here."

"I didn't think we'd ever see you again," she sobbed.

"I'm here now," I replied as I hugged her tightly.

She hugged me firmly again. "I'm just so happy to see you.

We talked about you often, wondering where you were, how you and the girls were doing. We were so worried."

"We've been fortunate. Very fortunate."

"You guys want something to drink?" Dad asked.

"I'm good," I replied and that was echoed by Sarge and Danny.

I took a quick minute to introduce the old man to mom. "Mom, this is Linus." I started to reverse it, saying, *Linus, this is Mom*. But I'd never used his given name and it just felt, well, weird.

He smiled and held out his hand, "Linus Mitchell, ma'am, pleasure."

"Karen," she replied. Then asked, "You're staying for dinner aren't you?"

"I figure we'd stay the night," I replied. "But, there's something we need to talk about."

"What?" Dad asked.

Several lawn chairs were sitting in the shade of the carport. It was just too damn hot to sit inside, so most people lived in the shade outside.

"Let's just sit down for a minute."

We all took a seat and Mom and Dad looked at me expectantly. Before I could say anything, Mom asked, "Are Mel and the girls ok?"

"Yeah, yeah, they're all fine," I said and looked at Danny. "We've had some losses. But for the most part, we're alright."

"What do you want to talk about?" Dad asked.

"I'd like you guys to come back with us. Looking at you both, I can tell things are hard. At home, we have food, lots of it. We have power and vehicles with fuel. Things aren't as hard there and I want you to come with us. That's the reason we came, to check on you, but really to bring you back with us."

Dad looked at Mom, but neither replied. "I want you guys to be there with the girls. I don't want to leave here and it be another year before I see you again."

"But, we have friends here," Mom said. "We've all been working together, and it's not been easy."

"Trust me, we can relate. It's not been easy for us and I know we had more going for us than you did. I realize you've got friends here. You've lived here forever. But you've got family that needs you guys too. I need you. I need to know you're alright."

"Butch," Sarge started. "We've had some seriously hard times. You asked how I met Morgan. He was carried into my house unconscious. He'd been shot in the head and a couple of his friends brought him to me."

Mom looked at me, her eyes wide as saucers. "I was in Tallahassee when this all started and had to walk home."

"You walked home from Tallahassee?" Mom asked. I simply nodded.

"How'd you get shot?" Dad asked.

"It was an accident. One of the people that carried me to Linus's house, a young woman, got scared and pulled the trigger. Luckily, it wasn't major."

Dad looked at Mom and said, "I know we have a lot of friends here, but Morgan is right. We have family and things aren't getting easier here. That last attack by the raiders nearly got in here. We may not be able to hold them off next time."

"You've been attacked here?" Sarge asked.

Dad nodded. "Yeah, twice. Everything was fine for a long time. No one bothered us. But we've been hit twice in the last month. Last time, they almost made it in. All we have is a bunch of old folks here."

"I'm sorry to hear that," Sarge replied. "And I hate to say it, but it's all the more reason you should come with us."

Dad looked at Mom and she shrugged. "I would like to see the girls, but I'd hate to leave everyone here," she hesitated for a moment.

"I get it, Mom. I understand community. If it weren't for the one we've built, we wouldn't be here now. As important as community is, the basis of it is family."

"You're right," Dad said. He looked at Mom and took her hand. "I think we should go." He looked over at me and then back at mom and continued. "I can't imagine what it took for them to get here and it may not be possible for Morgan to get to us again. I think we should go."

Mom looked around, "We have so much here. What do we do with it? How much can we take?"

It made me smile. The way her mind worked. Her first concern was for her house. Mom and Dad aren't very materialistic. They have things they need, and everything they have has a purpose. So, Mom was curious what she was going to do with it all.

"Mom, you pack what you need. We'll make room for it. There's plenty of room."

"So, you want to leave in the morning?" Dad asked. I nodded. He took a deep breath and thought for a minute. Looking at his watch, he said, "We've got a couple of hours before supper. Why don't you fill us in on what happened."

"It'll take a couple of hours," I replied.

Mel placed the jar of broth and homemade crackers into a small basket. Kay handed her a small Altoids tin filled with butter, saying, "Take this too. She could use the fat."

"Good idea. I know the crackers will be appreciated. They worked for me when I was pregnant."

Kay laughed, "It was hot pastrami sandwiches and ice cream that worked for me."

"I don't think we're going to find either of those," Mel replied with a smile.

Kay paused and leaned against the counter. "Why not?"

"I don't know how to make pastrami," Mel started before Kay cut her off.

Waving her comment off, Kay said, "Not the pastrami. The *ice cream!* Think about it. We have whole milk, real whole milk. We have sugar and we have some bottles of vanilla that we brought back from the houses here, and we have ice. We have everything we need!"

"But how would we make it? We don't have a churn."

"Oh, honey," Kay smiled, "there's more than one way to skin that cat. You don't need one of those silly little churns. We can make it with a blender."

"I never thought of that. But I think you're right; it could work."

With a hearty chuckle, Kay replied, "I know it will work because I've done it!"

Mel was getting excited at the prospect. "Let me take this to Fred and I'll be back so we can get started. But let's keep it a secret; it'll be a big surprise."

Kay gripped Mel's arm in a conspiratorial embrace, "That's a fantastic idea. I say we save it for when Morgan gets home."

"Besides," Mel replied, "It'll probably take a couple of days to make enough for everyone."

"It might. Go on, take that and get back here."

Picking up the basket, Mel replied, "Ok. I'm taking Ashley with me. Can you watch the other two?"

"Go on. I can handle those two."

Mel went out onto the porch and called for Ash, who came running immediately. "What's in the basket," she asked.

"Some things for Fred. You want to walk to her house with me?"

"Yes," Ashley replied and took Mel's hand. "She's going to have a baby, isn't she?"

"She is."

"I can't wait. Babies are so cute!" Ashley gushed.

"They are cute. You were very cute when you were a baby. Everyone said so."

Assuming a very upright stride, Ashley announced, "I'm still cute!"

"Yes, you are," Mel replied with a smile.

As they rounded the corner at the end of the road, a large Lubber grasshopper was walking across the now nearly grass-covered bed of the disused road. There was so little vehicle traffic back here now that the grasses and weeds were retaking what was once theirs. Seeing the insect, Ashley shrieked with excitement and ran towards the large lumbering arthropod.

Finding a stick, she knelt down and began to try and get it to crawl up onto it. As she talked to the large bug, it suddenly started to hiss. With a scream Ashley jumped up and ran back to Mel, who was waiting for her. It was good to indulge a child's curiosity of the natural world. Especially now that they lived so much closer to it.

"Did you remember what Daddy said about when they hiss?" Mel asked.

"Yeah! He was about to spit at me!"

Tussling Ashley's hair, Mel replied, "That's right. You're a smart girl."

The little girl looked up at her mother and added, "And cute!"

"Yes, you are indeed."

Aric was outside cutting back some large weeds from the walkway leading to the house. He paused and wiped sweat from his forehead with a rag pulled from a pocket. "Hey, Mel, Ashley. What brings you out this way?"

Holding the basket up, Mel replied, "Bringing some things over for Fred. How's she doing?"

Fred appeared at the top of the steps leading to the porch and replied, "I'm fine. I was just sitting in the shade up here. Too hot to be out there. Come up and sit on the swing with me."

Looking up at Fred, Aric replied, "Yeah, too hot," as he swung a machete.

"You hurry up and finish that and you can come sit in the shade," Fred replied. Aric wasn't smiling, he just shook his head and went back to chopping.

Harkening back to another era, Mel went up onto the porch and sat on the wide swing hanging from chains tied to the ceiling. Ashley preferred to *help* Aric with his work. "I hope she doesn't get in his way," Mel said.

"He needs the experience," Fred replied. Patting her belly, she added, "He's about to have that full time."

Mel looked Fred over. She was wearing a simple sun dress, the type of thing a lady would just pull over. She was barefoot, and her hair was up in a ponytail. "You look comfortable at least. How are you doing?"

With both hands, Fred rubbed her protruding belly. "I'm ready to evict," she replied with a smile.

"I can remember that. But at least you're not having to try and work while this is going on."

"Work? I'm lucky to be able to walk out here and sit down!

I can't imagine trying to work." She stared at her belly as she spoke, then looked at Mel and asked, "Is it always like this? Is pregnancy always this miserable?"

"No. It'll be easier next time."

"Pffftttt, there won't be a next time. Nope, one and done!"

"Yes, there will be!" Aric shouted. He was obscured by a large unruly hedge that had taken over the front of the house.

"One and done!" Fred shouted back.

Mel grinned and said, "It'll be easier next time."

The fire burned down enough that the rolling boil stopped. Jess used a large slotted spoon to scoop the scum from the top of the broth. Once the top was cleaned, she used a plastic pitcher to transfer the broth to a clean five-gallon bucket. The kettle was just too big to tip and pour. Once the bucket was about half full, she carried it inside.

Chris Yates, the medic that took the lead after the rocket attack, was tending to the wounded when Jess came in with the bucket. She told him what it was and asked where he wanted it.

"Put it on this bench over here," he replied, pointing to a long bench against one wall. "This will be great. Whose idea was this?"

"Mine. I figured since they would be out there smoking that beef all day, I could use the time to make this broth. It's really good for you and these people in here need all the help they can get."

"You're right about that," Chris replied. "Hang on a sec. I've got something for this."

He disappeared and returned a moment later with a plastic bag full of Styrofoam cups. "I found these in a desk drawer the other day. Figured they'd come in handy." He pulled a rolling cart over and Jess started filling the cups with broth and placing them on the cart. Once they were out of broth, Chris started to wheel the cart around the gym, offering broth to anyone that wanted it.

In some cases, it was a family member that took it to slowly and carefully feed a loved one. It was eagerly accepted by all and soon there were calls for *more!* The poor people in the gym were only eating what their family members could bring or what the limited staff could come up with. All they were able to muster was one meager meal a day and it was having a severe impact on those trying to recover. So, the broth was having a tremendous effect on all.

"I think they're liking it," Jess said.

"They'll like anything they can get right now," Chris replied.

"I have more out there and I'm going to start another batch. You want to throw some pieces of meat in this one? We have plenty. The guys are out there smoking some, but that will be a while before it's ready."

"If it's cut small; these people can't handle big hunks of beef. But I can, and I can't wait for some of that beef to be done! I haven't had beef since *The Day* and my stomach is grumbling for it. I'm not even going to go out there. If I smell it, I'm done."

"I gotcha," Jess said and picked up the bucket and left the gym. She went out to the smoker and leaned on the table where the guys were deboning and said, "Is there any way you guys can get a small piece, or a few small pieces, and like grill them? The staff in there is really hungry. It'd be nice to give them a little something."

"Sure thing, Miss Jess." Cecil said. "I'll cut a few pieces and cook them over the firebox. Have them ready shortly."

"Can I also get some small scraps to throw in the broth?"

Thad smiled broadly, "You just causing all kinds of work."

"It's for the people inside, Thad. I just feel so bad for them."

"I know who it's for and it's not a problem. Give me a few minutes and I'll chop a couple of pounds up."

"Great! I'm going to take the rest of what's ready inside and I'll be back in a few minutes."

We walked down the street towards the clubhouse. It was supper time and Mom and Dad were hungry. "We have community meals," Dad said. "It's just easier that way. I do a lot of fishing and we have a couple of nets we made. It keeps us in fish. There were gators early on, but I haven't seen one in months. But we do get turtles from time to time too."

"You're lucky to have the river. I lived on Suwannee when it all went down, and the river kept me and my neighbors fed as well," Sarge said.

"When we had to move out to Alexander, the river fed us pretty well too," Danny added.

"Yeah, I kind of miss those mullet," I said.

Getting to the clubhouse created quite a stir. Everyone there wanted to talk to us, to hear what we've seen and heard. We were swarmed by people. An old man ushered us to the front of the line, saying, "Here, you boys go first."

I held my hand up. "No, no, we're not going to burden you folks. We have our own food. You folks go ahead, and we'll eat what we brought."

Danny had gone to the boat earlier and filled a pack with MREs with this very situation in mind. He'd also made sure the boat was secure. As it turned out, the community had assigned someone to watch it, so it wasn't an issue. Danny slid the pack off his shoulder and opened it. Taking an MRE, I said, "See. We're good. You folks go ahead. We'll go take a seat."

Sarge grabbed a meal as well and looked at Mom and Dad. "You folks want one? We've got plenty."

"Why not," Dad said. "This'll be interesting."

As we walked to a table, several people asked, "Where did you get those?" We were a little elusive about how we came to have them. Simply saying they were *found*. The four of us helped Mom sort out what to do with the package and soon we all had something heating as we nibbled on some of the other contents.

"There's a lot here," Mom said.

"Better than C-rats," Dad added.

"Anything's better than those damn cans!" Sarge nearly shouted.

"You guys could have eaten what was fixed," Mom said.

"I know. But it didn't look like they had a lot there. And three of us bellying up to the buffet wouldn't look good in my opinion. Every bite we take is one less that someone here can have."

Mom smeared cheese spread onto a cracker and looked at Danny, "I'm so sorry about Bobbie. I was looking forward to seeing her."

"Thanks. There was nothing we could do. It happened pretty fast."

Mom picked at her cracker. "I'm very sorry."

As we were eating, an old man at the table beside us turned and asked, "How did you get gas for that boat?"

"We did something with the government," Sarge said. "They gave it to us."

"What's the government doing?" The man asked. "I haven't heard anything out of them."

Hearing that made me realize I hadn't listened to the radio in a long time and knew nothing of what may be going on. But with the old man's contacts, I'm sure if there were something I needed to know about, I would.

We spent the rest of the evening telling the group some of the things that had happened, as we know them. We made a point to not engage in speculation with any of the crazy theories some had. These people have been in a total vacuum since *The Day*. And here we were, from the outside with tales they couldn't imagine.

"What do you mean the Russians invaded?" A woman asked.

"They didn't invade, at least according to them," Sarge replied. "They claimed they were here to help. Purely humanitarian."

"What are we going to do about them?"

"They've already been dealt with," I replied.

As surprised as the people were hearing about the Russians, they were shocked when they were told that we nuked a Chinese fleet and they retaliated against Tampa.

"Did we strike them back?" A man asked.

"No," Sarge replied, shaking his head. "It was decided it was best not to. No sense in turning it into a full exchange; we have enough trouble."

"I agree with that," a woman replied as she took a bite of fish.

Another man walked up and surveyed our group. "What I want to know is, what the hell is the government doing? We haven't seen a soul from the government since all this started. What the hell are those people doing?"

"All we know is, the Department of Defense is in charge now. The President invited the foreigners in and the DOD kicked them out," Sarge replied.

"So, where's the President?"

"In a hole underground," I replied.

"Not anymore," Sarge replied, surprising me.

"What?" I asked.

"Yeah. I got word right before we left. They got him out last week. He's in custody now."

"That's not right! With everything that's going on already and now there's a coup?"

"It was for the best," Sarge replied.

"For the best? It's as wrong as it could be!" The woman shouted back. "We shouldn't be living in a police state!"

This made me laugh out loud. "A Police State? You've already said you haven't seen a soul since things changed. If you think about it, what does it matter who is in charge?"

"So, what?" The woman asked. "We just wait here to be hauled off to camps then?"

"Ma'am, why would anyone want to haul you off to a camp?" Danny asked.

"What else does a Police State do?" She replied.

"We haven't seen one lately," I replied. "We did take one down months ago and freed all the people."

The woman looked incredulous. "I don't believe that."

A man came up behind her and put his hands on her shoulders. "Come on, Maureen. I think you're worked up enough now. Let's go home."

The woman leveled a finger at me. "I don't believe you. And what's with that badge? You part of this coup?"

"No ma'am. I try to provide the people of my community with some level of law enforcement. My days are spent dealing with stolen chickens and theft in general. It's not fun and I didn't want the damn job."

Sarge reached out and slapped me on the back. "But you're doing a hell of a job!"

Thankfully, the man managed to pull Maureen away as she was about to spout off again. My head was starting to hurt, and I told Dad I was going outside. Mom started chatting Danny and Sarge up as Dad and I walked outside. We wandered down to the river and stood at the edge of the dark water. I reached into my pocket and took out the can of Cope. It was now less than half of a can I noticed as I lifted the top.

I turned on my flashlight and held it out. Dad looked at it in utter disbelief. As he took a pinch, he asked, "Where in the hell did you get that?"

"It came from Eglin. We have a couple of first rate scrounges in our merry band."

He held the can back out and I took a pinch for myself. "Let me see that light," Dad said. I handed it over.

He clicked it on and shined it at the far bank of the small cove of the marina. He laughed and clicked it off. Then back on. "I haven't seen an artificial light in, well, I can't remember."

"That's why I want you guys to come with me. Life is much better back at home, I promise."

Dad spit into the water, the slight splash the only indication he did. "How in the world do you have power?"

"You remember that little solar setup I had?" Dad nodded, and I continued. "Well, it's been a lifesaver. But it shouldn't matter soon."

"Why not?"

"We're working to restore power. That little gas turbine at the orange juice plant is up and running. It took us some time and the help of a bunch of Army engineers, but it's functioning now and we're clearing lines and moving it out our way. We restored Eustis right before the attack. I mean, we had the power there, but hadn't turned in on yet. But everything was damaged so bad, we had to abandon that idea."

"Hard to believe. When this shit started, I figured it was the end. But if you guys can manage to restore power in your little town. Maybe there's a chance."

"There's always a chance. Unless you're dead; and we ain't dead yet. So, we keep going, trying. What else is there to do?"

We stayed at Mom and Dad's that night. Being a nice guy, I let the old man have the spare bedroom and I took the couch. We used a manual pump to inflate an air mattress for Danny and laid it out on the dining room floor. The house was hot and humid. The air hung thick like old drapes and had a presence of its own. Then there was the silence. It was quiet as a tomb. It made me really miss home where there was a fan to at least move the air and more importantly, provide some white noise. Tonight, all I had was the ringing in my ears.

The still silence wouldn't last long though. Sometime around midnight, we heard a gunshot. Bolting upright, I had to wonder if I really heard it, or if it was just my imagination. The answer came quickly in form of fusillade of gunfire. I turned on my light, keeping it cupped in my hand to prevent it from lighting up too much, and moved towards the door. Dad, Sarge and Danny were all there. Mom was in the hallway, a small Smith and Wesson pistol in her hand.

"We're being raided again," Dad said.

"You've got help this time," Sarge replied as he picked up the Minimi.

I grabbed my pack and took out the PVS-14. Unstrapping the helmet secured to the pack, I snapped the device into its mount. "Yes, you do," I replied as I picked up the AK and messenger-style bag with spare magazines and VOGs. I handed my AR to Dad along with several magazines.

"Where are they coming from?" Danny asked as he adjusted his night vision.

"Sounds like the shooting is up front. But I doubt the main assault will come from there. This is a diversion," Dad replied.

Mom and Dad's house was in the center of the small community. We walked outside and could hear gunfire towards the gate that led out of the neighborhood. Even with the night vision, we saw nothing from our location so deep in the houses.

"With the weapons you guys have, I think we should hang out here and see where the main attack comes from. Then go there," Dad said.

"That's what I was thinking," Sarge replied. "Then go there and kill every fucking one of them."

It didn't take long to figure out this was the main attack. The raiders had an old truck they'd armored in a haphazard fashion with whatever plates of steel they could find. As the sound of the shooting near the gate grew, we ran towards it. We encountered several of the residents moving in the same direction. Before long, we were a sizeable force responding to the attack. When we got to a point we could see the gate and the defenders doing their best to hold back the assault, we split up into groups.

Sarge and Danny ran to take up positions opposite the gate where the community had built fortifications of sorts. Dad and I, along with several others, moved to a flanking position to the left of the gate. There was a lot of gunfire coming in.

"Must be a damn pile of them," Dad said as bullets cracked in the air over our heads.

"Let's see if we can even the odds," I said as I snapped a grenade into the launcher. It seated with a *click* and I held the weapon at an angle and pulled the launcher's trigger. It went off with a *shtock* sound and moments later detonated outside the gate.

As soon as the grenade exploded, the old man opened up

with the Minimi. He fired in long bursts, the tracers racing out and slapping into the truck, ricocheting and arching up into the night sky like cheap fireworks that never detonated. All incoming fire ceased. I took off at a trot in the direction of the fortifications. They were opposite the gate and offered a view down the road.

Falling in beside Sarge, I had to stick a finger in my right ear. That damn Minimi was loud! I looked over the top of the sandbags to see the truck backing down the road away from the gate. The raiders were attempting to take cover, keeping the retreating truck between them and us. Snapping another grenade into the launcher, I propped the AK on top of the bags and held it at a very slight angle, *shtock!*

The grenade impacted on the hood of the truck and detonated; these fireworks worked! But the impact wasn't like in the movies; most things never are. There was no enormous blinding flash or massive fireball. The raiders had armored the front of the truck and the windshield, but not the hood. The detonation ripped into the hood and blew the steel plate over the windshield off. The blast started a fire in the engine compartment, which quickly grew as a result of a ruptured fuel line. All the windows were blown out as well.

I watched the truck. Sarge made short work of anyone that tried to run from it, but I never saw the driver exit. The shooting soon died down and it was quiet, except for the fire consuming the truck, which was now fully engulfed. We came out from behind the barricade and walked towards the gate in the light of the dancing flames but didn't go through it. People from the community began to gather at the gate and all of them wanted to know what the hell just happened. The crowd stood in silence as the truck burned. The sound of glass breaking and things popping.

A couple of people that saw me fire the grenades came over and asked how I did it. I showed them the AK with the launcher on it and more than one commented, *they didn't expect that! That'll teach 'em!*

"I don't think they'll be back," Sarge said.

"I think you're right," Dad said. "This was way more than they expected, considering what happened the last two times."

An older man sidled up to me and asked, "Can I have that? Can you leave that with us?"

I looked at the rifle, then at Sarge. He shrugged, and I asked the man, "You know how to use this?"

"I spent three years in Vietnam in the Corps."

I handed him the rifle and he expertly removed the magazine and cleared the weapon. He replaced the round from the chamber into the mag and reinserted it into the weapon, charged it and put it on safe. I figured, what the hell, we've got plenty of them.

"Looks like he knows what he's doing with it," Sarge laughed.

I unslung the bag and handed it over. "There are mags in here and a bunch of grenades. You know how it works?"

"They didn't have those back then."

I demonstrated how to load the launcher and fire it. It's a simple process and he understood it immediately. "That's easy enough," he replied when I finished.

"I hope you don't need it. But if you do, you'll have it."

"Damn straight," he replied.

Several men, including the one I had just given the AK to, said they would stay up for the rest of the night in case the raiders came back. With more than enough volunteers, we decided to go back to Dad's and get another hour or two of sleep.

Dad pointed at the burning truck and said, "You may want

to stay away from that truck. If there's any ammo or anything in it, it's going to cook off and possibly explode."

"We're staying behind the sandbags," one of the men said.

Before we left, Sarge looked at the men staying and said, "Don't go out that gate tonight. We'll go out there tomorrow and clear the area. Safer in the light of day." The men were all eager to stay put; there was no way in hell they were going out there in the dark. With that settled, we headed back to the house.

As we walked, Dad asked, "What is that thing, Linus?"

Sarge looked at the short machine gun slung under his shoulder. "It's a Minimi. The Army calls it an M249. This is a paratrooper version, so it's shorter and lighter."

"What's it shoot?"

"The 5.56. It's a light weapon."

"It shoots like a damn firehose," Dad replied.

"That's why I like it. Better than an M4. Carries more ammo and fires at a higher rate."

With a nod, Dad said, "I like it too. Looks lighter and easier to shoot than the M-60 that I carried."

We made it back to the house and Dad told us to wait a sec. He went to the door and knocked out an odd pattern. The door opened, and Mom peeked out. She'd sat in a chair looking at the door since we left. We came inside and gave her the details of what happened.

"That's why I'm afraid to leave. These are our friends," Mom said.

"I gave them a weapon that will more than equalize the situation for them," I said.

Dad laughed. "Yeah you did. Blew that truck all to hell."

Mom fidgeted for a moment, then said, "I don't think I can go back to sleep."

"You're safe now," Sarge said. "They were running for the

hills, and I think we at least took out several of them. No way those who escaped will be back. Ever."

"Come on," Dad said as he took Mom's hand. "I'm tired. Let's try and get a little sleep. I have an idea that tomorrow will be a long day."

Reluctantly, she followed him and we all returned to where we were before the shooting started. Even with the heat, humidity and adrenalin, I fell asleep quickly. Stirrings in the house woke me before dawn. I sat up to see Dad and Sarge in the kitchen.

"You want some?" Sarge asked.

"Where in the hell did you find real coffee?" Dad asked.

"We've made a couple of trips to Eglin. There's aid coming in from Europe and a couple other places. Canada is doing a lot. Mainly to stop the refugees at the border from trying to go north."

As I walked into the kitchen, Dad took a coffee cup down from the cupboard. Blowing the dust out of it, he held it out, "I haven't seen coffee in months."

As Sarge filled the cup from his thermos, I said, "Dad, I thought you drank a lot of coffee," then pointed at Sarge, "Then I met him."

"One of these days, you'll grow up, your nuts'll drop and you'll learn to appreciate coffee," Sarge replied.

"He's just never spent time in a place where the only thing that kept you going was coffee. We didn't just drink it, we lived on it," Dad replied.

"Maybe not," I replied as I twisted the top of my jug of tea. "But I live in Florida where it's a million degrees in the summer. And I know that a cool drink will always beat a scalding cup of coffee any day."

"You don't know nothin' about nothin'," Sarge replied.

After I filled my glass, sadly there wasn't any ice. I asked, "You want to go down to the gate and take a look at what's left out there?"

"Yeah, let's get out there and see what it looks like," Sarge said.

Danny came out of the dining room, rubbing his face. Sarge looked at him, saying, "Well, if you can't get here on time, get here when you can."

I offered him the bottle of tea and he took a long drink. Looking at the bottle, he said, "Still cold."

"Gotta love Yeti bottles," I replied.

"You two done making out?" Sarge asked. "We got work to do."

I shook my head and collected my gear as Mom came out. Opening my pack, I took out an MRE and handed it to her. "Here, this is a breakfast. Not the best, but it'll fill a hollow spot."

She took it and looked it over for a long time. "It's strange to be holding a package like this. Haven't seen packaged food in so long. The one last night had so much food in it."

"You eat it and enjoy it."

"We're going to go look at the gate," Dad said. "Go ahead and pack everything you want to take."

Taking a knife from the block on the counter, Mom cut the bag open and replied, "I will. But I'm going to have something like a real breakfast first."

We left the house and started towards the gate. It was still dark, but the air was heavy. It must be eighty degrees already; it was going to be a hot day. The streets were dark and empty, and we walked in silence. Rounding the end of the block, we could see the gate. The men from the night before were still on duty, manning the same positions behind the sandbag emplacements.

Sarge stopped in front of the position, looking at the gate. "Any of you boys wander out there for a looksee?"

"Hell no," the man I gave the AK to replied. "We're not about to run out there and get our asses shot off."

Sarge gripped the Minimi and said, "Well, there's enough of us now."

"I don't think anyone is going to be out there," Dad said. "Last night was a hell of a surprise for them."

"That's all it takes," Sarge replied. "Make the investment not worth the return."

We formed a line and started advancing towards the gate. The sky was just beginning to turn purple as the sun was waking. One of the men began opening the gate as we covered him. Swinging the gate fully open, we stepped out onto the road.

The acrid stench of fire hung heavy in the air and smoke still drifted in faint wisps straight up into the thick still morning air. I passed on the driver's side with Dad. Danny and Sarge went up the other. The men from the neighborhood provided "cover" from behind the sandbags. I was more worried about them accidentally shooting me in the back than anything else.

We found three bodies and two blood trails leaving the area. We collected the weapons that were left behind. I walked over to the driver's door of the truck and looked in. The driver was still behind the wheel. Or at least his blackened form was. A burned human is a horrible thing to see. What was left of the lips was pulled back into a sneer, showing the bared teeth that hung open in an eternal scream with no sound.

"Doesn't look like there's anything to worry about here," Sarge said. He waved for the men to come out from behind the sandbags and called out to them. "Come on out here and search these bodies. Take anything useful, and then you'll need to bury them pretty quick too."

The men came out, and the one with the AK looked down at the bodies. "We should have thrown them into the truck last night."

"Maybe," Sarge replied. "But it would've stunk to high heaven."

Dad was looking at the charred truck and said, "And that smell will never leave you."

The man with the AK nodded. "No, it won't."

Mel looked out the window at the kids in the backyard. Aric and Fred were sitting on the porch watching them play. She was feeling better, her pregnancy progressing to the stage that morning sickness was waning. Mel smiled as the kids ran through the sprinkler and took to their bellies to slide down a piece of long black plastic that served as their impromptu slip-n-slide.

"Hand me that other jug of milk," Kay said.

Mel picked up the half-gallon jug and handed it to her. "Here, I'll measure the vanilla."

As Kay poured the milk into a large bowl, Mel measured out a tablespoon of the real vanilla and poured it in with the milk. Kay added the sugar to it and started stirring.

"When this one's done, we'll have nearly two gallons ready," Kay said.

"This will make for a really nice surprise when they get back," Mel said.

Kay glanced over at her and asked, "You think his folks are still alive? It's been a long time."

Mel took a deep breath. "Morgan's dad is a tough man. He's spent a lot of his life fishing and hunting. He worked for the state in the woods and on the water. If anyone is alive. He is. Morgan learned a lot from him."

Kay offered a reassuring smile with no conviction behind it. "Then this will be a really nice homecoming for them."

Dalton came into the house, announcing, "Ello ladies!"

"Hi, Dalton," Mel replied. "What are you up to?"

"I came to get food for the prisoners."

"How are they doing?" Kay asked.

"They're enjoying the food. Can't understand how they're being fed so well."

Kay smiled at the light compliment. "I do the best with what we have."

"And a smashing job you ladies do!"

"Thank you," Kay replied as she picked up a cloth bag and handed it to him.

"Ah, thank you," Dalton replied.

"How much longer are they going to be here?" Mel asked.

"No idea. When the old man gets back, we may know. He's the only one talking to anyone up the food chain."

"I'd just like them to go away. I don't like having them here. Having to feed them. They should be shot. Not fed."

"Oh, I agree," Dalton replied. "But some think they have a use yet. So, it isn't up to us to make that call."

Mel turned and leaned against the counter. "Yes, we could. Who's going to stop us?"

"Now Mel," Kay started. But Mel cut her off.

"Why not? No one has the right to tell us anything. We're the ones that paid the price for them being here. Not someone up in Eglin or wherever they are. It's not their friends and family that have been dying."

"I know how you feel, Mel," Dalton replied. "But if we do what you're suggesting, they'll all have died in vain. We're trying to rebuild our lives, community and nation. And it's a hard road. We could take the easy road, but anything worth having requires hard work."

Kay stopped stirring the creamy concoction in the bowl and said, "Oh, honey, he's right, you know. The hard thing is almost always the right thing."

Mel sighed, "I know. I'm just irritated."

"Mel, don't worry about Morgan," Dalton said. "I've met a lot of interesting characters in my life. I've done a lot of uh, interesting things in that time as well. Morgan is a guy I can't quite put my finger on. He's either the luckiest son of a bitch on the planet, or he's just damn good."

Mel laughed, "He'd disagree with you."

"Facts are facts," Dalton said as he shouldered the bag. "Just remember, like Kay said, the right thing is usually the hardest choice. I'm going to run down and feed these guys. I'll see you for dinner." Then he looked at the bowl and the items sitting on the counter and asked, "What are you two up to? What are you making there?"

Kay came out from around the island and began pushing Dalton towards the door. "It's nothing you need to know about. Now, go on."

Dalton left the house and returned to the old man's place. Coming into the garage, he saw the two men were lying on the ground right where he had left them. A Guardsmen was standing outside the door; they weren't going anywhere.

Seeing Dalton, the Colonel sat up. The only real interruption to his routine was when his meals were brought twice a day. Crossing his legs, he waited eagerly for the food. Dalton put the bag on the counter and started taking out the food.

"What has your cook prepared for us today?" Aleksei asked.

"Boiled socks," Dalton replied as he carried the plastic dishes over and placed them in front of the men.

"Your cook does a wonderful job with them. Pass along my compliments."

Dalton set the food down and replied, "One of those cooks wants to kill you. And I believe she would do it herself if she had the opportunity."

Aleskei took the meal with enthusiasm. As he ate, he said, "We all have reasons for blood lust."

Dalton pulled a bucket out and sat down on it. "Maybe. But I would say we have more of a claim to it at the present moment."

Aleksei shrugged. "The reason doesn't matter. Blood lust is blood lust. We will kill one another. That is the way of it." He looked up at Dalton and motioned with a crust of bread he'd just dredged through the soppings left in the bottom of the bowl. "What about you? I cannot figure you out. Your Russian is good. But your accent is peculiar. You've been to Russia, yes?"

"No. Just worked with some."

Licking his dirty fingers, Aleksei asked, "What sort of Russians have you worked with? What did you do with them?"

"Hunting men."

Leaning back on his hands, Aleksei replied, "I knew you were different. I could tell," he paused, "you are a dangerous man, I think."

"We all are. All of us here."

Aleksei laughed. "Yes, yes, of course you are. Especially your cowboy, yes?"

Dalton considered the man for a moment. "Why are you here? Why did your government send you here?"

Aleksei wiped at the beard that was now long enough to be in the itching stage. "Because I am a soldier. I should think then, that you understand why we are here." Aleksei waved a finger at Dalton. "But, you know the proper answer. Your president asked us to come. We are here to help the poor people of this country."

"Help with a Grad, huh?"

"You Americans have such a sense of superiority." Aleksei sat up and focused intently on Dalton. "But, that is not the truth, is it? You people are weak. You're fat and lazy. You feel you are, what is the word," he struggled for a moment for the right word. When it didn't come, he said, "that your government owes you. That everyone owes you, that the world owes you." He leaned back again and smiled. "But look at you now. How you say, your chickens have now come home to roost."

Dalton rose and walked over to Aleskei. The Russian observed him with mild disinterest. Dalton squatted down in front of the man. "You think we're weak? Look around you. You're chained to the floor. These weak and fat people managed to destroy all of your men. And we chained you to the floor."

"This is true, yes. But you didn't do it on your own. If not for your bombers, we would have eliminated the rest of you in your little town. Your country is going to change," he laughed; "it has changed already, only you don't see it. How you say, dead man walking? You are already dead and don't even know it."

Dalton looked over at the other man. He sat listening, but not saying anything. He was young, probably no more than eighteen. His Colonel probably told him to keep his mouth shut. Looking back at Aleskei, Dalton said, "You will find that I am hard to kill."

Aleskei laughed. "I am Russian. We know how to deal with peasants such as you. All of you. Soon, it will be you in chains. I will see to it."

"Suka!" Dalton shouted as he viciously slapped Aleskei, toppling the man to the floor. Dalton leapt onto the man, gripped his shirt and lifted him from the floor, delivering a punch to his nose. It busted like an overripe tomato. Standing up, Dalton kicked him in the ribs. He never said a word as he did this, and he decided in that moment he would never say another word to the man. But this would not be the last time Aleskei would feel just how "weak" these Americans were.

"What the hell did you do that for?" The Guardsmen asked.

"It's the only language he understands," Dalton replied as he walked out of the garage.

Thad closed the lid of the smoker. Wiping his brow, he said, "That's the last of it."

Cecil dropped a handful of beef fat into a bucket. "Now all we have to do is wait. I'll stay here overnight and watch this if you want. You go on home. It's been a long day."

"I can stay here," Thad said.

"I got nothing else to do, Thad. You go back home to Mary. If I had a pretty woman at home waiting on me, I'd want to be there."

Thad smiled. "If you're sure."

Cecil stepped around the table, wiping his hands on a rag. "I'm sure. Besides," he pointed at Perez sleeping on top of a picnic table moved under the covered walkway, "you need to get him home."

Thad shook his head. "He's somethin' else."

Without lifting his head, Perez shuffled through a pocket and fished out a pack of smokes. Shaking one out, he replied, "I can hear you." He lit the cigarette and let it dangle from his lips.

"See?" Thad said with a laugh.

"Oh, I recognize the type," Cecil laughed.

Jess came walking out of the gym with Doc in tow. They were holding hands as they walked towards the smoker. "How's things in there?" Cecil asked.

"I think all the ones that were going to die have. The rest will need a lot of help and time. But they should make it," Doc replied.

"That's good. Chris need anything in there?"

"No. He's in good shape now. There are fewer people to take care of. They're actually able to get some sleep at night now. Only one person is on shift at night. So, things are improving."

"You two ready to go home?" Thad asked.

"Yes, we are," Jess replied.

Mike and Crystal sat on the dock with their feet in the water. Crystal made lazy circles in the water with her toe. "How'd you get down here?" Mike asked.

She sighed, "Mother sent me down here. Said I needed to get away from the city for a while. I think she just wanted to get her kink on and wanted me out of the way to do it."

Mike pulled his shirt off and lay back on the dock. "You're lucky she did. Being stuck up north wouldn't be good."

"Maybe. But now I'm stuck in this Godforsaken swamp. It's so damn hot here."

Mike quickly sat up, "Oh, sorry, I'll put my shirt back on." He was smiling devilishly as he said it.

Crystal raised her eyebrows, "No, you're fine." She turned and lay down alongside him. "You're the best-looking thing I've seen in a long time."

"So, what are you going to do?"

Crystal traced a finger along his chest. "I don't know. Just wait and see. That's all I've been doing, waiting to see. I want out of here though. I'm bored."

"You should come over for dinner. Kind of like a date."

She laughed, "Janet will not let me leave here." She rolled onto her back and looked up into the clear sky, "it's like a prison."

"It could be worse," Mike replied. "At least here you've got food and people looking out for you. You're safe. And trust me, there's a lot to be said for that."

"Maybe."

Ted and Janet sat on the porch overlooking the lake. "They're getting kind of cozy with one another," Janet said.

"Good for them," Ted replied.

Janet sat up in her chair and looked at him. "Why do you say that? I'm trying to keep her out of trouble."

"Why? You worried about her reputation? Someone going to talk about her?" He looked over at her, "Those days are gone. Everyone needs to find a little happiness and it's in short supply at the moment. Let 'em have fun."

She sat back in her chair. "I suppose you're right. It's been rough, being stuck on the ranch. Worst of all for her. She's young and used to traveling and being in cities. She's had a hard time adapting to this."

"Shit, we've all had a hard time adapting to this. I'm bored out of my mind too. But this is life now, so I'm trying to make the best of it."

Janet's eyes flickered towards him, "That why you're here today? Trying to make it better?"

Ted looked at her for a moment. "It's nice here. A change of scenery is good. You and Crystal should come over for dinner. You can stay the night. We have plenty of room."

"Slow down, cowboy," she replied. "I'm not looking to be bedded yet."

Ted was flustered. "That's not what I meant. We have a house where Miss Kay cooks and we all hang out. You can stay there. It's Danny's house and he has the kids there. I don't stay there."

"Keeping up appearances, is that the idea?"

"Not that. Just no expectations. It would just be nice to hang out a little. Get to know you better."

"And what's the end game to that? We going to play house in some little trailer?"

Ted shrugged, "Doesn't have to be a trailer. Jus sayin'."

Janet laughed and stared out at the lake. After a moment, without looking over, she reached over and took Ted's hand. He didn't say anything, nor did he look over. He simply took the small gesture and the two sat rocking together.

CHAPTER 10

IT ONLY TOOK ONE TRIP to get Mom and Dad's stuff to the boat. We used Dad's surf cart to move it all to the river; there really wasn't much. Many of their neighbors gathered at the ramp to wish them well and say their goodbyes. Mom was pretty upset. She had a lot of friends here and would miss them terribly. But they all insisted she go. That it would be better to be with family during these times.

As they said their goodbyes, we waited at the boat, to give them the room and time. Once the hugs and handshakes were done, they walked down the ramp to the boat. I helped Mom in and Dad quickly stepped in as well. Danny held the boat as I got in and the old man followed me. He gave the boat a shove and hopped over the side as it drifted out into the small marina.

The ramp was full of people waving and wishing well. I made my way to the stern and started the motor. In a moment, the little community on the side of the river was out of sight and the broad slow St Johns was all we could see. Dad stood looking towards Sanford, at the railroad bridge that crossed just upstream. He took it all in. He'd lived here for decades and loved the river and now he was leaving it.

I kept the boat at an idle while he made his peace with leaving. I knew it would be hard on him not having it. Mom too. I saw her wipe tears from her face as she looked back towards where we'd come from. Dad finally sat down, and Mom laid her head on his shoulder. I took it as a sign they were ready and opened the throttle and we started up the river towards Crow's Bluff.

It was a clear, warm morning. It would be a hot day for certain. But on the river, it was cooler; and the boat racing down the river provided plenty of cooling breeze. I stood, holding onto the handrail as I guided the boat. The river was empty this morning, save the birds and occasional gator that would immediately submerge at the sight or sound of our boat.

I saw Sarge pour the last of his coffee from the thermos into a cup. He took a sip and offered it to Dad, who gladly accepted it and took a long drink. It made me smile. I wondered how Dad's arrival would affect Sarge's coffee stores. The two of them easily drank a pot a day, each. I was sure it would prove interesting to say the least.

Sarge took out his radio and made a call. I couldn't hear him over the motor, but I guessed he was calling the guys to tell them we were on our way. I didn't much care one way or another. I was enjoying the novelty of the river. Of being in a boat speeding down the slow-moving trail of black water.

Holding the tiller under my arm, I took a pinch from the can in my pocket, then gave it to my dad. He opened it and looked in, it was nearly empty, one pinch left. He closed it and went to hand it back, but I waved him off, telling him to take it. He did, the last pinch of Cope as far as I knew even existed and dropped the empty can in the bottom of the boat.

Then Danny took a can out and opened it. He put a pinch in too and smiled as he showed it was nearly half full. I gave him the finger; the bastard had been taking from mine when he had his own the whole time! He laughed and put the can back in his pocket.

When we got to Lake Beresford, I knew we were almost to the ramp. A sense of both relief and sadness came over me. Relief that we were nearly back but also a lament that we would leave the river and I didn't know if we'd ever see it again. I could only imagine how Mom and Dad were feeling. Dad knew the river better than I did by a long shot. He knew where we were and where we were going.

As we passed Mud Lake and the bridge over the river came into view, I slowed the boat. There were a few houses along the river here and people were out in skiffs, Jon boats, canoes and kayaks, tending lines, nets or just fishing. All in pursuit of their breakfast.

Pointing to the east side of the river, Danny asked, "What are they doing?"

I looked over to see two men wading in the brown water at the shore. One was dragging a small Jon boat on a lead behind him. Both men rooted around in the mud and from time to time would reach down and pull the large root of a pond lily up and toss it in the boat.

"Looks like they're harvesting the roots," I replied.

"You can't eat that shit," Dad replied.

"No. you can't," Mom echoed. "We tried, there's no way you can make that edible."

"Well," I replied, "you can. You just have to process the shit out of it. Takes a lot of soaking and water changes."

"Say what you want," Dad replied, "I don't think there's any way to make it edible." He shook his head and shivered, "stuff's horrible."

"Luckily, we don't have to worry about trying to eat that kind of trash," Sarge offered. "We've got plenty of food. And none of it comes from the bottom of a nasty river."

"Hey now, leave my river alone," Dad said with a chuckle.

Sarge smiled. "I know how you feel. I lived on the equally nasty Suwannee and miss it terribly."

Passing under the highway bridge, the trucks weren't there yet. I pointed the boat towards the ramp and Danny caught the pole and tied us off. Mom and Dad got out and we followed them up the dock to the overgrown grass lining the seawall. Two old black men sat there with cane poles in hand, their light lines disappearing into the murk of the river.

"Doing any good?" Dad asked.

One of the old men tilted a bucket to show one small catfish. "Not much this mornin'."

"It's getting harder."

"Yes sir, it is."

The other man looked down at the boat. "That's a nice boat. Where'd you get the gas, ain't no gas anywhere."

"We had some saved up," I said.

"Y'all waiting on something?"

"Our ride," Sarge said as he plucked the mic from the plate carrier. He called Ted, who replied immediately that they were a few minutes out.

"You got trucks too?"

Sarge nodded. "We work for the government."

The first man laughed. "Government! What government? Ain't no government."

"There still is some. They're trying to get things sorted. But there's a lot that needs to be done."

Presently, the trucks rumbled over the drawbridge, garnering the attention of the two men fishing. One of them looked up at Sarge and commented, "You wasn't shittin' when you said you worked for the government, were you?"

The two big trucks swung around into the parking lot. Ted lined the trailer up on the ramp and Mike parked the other one and got out. Then the passenger door opened and a young lady stepped out. Sarge gave him the stink eye and walked quickly over to him. He looked at Crystal and asked, "What the hell is she doing here?"

Mike shrugged, "She wanted to go for a ride."

"This ain't your daddy's car to take out to try and get a little stink finger in."

Mike patted him on the shoulder. "Relax. We're just here to pick you guys up. Nothing's going on. They're going to come over and hang out with us today and maybe stay the night."

"They?"

Mike pointed at Janet. "She came too."

Sarge shook his head and leaned in close to Mike. "You two fuckers better not do anything to stir up shit between us and Dave. I'll be the first to lead you at the end of a shotgun to your wedding."

"Look, Top, I promise you. We're not up to anything like that. I like her, and I think Ted and Janet are getting on really well too. You have Miss Kay—" Sarge cut him off.

"Watch what you're about to say."

"Calm down, would ya? Listen for a minute. I know you think I'm just a wild ass, but I want what you, Thad, Morgan and Aric have. I want someone around, to be with someone. And, so does Ted. This is for real."

Sarge looked at Crystal. She was standing with Ted. "I'm calling bullshit." He looked at Mike. "But I couldn't think of anything better than you two boys settling down." He looked at Ted again, "But until I see it," he looked back at Mike, "I'm calling bullshit."

Mike smiled and quickly wrapped the old man up in a hug. "Thanks, Dad!"

Sarge slapped him in the side of the head, "Get off me, you damn idjit!"

Mike laughed and ran off towards Ted. I introduced him to Mom and Dad and he in turn introduced Crystal. We were chatting for a moment when Sarge shouted, "Let's get this scow loaded and get the hell out of here!"

We quickly loaded the boat and I was strapping it down when Dad walked up. "What kind of situation have you gotten into?"

Removing the plug from the boat, I replied, "What do you mean?"

"All this," he replied, indicating the trucks. "Where the hell did all this come from? What exactly are you doing? I mean, how in the hell did you get all this shit?"

I stood and leaned on the gunnel of the boat. "Some of it we took from the DHS. Some of it the Army gave to us. Remember, I told you we've been working with the DOD. The old man there, he's been promoted to Colonel. We were working with the local National Guard unit; I told you what happened to them. But during all this, we've acquired a lot of gear, food and other supplies. We've been trying to support the community, helping who we could." I shrugged, "Just living."

"Looks like you've done alright."

"Come on, let's go home."

I got in a truck with Mom and Dad. Ted was driving, and Janet was there as well. Mom and Janet chatted, the excitement of someone new to talk to taking hold of them. Dad sat looking out the window as we rumbled over the bridge. When we turned onto 42, the trucks sped up. After a couple of miles, Mom sat back in her seat. She didn't look too good.

"You feeling alright?" I asked.

"I suddenly don't feel so well."

"Hey Ted, slow down a little. I think Mom's getting a little car sick."

"I feel it too," Dad said. "We haven't moved this fast in almost a year. Kind of an overload."

Ted called Mike on the radio and told him to slow down some and why. Both trucks slowed to about thirty. Dad suggested Mom not look out the windows. She leaned back against the side of the truck and closed her eyes. "I think I'll just rest a little," she said.

We didn't talk much for the rest of the ride. Though, Ted and Janet chatted some. I was eager to get Mom and Dad home so they could relax and, more importantly, to get them a good meal. Left to my thoughts, I began considering where they would stay. I knew they wouldn't want a large place. I hadn't given this much thought and probably should have had something set up beforehand for them. But then, they may find a place they prefer, and any work done would simply have been wasted.

But we had time, now. Plenty of it. I sat with my back against the bulkhead of the truck and looked at Mom. She was rocking with the rhythm of the truck and her color looked a little better. Aside from being thin, she looked good. They both did. Their skin was now a dark mahogany from so many hours spent in the sun. Even in the Before, they spent most of their time on the river and current events dictated they spend even more trying to eke out a living.

It made me feel better to know that their lives were about to get a lot easier. At the same time though, I felt a sense of failure, of having let them down for so long. The fact that it took me nearly a year to get to them weighed on me. It was tempered with the fact they were both well and sitting in the truck with me. I couldn't imagine any other outcome to this expedition. The alternative was just unthinkable.

When we turned onto highway nineteen, Dad sat up and looked out the windows again. The market was bustling with activity and he commented on it.

"What's going on over there?" He asked.

"One of the local markets where traders go to try and sell their wares. There's a couple of them. This one, one in Umatilla and there used to be one in Eustis," I replied.

"How is Eustis now?"

I shook my head. "Gone, for the most part."

He sat back. "Still good to see people out like that. We never left the subdivision. There was nothing close you could walk to and paddling a boat into Lake Monroe was a hell of job and dangerous."

Mom sat up at the comment, "We lost a friend who tried. He left one day to try and go to Sanford. He never came back. No one knows what happened to him."

"You won't have to worry about that sort of thing anymore," Ted said over his shoulder.

Janet turned in her seat, "It's mostly quiet around here now. These guys have pretty much dealt with everything that's been thrown at them."

"Quiet for now," I sighed. "Subject to change without notice."

"Ah, come on, Morgan," Ted countered. "We're finally on the downhill slide, man."

"I'm not worried about the slide," I said, "but what's at the bottom of it."

Ted looked back over his shoulder at Dad. "He always been like this?"

Dad smiled. "Reality is a bitch."

"Yeah," I replied, "and I live in Realville."

"We all do," Dad added.

As the trucks slowed and navigated around the burned-out wrecks in the road in front of the turn to the neighborhood, Dad asked, "What the hell happened here?"

"Just DHS wrecks. Some lessons gotta be learned the hard way," Ted answered.

Mom looked at the rusted hulk of one of the MRAPs and asked, "You did this?"

"We did," I replied.

"They were government trucks?" I nodded that they were. "What were they doing? I mean, why did you have to do that to them?"

"Because they were shooting the hell out of us. Trust me, they weren't here offering relief."

"No, they weren't," Ted added. Then he asked, "Did you tell them about the camp?"

"No, but there's plenty of time for that," I replied as we rolled down the road towards the bunker.

"We passed your house," Mom said.

"We don't live there anymore. Those same government helpers who manned the burned out trucks you just saw on the road up there trashed our house. We had to move."

"Where do you live now?" Dad asked.

"Next to Danny. We all congregate at Danny's house most of the time anyway, so it puts us closer."

The two trucks parked at the end of Sarge's street, near the bunker and we all climbed out. Sarge walked up to Dad and asked, "Well, what do you think?"

Dad looked at the bunker and the Guardsmen standing around it. "Things that bad?"

Sarge looked over his shoulder at the bunker, "Not

anymore. We had a rough time for a bit. But I think that's all behind us now."

"Where are Mel and the girls?" Mom asked.

"Come on," I said, "let's walk down to the house."

"Morgan, I'll catch up later. I need to go check on our prisoner," Sarge said.

"You need any help, boss?" Mike asked.

Sarge glowered at him. "Hell no, I don't need your help!"

"You have a prisoner?" Mom asked.

I nodded. "It's a Russian Colonel. We're holding him until Eglin can send someone to get him."

"You better hurry with that," Wallner said. He was sitting in a chair under the tarp at the rear of the bunker. "Dalton kicked the shit out of him."

"Why?" I asked.

He shrugged, "I wasn't there. Just heard about it. I guess Ivan said something that made him mad. Bert said Dalton never said a word, just kicked the crap out of him."

"He probably deserved it," I said. "Either way, I really don't care."

We turned and started down the road towards the house. Mom and Dad were looking around and Mom asked, "How many people are here?"

"We have about seven houses occupied and many others available. So, you guys can choose the one you like. We've got around, thirty-ish, I think."

"Between the National Guard guys that we have and us, plus the two prisoners, it adds up quick."

"What exactly happened to your house?" Dad asked.

I told him the story of us getting tangled up with the DHS and how we were forced out and had to go live on the river for a while. How we then managed to overthrow the camp setup at the bombing range and were then able to move back.

"When we got back, we found they'd destroyed our house. Just ridiculous vandalism really. What bothered me the most was the fact that they knew where I lived. They didn't bother any of the unoccupied houses. Did a number on Danny's house too, but not as bad."

"It's hard to imagine that our government would do this kind of crap, considering what the country has been through," Dad said.

"Oh, it was all for our own good of course. They were rounding people up and moving them to camps where they could get medical treatment, food and shelter. What they didn't tell people was that it was Hotel California. You could check in, but you couldn't check out. They were splitting up families; even in the camps, men were separated from women and kids. Naturally, this led to all manner of trouble, sex crimes committed by the staff, physical abuse. We finally had to do something."

"So," Mom started, "you and your friends just attacked the camp? Weren't there a lot of government people there? How'd you do it?"

"Well, this little group is pretty skilled. We have some special forces types here and that is the sort of thing they did all over the world. Don't get me wrong, it was tough. But we managed to succeed." I looked at Dad and said, "You know what the craziest thing was? Some of the people locked up there were upset when we took it over and freed them. They didn't know how to act when there wasn't someone around making their decisions for them. It was nuts."

"The evil you know versus the unknown," Dad replied. "Once they adapted to the new conditions there, they resisted the change, even if it meant freedom."

"Exactly. I couldn't wrap my head around it."

We were approaching my gate, but I pointed to Danny's and said we should go there, figuring Mel and the girls would be there. As we passed the gate, the dogs came trotting out. We stopped the truck and got out. Dad knelt down. He'd always had a soft spot for dogs, so we waited while he scratched and petted them.

"Where'd this guy come from?" Dad asked, scratching Drake behind the ears.

"We found him. He seems to like it here and he's really smart," I replied.

"Didn't you have a little female too? Like this one here?" Mom asked, pointing at Meat Head.

"We did," I replied. "She's dead though."

"What happened?" Mom asked.

Without looking up, I simply replied, "She died."

Dad looked up but said nothing. He rubbed Meat Head's ears and stood up. We walked through Danny's gate and I half expected to see people sitting on the porch. But the chairs were empty. Danny went up onto the porch and in through the door. We followed him in and I saw Mel and Kay standing in the kitchen. Mel's face immediately lit up and she rushed over. I hugged her and gave her a kiss. Then turned to Mom and Dad.

"Well, here they are," I said.

She gave Mom a long hug as the two said words I couldn't make out. Then she hugged Dad. When the greetings were over, Kay looked at Mom and Dad and said, "You two look like you could use a cold drink and something to eat!"

Mom and Dad sat at the counter and Kay poured them a glass of tea. As she set them down, Dad asked, "Do you have any coffee?"

"We sure do!" Kay responded and quickly poured him a cup.

Ignoring the tea, Dad took to the coffee. He drained the cup quickly and Kay refilled it. "Take it easy now," Kay said as he sipped on the second one.

"It's been a while since I've had any. Where in the world did you get it?"

"Morgan and Linus brought it back," she replied. "They're always coming up with something."

I introduced Mom and Dad to Kay and they sat chatting while Mel prepared them a plate. Mom was looking around the kitchen and asked, "Do I smell bread?"

"Whatever it is, it smells amazing," Dad added.

Kay jumped, "Oh! Yes, there is bread. I need to get it out of the oven!"

Kay removed the loaf from the oven and tipped it out of the pan. The smell was incredible, and I could only imagine how it made Mom and Dad feel.

"Give it just a minute and I'll slice some up for you," Kay said as she set the jar of butter out on the counter.

Picking up the jar, Mom asked, "Butter?"

"A man in Altoona makes it. We trade for it," Kay said.

Mom looked at Dad wide-eyed. "I told you it was better here," I said.

Kay went ahead and sliced the bread, even though it wasn't yet cooled. She placed a thick slice in a plate for each of them and slid it across the counter along with a butter knife. Mom took the knife and spread a generous amount of butter on the steaming piece of bread on her plate, then handed the plate of bread to Dad and he did the same.

I watched Mom as she took the first bite of the bread. Her eyes were closed, and she had a look of sheer ecstasy on her face.

She even let out a little moan as she chewed. Mel slid bowls in front of each of them with leftovers from the previous night's supper. Mom and Dad both quickly ate, savoring every bite and commenting repeatedly about how good it was. Naturally, Kay dismissed the compliments. I went to the fridge and took the tea jug out and kept their glasses full. We talked as they ate, sharing stories about what we'd all been up to since the Day.

In between bites, Dad told of how they were at home on the Day. That when the power first went out, they just assumed it was another routine outage. They realized it was something more when they went out to Mom's car for a trip to town for dinner out at Cracker Barrel, figuring with the power on the blink that they might as well eat out. But the car wouldn't start, nor would Dad's truck.

"That's when we realized there was something major wrong. We knew it wasn't just the usual temporary power outage," Mom said.

"I went around to the neighbors," Dad said. "No one's car would start. I started thinking about you talking about the EMP and what that would look like and I knew that must be it."

I nodded. "It took me a minute to figure it out too. And I was standing on the side of I-10. At least you were at home."

"How'd the people in your neighborhood react?" Danny asked.

"They came together." Dad replied. "We had a couple of issues early on, but once we got rid of those trouble makers, it was good. Everyone banded together. Worked together, shared what they had."

"It wasn't like that here," Mel said.

"Nope," Danny added.

"You guys had trouble?" Dad asked.

Danny nodded. "For a long time, actually. We had some

people that wanted to try and take charge. But their idea of taking charge was just to try and take advantage of the situation."

"We had to fix that," I said. Dad looked at me but didn't say anything.

"How long did it take you to get home?" Mom asked me.

"About a month, I think. Give or take."

"And there were still problems when you got here?" Mom asked. I nodded, "Oh yeah."

"We had a couple of neighbors that wanted to come into the house and *inventory* our food and supplies," Mel said. "I wouldn't let them in," she nodded at Danny. "Danny helped me. It was scary though."

"Were the girls at home when that happened?" Mom asked.

"No, they were at school, in programs. I drove the Suburban up there to get them. That was a problem. Not only because I had a truck that ran, but because the school didn't want to let them go. But I got them out and we came home."

Dad looked at me, "That old Suburban still runs?"

I nodded. "Oh yeah. That old Cummins runs just fine. She's a little worse for the wear now, seen some hard days. But it runs, and we still use it."

"The benefits of a diesel," Danny added.

We talked for a while, filling in more of the blanks. Mom and Dad ate their fill, which was considerable for the two of them, and drank a gallon of tea. Mom commented on the tea and asked how we sweetened it. I told her how we got the sugar.

"I just can't believe there's help out there and nobody is getting it," she said.

"People are getting it. We gave a lot out. We were giving out food and all manner of supplies at the park in Eustis when we were attacked once. A lot of people lost their lives that day," I said.

Danny held up his hand, "And a lot were injured. That's the day we lost Bobbie."

Mom got a worried look on her face. "Is it safe here? We had some trouble back home, but nothing like what you're talking about."

"It is now," I replied. "We've eliminated all the real trouble. After our last little mission, we now have enough firepower to fight off anyone. So yes, it's safe here now."

Mom looked out the kitchen window and saw Little Bit and kids playing in the yard. She stood up and walked to the door and stepped out on the porch. We all followed her and stood, watching them play. After a moment, Mom and Dad went out the screen door into the yard. The kids looked up. Naturally, Jace and Edie didn't know who they were, and it took a moment for Little Bit to recognize them. But when she did, she screamed and ran towards them.

"Grandma! Poppee!" Mom knelt down and caught her as she crashed into them. She picked the little girl up in a tight hug.

"Look at you! You're so tan and you've gotten so tall!" Mom said.

Hugging Mom's neck, Little Bit replied, "I've missed you so much! Where were you?"

"We were at home, honey."

Little Bit kissed her on the cheek, then leaned out and kissed Dad on the cheek and wrapped her arms around his neck as well. "Poppee!" She shouted. "I'm so happy you're here!" She released him and leaned back, a look of surprise on her face, "I have a baby squirrel! His name is Ruckus! He fell out of a tree and daddy caught him in his hat. You want to see him?"

Dad tussled her hair and said, "I sure do. Are his eyes open yet?"

Wiggling to get set down, she took Dad's hand. "No, they're

not. I have to feed him anyway; you can help." She grabbed Mom by the hand and led them back up to the porch.

I sat down and watched them. Little Bit opened the box and took the little rodent out. She cupped it in her hands, then handed it to Dad, reminding him to be careful, *he's just a baby.* I sat and watched them with a proud smile; it was as if nothing bad had ever happened. Like she'd just seen them last weekend and it was a normal thing for them to be here today. Such is the mind of a child, and I envied it. Mom and Dad sat down, Little Bit climbed up into Dad's lap and sat there while she fed Ruckus.

The three talked, about the things a seven-year-old finds interesting, naturally. But it wasn't about the conversation. It was about being there with her. Because while Little Bit acted the way she did, I could see it on Mom and Dad, the weight of the time lost. Of the uncertainty of ever seeing her again. Tears ran down Mom's face as she ran her hand through Little Bit's hair.

"Where are the other two?" I asked Mel.

"They took some stuff down to Fred's. They should be back soon."

Jace ran up to the edge of the porch and called to Little Bit, "Ashley, come play with us!"

She looked at Dad and asked, "Can you wipe his butt?"

He smiled and took Ruckus as she scampered down out of his lap and jumped from the top step into the yard. She was at a full run when she landed. Mel went over and took the squirrel and I sat down beside Mom and Dad.

"Who are these two?" Mom asked looking at the kids.

"They came here some months ago with their parents. But the parents were killed. We just barely managed to save the kids. Danny and Bobbie took them in."

"Danny always did want kids," Mom replied. "Sad that they lost Bobbie as well," she added.

"It was sad for all of us," Mel said.

Mom looked up at her. "I know it was and I'm so sorry."

Mel looked out at the kids. They were back to the slip-n-slide and she said, "She's still here though. We have to be grateful for what we have and not dwell on what we've lost."

"Aint that the truth," Dad said.

A noise in the house got our attention and Mel went inside. She returned quickly with Lee Ann and Taylor. When the girls saw their grandparents, they both started to cry and rushed over to them. The emotions started again as they were all a knot of hugs, muffled words and tears. I left them on the porch, to give them all some time. Mom and Dad were here now and there would plenty of time to spend with them. I wasn't in a hurry.

As the afternoon turned into early evening, the house began to fill up. Everyone made their way to Danny's in ones and twos. Crystal and Janet arrived with Mike and Ted. Dalton came in alone, as was usual. Fred and Aric showed up with Jess and Doc. The house was getting packed. I was sitting on the front porch with Dad and Sarge. They were trying to see who could drink their coffee the fastest I think. I sipped on some tea and listened.

There were voices everywhere. I could hear people on the back porch and the kids were running laps around the house in an unending game of tag. Kay came out of the house and refreshed the coffee. It made me so happy. To be sitting on the porch with Dad on what seemed like an ordinary day in an ordinary life.

Mel and Kay had prepared a massive pot of beef stew, the last of the cow we'd found on the road. I guess the arrival of the heifers was a sign that it wasn't to be the last beef we'd ever eat, and it was put to good use. It was paired with fresh biscuits and everyone enjoyed the meal and the company.

I was getting up to carry my plate into the house when a Hummer drove down the road. I stopped to see who it was and was surprised to see Scott step out. As he came up to the house, I asked, "What's up? Something wrong?"

"No, no, nothing is wrong. I just need to talk to Danny and Thad."

"They're on the back porch," I said, curious what he needed.

He went into the house and I followed him in. When Kay saw him, she immediately thrust a bowl into one hand and a biscuit into another. Scott pretended to protest, but not very hard or convincingly.

"Thank you, Miss Kay," he said as he stuffed half a biscuit in his mouth.

"You just eat all you want. Now go out back and sit down. I'll bring more biscuits."

He went out the back door and I stepped into the kitchen and rinsed my bowl and put it in the sink. By the time I went out the back door, Scott's bowl sat empty on the table and he, Thad and Danny were walking around the side of the house.

"Where are they going?" I asked Mary.

She shrugged, "I don't know. Scott said he needed their help for a minute."

I walked around the porch, trying to catch up with them. By the time I got out front they were already in the truck and backing out.

"What the hell are they up to?" I asked no one in particular.

"Sit down, Morgan," Sarge said. "He needed a hand for a minute. Your mom and dad are here tonight, let them handle it."

"Whatever. Would just like to know what's going on," I replied as I dropped back into my rocking chair.

"This is real nice," Dad said looking out over the yard.

"You get enough to eat?" I asked.

He patted his belly; I could see it under his shirt. "I sure did. First time I've actually said that in nearly a year."

"Told you it was better here."

He looked over at me. "It is. But Linus has been telling me some of what you all have gone through. It took a lot to make this happen."

I nodded. "A lot of work. A lot of lives too. All we can do is stay at it. No one is going to do it for us."

"Well, you've done a hell of a job, son."

"It wasn't just me. I just did my part. Everyone here did theirs. That's why we're all here."

"Told ya," Sarge said and Dad smiled.

"What?" I asked.

"He said you wouldn't take any credit. But that everyone is here because of you."

I shrugged. "I don't see it that way."

"Morgan," Sarge started, "you may not see it. But you have, like a gravitational pull that draws people together. Name one person here that you didn't bring here. Everyone here owes all of this to you."

"Not true," I replied. "Danny was here."

Sarge's face contorted, "Would you quit being an asshole and just take the compliment!" Then he looked at Dad. "Don't know how you did it. I could only imagine what a pain in the ass he was when he was young."

Dad smiled, "He wasn't that bad. And he's really making up for it now."

"Ha! There!" I shouted back at Sarge. He shook his head and Dad and I started to laugh. We got to the old man and he soon joined us.

It was dark when we saw the lights of the Hummer coming back down the road. "About time they got back," I said. But it stopped and turned into my driveway. "What the hell are they doing?" I asked as I got to my feet. As I started to step off the porch, the lights started moving again and the Hummer pulled back into the yard.

Scott, Thad and Danny all got out of the truck and walked towards the porch. They all had grins on their faces and I looked them over and said, "You're all grinning like an ass eating briars. What's up?"

Danny didn't respond; instead, he walked past us and disappeared around the corner of the porch. When the lights went out, I looked over my shoulder and said, "Shit, now what?"

As I turned to go see what was wrong, Scott grabbed my arm. "Hang on a sec there, boss." He raised a radio and called, "Go ahead and close it"

"Close what?" I asked.

It's closed. Came the reply. Danny had appeared at the corner of the porch and Scott looked at him and nodded. He disappeared again, and the lights suddenly came back on. As well as another sound, it was loud and obnoxious. But a cheer erupted from inside.

"What the hell is that?" I asked.

Danny came around the side of the house. He was grinning from ear to ear. "It's the AC. It's on."

"What? How?" I asked, then I looked at Scott. He was almost vibrating with excitement.

"We got the line back up out here. And we powered up the Kangaroo store in Altoona on our way out, the lights are on there too." I looked over at my house; it was dark. "Come on," he said, "we turned the mains off on all of the houses."

"You have the power on all the way out here?" I asked.

He nodded. "Yep. Since we had to disconnect Eustis, we focused on running it out here. The Kangaroo in Umatilla has power now too, and the lights are on there as well. Come on, let's go turn your power back on."

Dad got up and the three of us walked over to the house. The big cable I'd connected the solar system to the house with was still plugged in, but the breaker for it was off. Scott nodded at the panel as he held a flashlight, "Go ahead, turn it on."

I flipped the main and nothing happened. The house was still dark. But then, we didn't leave lights on like we used to. After a moment, the AC hummed to life. "Well I'll be damned," I said as we walked around to the front of the house. I went inside and flipped the switch for the porch light, it came on and I walked over to the thermostat. It read eighty-six degrees. The LED screen worked. I checked it and adjusted it down to seventy.

Turning around, I grabbed Scott in a hug, "Holy shit, man, this is awesome!"

"Baker is on her way down. We're going to make sure that all the houses in use are good to go. You guys will be able to sleep in AC tonight."

Already there were trucks and ATVs zipping around the neighborhood. Mel and Mom showed up at the front door and came in. "Is the electricity really on?" Mel asked.

I nodded. "Yep and the air's running too."

With tears in her eyes, she wrapped her arms around Scott, "Thank you, thank you, so much. Thank you."

"Oh, it's nothing, Mel. We've been working on it for a while now," he replied.

She turned to me suddenly and said, "This means we won't sweat at night anymore!"

"Yeah, I cranked it down to seventy," I said with a huge smile.

"Is that as low as it will go? Turn it all the way down!"

"It won't do any good. The AC has to pull all the moisture out of the house and that's going to take a while. We won't feel any real difference until tomorrow probably."

"I'll take anything I can get. We need to go back over to Danny's. We have a surprise for dessert tonight."

As we walked back over to Danny's, a large bucket truck rumbled down the road. It pulled up in front of Danny's house and then Baker, Terry and Eric got out. Baker was smiling from ear to ear and asked, "Well, what do you think?"

Kay was on the porch and practically ran out to her. "You are a sweetheart!" She shouted as she wrapped her arms around Baker.

"We were trying to get it here sooner. It really all came together today," she replied. "We got power on in a couple of places in town as well. There's still people at the Kangaroo in Altoona. They're all standing around under the lights of the gas island like cavemen looking at a fire. Pretty funny."

Sarge came down off the porch as well and held his hand out. "Hell of a job. Hell of a job." He shook Baker and Terry's hands. Having been harassed by Sarge way too many times, Eric wouldn't get close enough to him to shake his hand.

"You all come up and get some supper. Then we'll all have dessert," Kay said.

"That sounds wonderful to me!" Terry called out.

The engineers came up onto the porch and were all served heaping bowls of stew. As they ate, people slowly started making it back to the house. All were excited that the power was now on and in all but one case, Thad's house, the AC was working.

"We can look at it tomorrow," Terry told Thad as he pushed a biscuit in his mouth.

"Ain't no rush. We're used to it. Just nice to have the well running and be able to take a hot shower," Thad replied.

"Holy shit," I said. "I hadn't even thought of that! A hot shower!"

It got a laugh from several of those gathered. Mike and Ted arrived back at the house to say their house was up and running as well. Then Mike asked Baker, "You think we could get power out to their ranch?" He pointed at Janet.

Baker looked at Terry and he asked, "Where are they?"

"Off forty-two, past the farm a ways."

Terry nodded, "It'll take a couple of days. We'd have to go out and clear all the lines. But I don't see why not."

"That would be amazing," Janet said.

"Yes, it would," Crystal added. "I'd like a hot shower too."

"We'll need to start making a list of people and the houses they live in. See how many houses we can restore power to. It would make a huge difference," I said.

"We already have power to the gym in Eustis," Terry said.

"That's good," Sarge replied. "The injured folks there have really been suffering, and this will help ease their pain a bit as they recover."

"Alright, enough of this," Kay said. "There's plenty of time tomorrow to discuss all this. It's time for dessert. Who wants some ice cream?"

There was a near universal shout in reply, "Ice Cream?"

"With grape syrup too," Mel added.

Mel and Kay went to the kitchen and began scooping out bowls and cups of ice cream. Nearly every container that could hold it was used. You'd take your bowl and drizzle some of the deep purple syrup made from the grape juice on top. It was heavenly. I got mine and sat down beside Mom and Dad.

Dad was eagerly eating the intensely sweet treat. "Not bad, huh?" I asked.

"This is amazing," Mom said.

Mel came up and sat with us after getting the kids a bowl. It was funny to watch Jace and Edie. I wasn't sure if they'd ever had it before. But they sure knew what to do with it and the kids sat giggling and getting themselves covered it in.

"When did you guys make this?" I asked.

"While you were gone. We had the idea and decided, *what the hell,* and made it."

"It's amazing," Mom said again. "I can't remember having anything this sweet, ever."

I laughed. "Your sweet tooth has gone dormant."

"Mine's waking up," Dad said.

I looked around the table at the people that mattered the most to me in the world. And they were all here, gathered together eating ice cream of all things. "Not a bad homecoming huh?" I asked.

Dad looked up, "Not bad at all."